# YOURS ROYALLY

A CINDERELLA LOVE STORY

KRISTA LAKES

ZIRCONIA PUBLISHING, INC.

## ABOUT YOURS ROYALLY

*Can a regular girl ever marry a real life prince?*

**Prince Marco:**

Royal life can be a royal pain, and Marco needs a break. A secret identity, just for a few weeks. A relaxing vacation in America, where nobody knows who he really is. Not even the girl he hires to be his personal assistant, Sabrina. But when Sabrina turns out to be the best part of his vacation, he finds it harder and harder to keep his secret from her...

**Sabrina Wise:**

Sabrina never imagined that any job could lead to paparazzi encounters and surprise trips to Hawaii. Who could have thought that her boss would turn out to be as charming as he was handsome? But, behind their sizzling sexual tension, she can't help but think there's something more to Marco. Who *is* this gorgeous man she's taking orders from, and why is he keeping so much hidden away? If she's willing to risk everything to find out, she might end up in her own Cinderella fairy-tale ending...

*What happens when Mr. Right turns out to be Prince Charming?*

∽

Marco started up the music. It began with a simple drum beat, but soon flutes and horns chimed in. The music was extremely complicated and sounded like a combination of jazz and blues, mixed with salsa. Underlying the melody, though, was a rhythmic beat that actually caused Sabrina to tap her toes.

"Do you like it?" Marco asked, as he stepped close to Sabrina and placed his hand onto her lower back. "I imagine it sounds quite a bit different from the music that is made here."

Sabrina nodded. Her bangs fell into her eyes and Marco reached up, pushing her hair across her forehead and behind her ear. It was such a simple act, but meant so much to her.

"My hair is a mess," she said, desperately filling the silence with anything she could think of.

"I think you look beautiful," Marco said, sliding his fingertips down her cheek. "The most beautiful girl in New York City."

Sabrina bit her bottom lip and looked at the ground, unable to fully accept such a compliment. How Marco saw her and how she saw herself were two entirely different things.

"That's really sweet," she said, bringing her gaze back up to his eyes. "Thank you."

Marco leaned in and kissed her. Her eyes widened at

first, surprised by the sudden affection. They resumed what they had started at the haunted apartment, though this time with even more passion and far fewer ghosts. Sabrina stood up from her stool without breaking the kiss. She brought her hands to the top of Marco's shoulders, pulling herself close to him. Her body tingled all over as their tongues danced.

Somewhere, in the very back of her mind, Sabrina knew that she was falling for this guy. And she realized that it put her at risk of getting hurt. She'd had her heart broken before, and she understood that it could likely happen again. But Marco was different. She wanted to believe that he would never hurt her.

She felt his hands slide down her sides, gliding easily along the smooth fabric of her shirt to the band of her pants. His touch turned her on, and a surge of excitement pumped through her. She breathed in, letting the soft scent of Marco's cologne fill her nose. She placed her hands onto his face. His beard stubble scratched at her fingertips as she drew her hands downward, all the way to his neck and then to his chest.

Marco slowly broke their kiss and looked into her eyes. Sabrina saw that his pupils had dilated and he was breathing harder now. Her hands were still on his chest and she noticed the rise and fall of each breath.

He wrapped one arm around her waist and lifted her from the floor, cradling the backside of her knees with his other arm. She was surprised by his strength as he carried her effortlessly away from the bar and to the darkened bedroom. It was as though she was in a trance, unable to take her gaze away from him. His masculine features, the beard stubble and his chiseled jaw, which were half-covered by his shoulder-length black hair. This was every woman's dream come true, and she was living it. Sabrina put a note in the back of her mind to pinch herself when this was over, just to make sure that it was all actually real. Until then, she didn't want to wake up...

Don't forget to join my mailing list as well for updates! (clickable link)

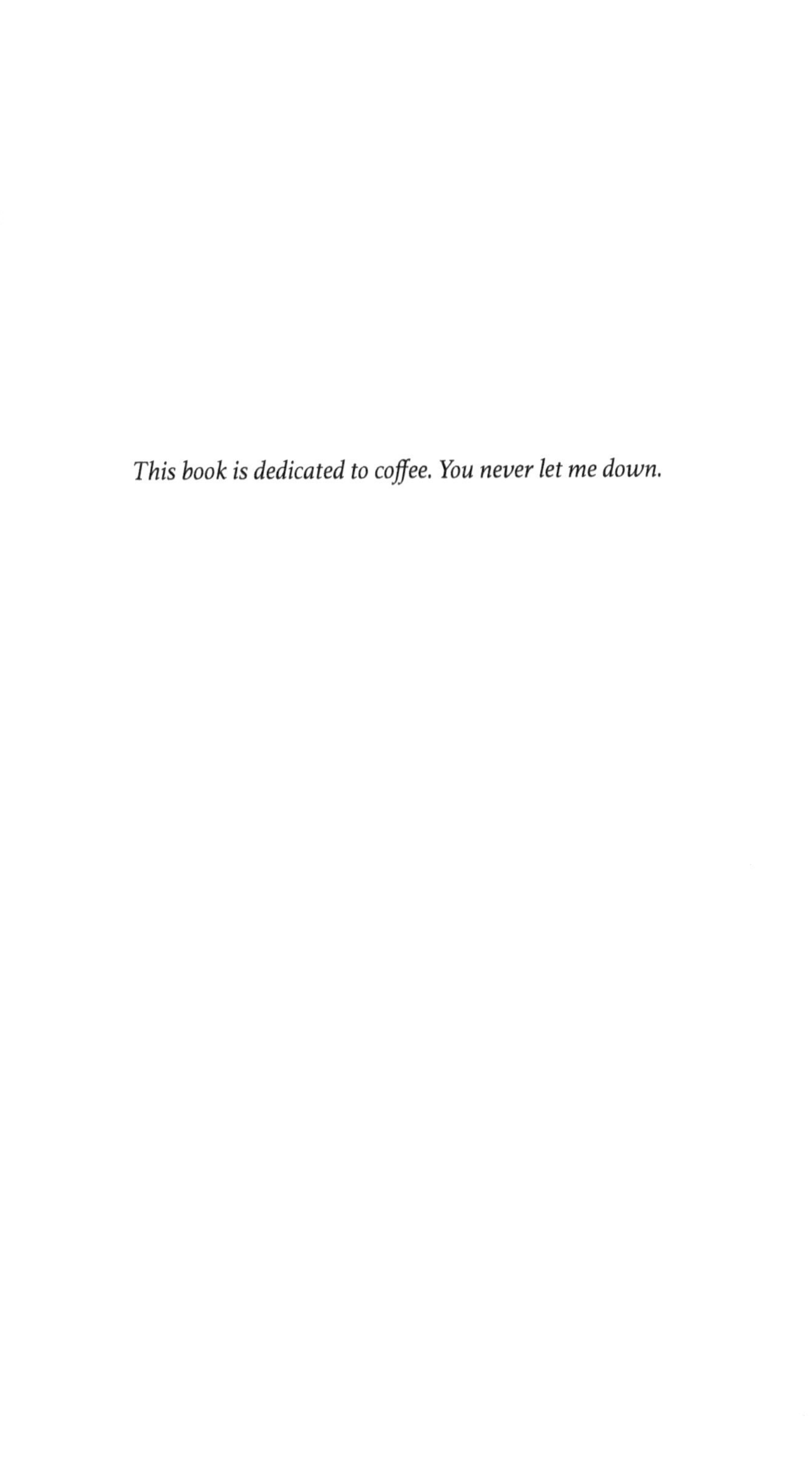

*This book is dedicated to coffee. You never let me down.*

# YOURS ROYALLY

# CHAPTER 1

 abrina

*O H   G O D, I hope I don't throw up. What a horrible first impression that would be.*

Sabrina swallowed down her nervousness and shifted a bit in her seat, twirling her auburn hair in her fingers. Anything to distract herself from the swarm of butterflies that was currently terrorizing the inside of her belly. The eggs and bacon breakfast had seemed like a good idea a few hours ago, but she began to question it now that she was about to face the most important interview of her life and it didn't want to stay down.

The air of the small square interview room was cold as the air conditioner refused to turn off. It was a stark contrast to the heavy, humid air outside and in a few more minutes, Sabrina thought she might be able to see her breath. She rubbed her arms, wishing she had worn more than a thin dress shirt. She hadn't brought a jacket, or even a cardigan.

Besides the fact that she didn't own one that was near nice enough for the occasion, she hadn't even thought about it until now, and why would she? Summers were exceptionally hot and stuffy in Memphis.

She'd arrived ten minutes early just to be safe, but those extra minutes were now passing painstakingly slowly. She wiped her sweating palms nervously against the fabric of her skirt. She'd worn an ensemble of some of the nicest pieces of clothing she owned: a long black pencil skirt, her favorite black heels with a silver buckle near the toe, and had even borrowed a slim, light blue blouse from her mother.

It was best to fill the time preparing, she'd decided, and had since spent the last several minutes running over some scripted answers to a few predicable questions.

*I'm an especially hard worker and it's one of my greater strengths, although I'm equally dependable and loyal. I found your ad online and immediately thought my traits aligned with the description.*

Then came her Aunt Faye's voice at an internal pitch louder than Sabrina's own thoughts. *Don't overthink it,* she'd said. *You're a smart girl with a good head on your shoulders, act like yourself and that alone will be enough.* A subtle smile formed in the corner of her mouth as she recalled her aunt's prep speech the night prior.

A dark table loomed in front of Sabrina. On it was an empty notepad and a single pen. On the wall behind the desk was a pane of glass that Sabrina recognized as a two-way mirror. She'd worked at a retail shop that had one in the security office. It had a different tint to it or something. She couldn't quite put her finger on it, but she knew that it was no regular piece of glass. Instinctively, she'd sat facing the mirror, wondering if there was someone on the other side.

For that reason, she tried to maintain a stoic expression as she waited, desperately doing anything to keep her nerves from showing on her face. It'd also kept her from checking the wall clock too frequently, not wanting to give off an anxious impression.

*Any minute now,* she thought, resisting the urge to check her watch.

The unhinging of the outside door handle was the first thing she heard before the door opened slowly. Whoever was behind it was concluding a conversation before stepping in. The voice was feminine.

"No, that is exactly what needs to happen," the woman said. "Take care of it, please."

A well-dressed lady stepped through the door and shut it delicately behind her. She was wearing black dress pants with a tight fit around her waist and thighs. She had a thin white shirt tucked into them, with long sleeves and a collar that lent her a business-like appearance.

"Hello," the woman said, while extending a hand. "I'm Valetta. We spoke on the phone."

"I remember you," Sabrina said, standing up to shake her hand. "It's great to meet you in person."

The first phone interview had mainly consisted of standard interview questions, but she knew to expect a much more thorough inquiry for their in person meeting. Her past interview experiences never involved anything too intricate and were always designed for simple jobs, ones where her personality wasn't much of a focus. Getting hired was always easy, but making enough money to pay for college was not. This job, however, would make the goal attainable for the first time in her life, and that was exactly why this interview was so crucial.

The job sounded simple enough. She'd simply be the

personal assistant for a traveling foreigner, but the pay for this position was several grades above any wage she'd ever made before. Since it was only for a limited amount of time, she could pick up with school immediately after. She couldn't have designed a better summer job.

"Please take a seat." Valetta spoke the words with a thick, but pleasing, accent. It was something Sabrina remembered from their first conversation, which made sense given the job description. "Make yourself comfortable."

Sabrina did as she was asked while Valetta sat down in the chair on the other side of the desk. Valetta set down some papers and her phone, and organized them before looking up.

"Thank you for meeting us here," Valetta said, a polite smile crossing her face. She was probably a few years older than Sabrina's mother, but with less worn features.

"Oh, of course," Sabrina said. "Thank *you* for meeting me."

"It actually worked out well for us to come to Memphis," Valetta replied. "This hotel had an open room and everything after the flight was pretty effortless. After the difficulties we've had setting up this trip, this was a welcome change."

"You've had a difficult trip? Is there anything I can do to help?" Sabrina asked, in an attempt to make the conversation a little less formal.

"Thank you for your offer. Our current trip plans changed, and we're having to hire a local instead of bringing our own staff," she said, shaking her head. "But, we couldn't be happier with the amenities here. Memphis seems like a wonderful city, at least from the small amount that I've been able to explore so far."

"It is a very fun city," Sabrina agreed. "The food here is

some of the best in the United States, not to mention the music. It's an amazing place, as long as you can handle the heat."

"Yes, it's hot where we come from too," she said, as she made an upward sweeping motion with her hand. "But you Americans love the A/C."

"It's true," Sabrina said with a chuckle. "We like air conditioning almost as much as we like Walmart and hot dogs. You know, the finer things in life."

Valetta bowed her head in a short laugh. "When we last spoke, you said that you grew up here in Memphis. Out of curiosity, have you done much traveling?"

"Not much," Sabrina said, instead of *not at all.*

"Perhaps that's about to change," Valetta said, fixing her gaze on Sabrina as she laid her palm on the folder in front of her. "I'd like to get started."

"Sounds great," Sabrina said, as her heart thudded behind her rib cage.

"Wonderful," said Valetta with a perfect smile. "I'd like to go over the job responsibilities again. I know we went over them over the phone, but it is crucial you understand them."

Sabrina nodded. "Of course."

"This is a temporary personal assistant position," Valetta started off her speech. "Above all, my client's privacy is the most important thing. Many of the position's responsibilities are designed to protect his identity and ensure that his whereabouts are not discovered. This means that you will be the face of almost all procedural requirements. Hotel, restaurant, and all other reservations will be made in your name. If room service is desired, you will order it, receive it, and do all the talking to staff members. You will also clean the room yourself so that no member of the house keeping staff enters my client's quarters. Just to be clear, this isn't a 'bodyguard' position. However, if a difficult situation should arise, you will be entrusted with prioritizing the security of my client's identity in every decision you make. Think of the job as something between a maid and personal assistant. Does that make sense?"

"Absolutely," Sabrina said with a nod. She'd never heard of a job like this, but she was ready to work.

"While all of this precaution may seem excessive, I promise you that it is not. People of all sorts, paparazzi especially, have been known to stalk and harass my client," Valetta said. "I don't want to turn his trip into a covert operation, but to simply to ensure that it can be enjoyed with the smallest number of incidents possible."

"Of course," Sabrina said, attempting to demonstrate that she was following more than she really was. The secrecy, the significance, the all-around mystery; it was all a little strange, she thought. Strange and intense. But the pay was equally as intense, and that's what mattered.

"Good. Then I want to confirm that you're willing to do everything I just mentioned," Valetta said, her expression stalling as she looked directly at Sabrina.

"I am," Sabrina assured her.

"Excellent," Valetta replied with a smile. "Then, the next thing I would like you to do is try to identify some photos."

"Okay," Sabrina replied, hoping her smile didn't show her nervousness. She had no idea that she was going to have to identify photos for a job. Her brain immediately went a million miles a minute, trying to recall every photo she'd ever seen and how it could relate to the job of a personal assistant.

Valetta opened the manila folder in front of her and removed nearly a dozen glossy photos. "I'm going to show you pictures of several different people and I'd like you to tell me whether or not you recognize them."

"I'll do my best," Sabrina said, overwhelmed with curiosity. She'd never had to do anything like this before on a job interview.

"I'd like to move through them fairly quickly," Valetta said. "So if you're able to identify the subject, say their name. If not, a simple 'no' will be just fine."

"Yes, ma'am."

Valetta slid the first photo across the desk so that it was facing Sabrina. It was a picture of a blonde man with a thick beard. He was wearing a grey suit with a black undershirt. He was handsome, and Sabrina could have pictured him as a model for something, but he definitely didn't look familiar.

"No," Sabrina said. "I'm afraid not."

Valetta pulled the photo back and immediately turned over a different one. This picture was of a different man. He had wavy black hair that fell to his chin and was wearing a white button dress shirt tucked into grey slacks. His features were striking, with dark almond-shaped eyes and Cupid's bow lips. Gorgeous, no doubt. But still, not familiar.

"No," Sabrina said again.

Valetta made no expression as she exchanged the photos again. This one was of an older man with a grey beard. He was wearing a fuzzy black robe, which could hardly contain his large gut. He was looking toward the sun and squinting. He appeared confident and proud, but there wasn't a single thing about him that seemed familiar, other than she could easily imagine him living at her family's trailer park.

*This has got to be the strangest interview process I've ever been a part of,* she thought. *And I must be failing miserably. I don't know a single one of these.*

"Nope," Sabrina said, her forehead hot and growing warmer. The cold air was harsh against her clammy skin and for the first time she noticed her back soaked in sweat. She wanted this job so badly that these photos were becoming frustrating.

Valetta retrieved another picture from her folder and instantly Sabrina's chest inflated. She knew this one, or at least she thought she did.

"Oh," she exclaimed. "That's, um, that's..." Her head fell into her palms as she racked her brain. "That's that actor.. he's Irish..." When Sabrina looked up again she was glad to see Valetta smiling, as if she was amused by the struggle for her to place the actor. "That's the guy whose daughter is always getting kidnapped in every movie."

Valetta laughed. "Liam Neeson?" she suggested.

"*Yes*," Sabrina said, allowing herself to join Valetta's laughing. "It was on the tip of my tongue."

"That's okay, you passed," Valetta said, and Sabrina wondered if that meant that she *hadn't* passed with the other pictures. She slid another picture so that it was facing Sabrina.

It was a picture of a young blonde woman wearing a red dress. She appeared to be dancing in a rainstorm in the middle of some city, with taxi cabs parked behind her.

"No, I'm afraid not." Sabrina's throat tightened and again she felt the presence of sweat on her hands. She had no idea if it was good or bad that she didn't recognize any of these people. She had to assume not.

Valetta retrieved another photo, this one Sabrina recognized instantly.

"Oh, that's the Queen of England," Sabrina said, proudly. More than the queen herself, though, Sabrina had recognized the dogs she was posed with.

*At least I got that one,* she thought.

Valetta continued with several more photographs. Several were of famous actors and celebrities, but many more seemed to be of ordinary people. Some faces were even repeated, but in different poses. Sabrina hoped that the fact that she had no idea who ninety percent of the photos were wasn't going to cost her this job.

"Good," Valetta said, collecting the photos and sliding them back into the folder. "I realize that this might seem like a silly test, but I assure you that we do it for a reason. There is a method to our madness."

"I'm happy to do whatever you need," Sabrina replied. She smiled and tried to ignore the feeling of failure weighing down on her shoulders.

"Now, I have some questions for you." Valetta tucked the manila folder under her pad of paper and poised her pen to write. " I know this is probably a very cliché question, but I'd like to hear you talk about your strengths."

It might have been cliché, but it was the exact question Sabrina needed. She knew how to answer this question, and it gave her confidence after the failure of the images.

"Certainly. I think my biggest strength is my work ethic. I come from humble beginnings, but it has only ever been a motivational tool for me. I've always believed that hard work pays off and I've approached every job I've ever had with a mindset that I'm going to give it my all, no matter what. I also believe that my work ethic naturally translates to being a loyal and dependable employee."

Valetta nodded and marked something on her pad of paper. "And being a hard worker, have you had any experience doing maid work or acting as someone's assistant?"

"I have actually," Sabrina said, recalling a summer many years ago between her junior and senior year of high school.

"I worked at a maid service for a few months one summer. We usually cleaned anywhere from three to five different homes a day." She paused, then added, "But you could pick up extra houses if you finished early, so I did that pretty often as well."

"Excellent," Valetta said. Sabrina exhaled softly, as if she'd just made it through the first of nine innings.

*One question down, a million to go. Remain calm and speak slowly,* she reminded herself.

"Can you tell me about other jobs you've had, Sabrina?"

"Of course. My first job was as a dishwasher while I was in high school, but I became a waitress when I graduated." She paused. Here was where she wished she could say she went to school or had done something with her life, but she hadn't. She'd just worked instead of going to college so that bills were paid and food was on the table. "I still work there, in addition to my retail position."

"You currently work two positions?" Valetta asked, her pen poised above the paper.

"Yes," Sabrina said with a nod. "I'm a hard worker and these positions have given me a fair amount of experience dealing with people and have taught me a lot about what it takes to make a customer happy."

"Quite the handy skill set," Valetta said, looking up from her notes. "And that's actually a great segue into my next topic. I'm going to ask you a few questions about hypothetical situations that might arise while on the job. Take a moment to think about it and then tell me how you'd respond."

Sabrina nodded.

"Picture this scenario," Valetta said. "Say you are out with my client, a local businessman, in a public place and a stranger approaches the two of you. The stranger claims to know my client, but clearly that is not the case. Also, this man happens to strike you as being slightly suspicious. What would be your response in a situation like this?"

"Regardless of whether or not the stranger seemed suspicious, I'd attempt to consult your client and follow his lead. If he's uncomfortable with the stranger, then that person is not to be trusted," Sabrina replied. "You said that I'm not a bodyguard, so in this instance, I would try to alert his security or find a way for us to get to a safe place."

"Good answer," Valetta said, her lips curling up into a pleased smile. "Let me give you another situation. While sightseeing, my client, a well-known public figure, sees a nice bar and decides he'd like to grab a drink and spend an evening downtown. You join him, but also notice that while enjoying himself he's become involved with a female who's had a bit too much to drink and is now drawing unnecessary attention to my client. How would you respond?"

Sabrina paused. This question was a potential minefield, but she felt confident she could answer it. She'd dealt with plenty of women like that as a waitress.

"It depends on what the client wants," Sabrina replied. "I'd hate to ruin an evening for him, so if he wants the woman to continue with him, I'd find a way to get them to a more private location. If he does not want the woman with him, I'd find a way to separate them. However, it is up to the client."

Valetta smiled slightly and her eyes flicked toward the mirror. "How would you separate them, if that is what the client wished?"

"First, I would pay the woman's bar tab and then tell the woman that she had something in her teeth and that she should go check the mirror," Sabrina answered. "While she was away, the client would leave the bar. I would have the bartender tell the woman an emergency came up and he had to leave."

"That would solve the problem." Valetta frowned slightly. "But why pay her bar tab?"

"If the goal is to avoid unnecessary attention, a happy customer is always better than one who feels that she has been jilted. In a drunken state, the woman could easily believe that he'd left her with the bill and would come looking for him," Sabrina explained. "You said he was a public figure, so this way, there would be no public backlash."

"Excellent answer," Valetta said with an approving nod. She smiled and turned to face the two-way mirror, obviously anticipating someone to receive her comment from the other side. "I have a few more questions for you-"

Her phone buzzed on the table with an incoming message, cutting her off. Valetta glanced at it and smiled.

"Actually, if you don't mind, I'm going to leave the room for a moment," Valetta said, pocketing her phone. "I'll be back shortly."

"Of course," Sabrina said, noticing that her palms were clammy enough that it was uncomfortable. She wiped them on her skirt under the table, but she wasn't sure it did much good.

*I blew it,* she thought and tried to tame her disappointment before it turned to tears. While she felt she'd answered the questions well, she knew she'd bombed the photo section. Plus, the fact that the interviewer was leaving in the middle of the interview was never a good sign.

*What the hell kind of interview is this anyway? Am I interviewing for a job, or a spot on a game show?* She tried not to think about it, since she knew it would make her cry.

Part of her wanted to stand up and leave before Valetta

returned to say that she didn't get the job because of her poor pop culture identification, or whatever it was that she had been trying to learn about Sabrina during the barrage of strange photos.

The floor was crumbling beneath her, or so it felt, and the prospect of finally getting a college education was actively shattering along with it. This job was her first real ticket to a better life, but she could feel it slipping through her fingers.

Valetta reentered the room and gave her a warm smile.

Sabrina clenched her hands in preparation for bad news.

Valetta took her time sitting down. She no longer carried the manila folder and instead had a large stack of papers. Sabrina hoped they weren't more photos for her to identify.

"Before we continue, do you have any questions for me?" Valetta asked as if she had never left.

"Um... no?" Sabrina's mind went blank. *Way to impress your potential employer,* she thought.

"Before we go any further, I need you to sign this nondisclosure agreement." Valetta slid the packet of paper across the table. "It's fairly standard, but it basically says that you won't tell anyone who you met here today."

"Okay," Sabrina replied. She read through the paperwork, trying her best to understand the dense legalese wording. It matched with what Valetta said, so after a moment, Sabrina signed the paperwork and sent it back across the table.

"Excellent." Valetta turned in her seat and gently tapped her knuckle on the glass behind her. Then she stood and went to stand by the door.

The door creaked open, and a man stepped into the

room. Sabrina recognized him instantly from one of the photos.

*It's the guy from the second picture. The one with the shoulder-length black hair and beautiful dark eyes.*

The man was tall and wore an expensive-looking white dress shirt tucked into a crisp pair of dark grey slacks. It was a similar outfit to the one he had been wearing in the photo. Immediately, it felt as if the room got smaller, his large persona crowding the space.

He nodded toward Sabrina with a smile that grew from the hard edge of his chin and curled into his lips.

"I'd like to introduce you to Marco... Smith," Valetta said. The way she said it made it obvious that 'Smith' was not the man's real name.

The man's smile grew even more as he neared the table and extended a hand while Sabrina stood to shake it. His grip was firm, but his skin gentle and smooth.

"Hello," he said with another nod. His voice was tuned with a deep accent that was as melodic as it was foreign.

"Hello," Sabrina said, a smile spreading across her face. "I'm Sabrina."

"I know who you are," the man said, still smiling. It was then that Sabrina realized she was still gripping his hand. She quickly released and sat back down. "I came in to offer you the job."

"Really?" Sabrina said, a little shocked that she was being offered the position on the spot. It was a good thing she was sitting, or her knees might have buckled.

"Really," Marco assured her, taking a seat in the chair Valetta had vacated a moment earlier.

"Marco and I feel that you would be great for the position," Valetta said and turned toward Marco, who nodded in agreement.

"I think you would be wonderful," Marco said, every word sounding like its own subtle, musical note. His accent had a slightly different ring than Valetta's, whose chipper voice overshadowed her inflections.

Marco was directly across from Sabrina with both forearms rested against the table. The sleeves of his white shirt were rolled up to his elbows, creating contrast against his tan skin. At the end of his wrist was a tightly fitted gold Rolex.

Sabrina's first thought was that she'd just been hired to assist some sort of model, a rather wealthy one, looking to spend some time in the United States in order to escape his fame. She also toyed with the idea that he was a foreign athlete. Although concealed, his frame and shoulders indicated a sturdy figure beneath a layer of expensive clothing.

"Wow," Sabrina said, taken aback both by the sudden offer and the aura of the man sitting in front of her.

Both Valetta and Marco smiled back at her, as though they anticipated her level of shock.

"Take your time making a decision," Valetta said. "But do keep in mind that we hope to begin traveling before the end of the week."

"Can I accept the job right now?" Sabrina asked, giddy with excitement.

Valetta's eyebrows rose with a smile. "Of course you can."

Sabrina allowed herself a soft laugh. "Is that okay or did I just make myself look incredibly desperate?"

This time it was Marco who answered. "It's *very* okay," he said. "I was hoping you'd say 'yes'."

Sabrina forced herself to meet his gaze, which was concentrated and direct. His dark eyes were highlighted by the definition of his facial features. They were large and carried a deep and intriguing intensity.

"Okay then," Valetta said, feeding off of Marco. "You're hired!"

A weight that she didn't even realize was there lifted from Sabrina's shoulders. For the first time that morning, she felt at peace. At peace and ecstatic. Her chest, which had once been crowded with nervous butterflies, was now filled with a delighted energy. She inhaled, feeling her breath all the way into her lungs. A goofy smile had slowly consumed her face, but she didn't care.

*I can't believe it,* she thought, her excitement spreading to each of her four limbs. *This is really happening.*

This job offer was a promise that in only three months' time she'd make enough for four years of college without another job in between. She could concentrate on her schoolwork and finally live the life she wanted. The reality of this amazing opportunity was just starting to set in.

"You said you're from around here?" Marco asked, a question that helped to bring Sabrina out of her daze.

"Yes, I am," Sabrina said. "Born and raised."

"Yes, you have a thick accent," Marco said, gesturing with his hands.

"Really?" Sabrina blushed. She'd spent most of her life trying to hide her southern accent. She'd worked hard to learn how to speak like she'd grown up on the right side of town rather than in a trailer park. 'Non regional diction', they called it.

Marco chuckled. "You do, but I like it. And don't feel bad, everyone in America has an accent to me. I'm sure you can hear my accent very clearly as well."

"That's not a bad thing," Sabrina said, scanning his beautiful features and taking them in all over again. "I like your accent, too. Can I ask where you are from?"

In her peripheral vision, Sabrina saw Valetta look to Marco, awaiting his response.

"I'm from the Mediterranean," Marco said, without returning Valetta's glance. "From a very small island."

With his finger and thumb he made an indication of something small.

"Welcome to America," she said enthusiastically.

"Thank you, Sabrina from Memphis," Marco said with his warmest smile yet.

She giggled. "You're welcome, Marco from 'small Mediterranean island'."

This time his laugh came from deep in his chest.

*His smile is going to consume me,* she thought. *How am I going to survive working for this hunk for the next three months? Making ridiculous money won't hurt, so maybe that'll keep me focused. What a wonderful combination, though. Am I dreaming?*

"Now I have some paperwork for you to sign," Valetta said, moving to put yet another set of papers in front of Sabrina. "This is your contract. If you'd like a lawyer to look over it, you are welcome to."

Sabrina knew she couldn't afford a lawyer. Besides, she didn't even know what kind of lawyer she would need to hire. The only lawyers she knew were the ones from TV and the car accident commercials, and somehow neither of those seemed like the kind to look over a contract.

"There are a couple of things that I would like to point out as non-negotiable," Valetta continued before Sabrina said anything. "First, my client is to remain anonymous. This is per his wishes. You are not to attempt to obtain outside knowledge about him. Any attempts will be met with immediate dismissal and legal action."

"You mean, I'm not allowed to Google him or look him

up on social media?" Sabrina asked slowly, making sure she understood.

"Correct." Valetta nodded. "Also, there is another nondisclosure agreement in there. You will be a part of Marco's life, and as such, you are never to reveal personal details without his permission."

"I never would," Sabrina assured them both. "I don't talk about people behind their backs."

Marco smiled and looked at Valetta like he had expected Sabrina to make such a statement. His dark eyes sparkled with an inner warmth that Sabrina couldn't help but smile back at.

"You came very highly recommended," Marco informed her. He held out a pen for her to sign with. "It will be a pleasure working with you."

Sabrina grinned and took the pen. It was a nice pen with a good deal of weight to it, but as she signed her name with a flourish, it felt like it weighed nothing. With the ink of the page, the door to her future opened.

# CHAPTER 2

PRINCE MARCO STROLLED across the floor of his hotel suite. It was a nice room, there was no doubt about it. It had the best amenities of any hotel in Memphis, at least that's what Valetta assured him. It was filled with big leather furniture, stainless steel kitchen appliances in the over-sized attached kitchen, and floor to ceiling windows along the outside wall. It also included a hot tub in the bathroom and a massive balcony that overlooked downtown Memphis.

Despite its grandiose appearance, the place was significantly smaller than his own bedroom at his palace on Orsino Island. He didn't mind, though. It made the trip feel more real. He didn't care if it was the biggest or the best because he was on his own. This was the last time his life would be his own and he was going to enjoy every moment of it.

He unbuttoned his white dress shirt and slipped it off of

his shoulders, tossing it onto the bed. It was still early in the day, but he already felt accomplished. He had just found the woman that would take care of him during his vacation in the States.

He shook his head and let out a sigh of relief. Valetta had almost insisted on canceling the trip when his original trip assistant had fallen ill, but Marco had managed to talk her out of it. He had assured her that an American girl could do the job.

He thanked his lucky stars that he'd found Sabrina. He had thought it would be easy at first, to find the perfect girl with all of the right qualities, the most important of them being that she couldn't know who Marco was. But that was a quality that was harder to find than he had imagined, being that he was the Prince of Orsino Island. They'd interviewed what felt like hundreds of girls and he was about to cancel the trip, but, luckily he had found her.

*Sabrina, what a beautiful name for a beautiful girl,* he thought as he plopped down onto the bed and put his hands behind his head. He stared up at the ceiling and let out a relaxed sigh. His new assistant, Sabrina, whom he had only quickly greeted after hiring her for the job, was still fresh on his mind.

He couldn't shake the image of her sweet smile, her smooth and silky auburn hair, or the way her blue eyes lit up the room. He knew the moment he laid eyes on her from behind that two-way mirror that she was the perfect candidate. There was something innocent and magical about her, something that he couldn't quite put his finger on. Whatever it was, though, he liked it.

He found himself looking forward to traveling with her. Every one of her job referrals had raved about her and how wonderful and easy to work with she was. He always wondered how truthful people were when they were picked by the applicant, so before this interview, he had sent Valetta to her waitress job to ask the other waitresses when Sabrina wasn't working. The only negative thing said about her was that she was too eager to pick up extra hours and she made the other waitresses look bad because of it.

He checked his watch and did the mental math to figure out the time change. His father, King Carlo of Orsino, should be back from the doctor by now. He reached into the pocket of his slacks and pulled out his cell, punching in the digits to his father's personal line. His stomach twisted slightly as he waited.

"Hello?" King Carlo answered, his voice gruff and scratchy.

"Hello, Papa," Marco replied happily, then changed the tone of his voice. "Father. How are you feeling?"

"I'm well, son," he said. "Or at least, I feel well."

"How did the doctor's appointment go?" Marco said. The tightness in his stomach spread to his chest. "Is it cancer?"

"They've run three kinds of tests so far, including an MRI and blood test," the father told his son. He paused before delivering the bad news. "They're certain that the tumor is cancerous."

Marco sat down hard on the bed as his legs gave out. They had both known for several weeks that the diagnosis would likely be cancer, but Marco had stayed hopeful the entire time. It seemed he had been hopeful for no reason.

"What now?" Marco asked. He was glad his voice didn't falter. He would be strong for his father.

King Carlo let out a slow, difficult breath. "I have another doctor appointment soon to discuss the options."

"Options?" Hope flickered in Marco's chest. Perhaps this cancer wasn't as bad as they had feared.

"Yes." He coughed for a moment before continuing to answer. "There are a few different things they can try. From what I've learned, surgery is the first thing they like to attempt, but surgery is not always possible."

"What do you mean it's not always possible?" Marco asked.

"It depends on the size of the tumor and its exact location, as to whether or not they can remove it surgically," King Carlo explained patiently.

"What if they can't?" Marco's voice almost cracked with the question.

"Then they'll probably start talking about chemo and radiation. And even if I do qualify for the surgery, I may have to face those things anyway. Surgery often isn't the only thing that needs done. It's likely just the first step of a long journey of recovery."

A ball of anxiety crept into Marco's gut. His father had always been so strong and vital. He had always been a giant in Marco's eyes. There was nothing the king of a country couldn't do, couldn't conquer. He was Carlo the Great. The very idea that his own body was destroying him from the inside out terrified Marco.

"I'm sorry, Papa," Marco said. He wished he were a small child again so King Carlo could pick him up and spin him around to make him laugh. That used to make everything better.

"For *what*?" he said with a raspy chuckle. "You certainly didn't give me cancer. I mean sure, you were a difficult teenager, but that isn't what did this to me."

Marco managed a half smile, happy to see that his dad hadn't lost his sense of humor.

"When do you see the doctor again?" Marco asked.

"They haven't made an appointment yet." His father

sighed, sounding more tired than Marco remembered. "It will be soon, though. They tell me that the earlier they do the surgery, the better the prognosis."

"I will come home, Papa," Marco said. "I don't need to stay in the States for this vacation. I should be there for you. I should speak to the doctors."

"Nonsense," King Carlo said. "I'm excited for you to get away from the island for a while. It'll be good for you to do some traveling and have some fun before you take the crown. I don't want you to worry about me or my meeting with the doctors to discuss surgery. I will be fine. You needn't worry."

"I *am* worried, though. I can't help it," Marco said. "You are my father."

"I appreciate the concern, my son," he said gently. "But even if you came home, there's nothing you can do. You are not a doctor, Marco. I don't want this disease to end up a burden for both of us. Let's not give the cancer that kind of power over our lives. You've been wanting to take this trip for a long time and there's no way that I'm letting my illness effect your plans."

"Are you sure?" Marco said. He stood from the bed and began to pace across the plush carpet. "I feel like I should be there, even if there's nothing that I can do."

"Marco, you'd be doing both of us a disservice for coming home early. You'd ruin your trip and I'd be angry at you for doing so," King Carlo replied. "Just stay in the states and enjoy yourself."

Marco sighed. He knew that there was nothing he could do, but he hated being an ocean away from his father during this. He knew being in the room with the doctors wouldn't change the outcome, but he couldn't help but feel a bit guilty.

"I know you are thinking of coming home," Carlo said, as if reading Marco's mind. "If you do, I will be quite angry. You must go on this trip. That's a royal command, Marco." For a moment, Marco felt the old strength that his father once had creep into his voice.

Marco sighed. His father only ever said that if he was serious. "I want you to know that I'm only a phone call away. If you need me back at the palace, I'll drop everything and get on a plane immediately."

"You are a good son," Marco's father told him. Marco's chest swelled with pride at his father's compliment.

"Thank you, Father," Marco said. He stopped pacing and instead gazed out the large window at the city below.

King Carlo cleared his throat. "So tell me, Marco, how did the interviews go today? Did you find someone to help you while on your sabbatical?"

"I did," Marco said. Sabrina's face flashed into Marco's mind.

"And...?"

"Her name is Sabrina. She's from Memphis, Tennessee, born and raised. In fact, she lives just a few miles from the hotel where I'm staying now." Marco couldn't hide the excitement in his voice and his father recognized it immediately.

"She's attractive, I take it," the old man said.

"Did I give it away?" Marco asked. He ran a hand through his hair and chuckled slightly.

"You always do."

"Well, you're right. She *is* very attractive," he told his father. He couldn't stop the smile as she pictured her face. "There's something about her that intrigues me. She's not flashy and vain like most of the women I encounter. She seems simple, but a *good* kind of simple. There's an innocence in her that I find myself drawn to."

The king chuckled. "She sounds lovely, Marco. But don't let your stepmother hear of your attraction to her. Magdalena would not be pleased to hear you've taken a liking to someone who is not royal blood. You know how she feels about commoners."

"I don't plan on marrying her after just hiring her, but I wouldn't tell Magdalena anything of the sort regardless," Marco said. "This conversation is between you and I, and hopefully it will stay that way."

"Of course, son. You can have confidence that our conversations our private. I just wanted to tell you to not mention anything about Sabrina to your stepmother, that's all."

"Understood, Father," Marco said, with genuine respect in his response. "I always appreciate your council."

"And I always appreciate yours as well," King Carlo said.

Marco opened his mouth to tell his father more about his plans, but it was then that his father began to cough. Long, deep and bone-shaking coughs that worried Marco more than he cared to say. The specter of death rattled through these coughs and it terrified the prince.

"I hate to end our conversation, but I'm a level of exhausted that I haven't felt in a long time," King Carlo said once he caught his breath. "I'm going to go take a bath and try to get some sleep tonight. I have a long day ahead of me tomorrow."

"Yes, of course, Father. Please, go and get some rest. I'll be thinking of you." Marco frowned and felt guilt lay upon him again. "And don't forget, I'm only a phone call away. If you need anything from me, I'll be at the palace within twelve hours. Faster if I can manage it."

"Thank you, Marco." King Carlo's voice wheezed as he took a breath in. "Have a good vacation and stay in touch. I'll let you know what I find out from the doctors about the surgery. Keep your fingers crossed for me."

"I'll keep them crossed forever, if that's what it takes," Marco said.

"Good boy," his father said, before hanging up the phone.

Marco set his cell onto the nightstand next to the bed. Then he drew in a long, slow breath and tried to relax. His father's cancer diagnosis shook him to the core.

He hoped so badly that things would turn out okay. He couldn't imagine a world without his father in it. King Carlo was Prince Marco's greatest influence. He was a powerful and honest man, and through example, had taught Marco to be the same way. He had shown his son that honor was not just a word but also a way of life. He was not only a good king, but a good man.

*I pray for you, Papa. I pray that this cancer goes away and that you can live the rest of your days without worry,* Marco thought.

He turned from the window and walked toward the bathroom to splash some cold water on his face. He thought of ordering a drink up to his room to help settle his nerves, but decided not to. Soon, he would just ask Sabrina to do this, and he wouldn't have to deal with room service or remembering how much was considered proper to tip here.

Despite his worry over his father, the image of Sabrina still managed to stay at the forefront of his mind. It gave him relief and he found himself smiling at the thought of her.

"What is it about Sabrina?" he asked himself, while drying his face off with a towel.

There was no way that he could have denied it. He was

attracted to the new hire. In and of itself, this was no big surprise. Marco was a wealthy playboy who lived in a palace on an island. He often met beautiful women he was attracted to. And just as often, he landed these ladies in bed. But this girl was different. She felt unique.

The idea of Sabrina in his bed made a fire grow inside of him. He immediately wondered what her figure looked like underneath her clothes, pondering if her innocence would be something that disappeared once she was beneath the sheets. A surge of excitement filled him as he let his imagination run wild. He pictured her fair skin, supple breasts and firm behind. He thought about what it would feel like to touch all of it, bring his lips to her, shower her in attention.

But he found he wasn't satisfied with this fantasy. He wanted to know what would make her smile. He wanted to know how to make her eyes dance with joy as much as he wanted to pleasure her body. It was strange for him to think these things, and he wasn't quite sure what it meant.

"I need to lay down for a bit and close my eyes," Marco whispered to himself, as he made his way back to the bed.

The long flight to Memphis had taken its toll and jet lag had managed to finally catch up with him. As he laid down, he found himself shocked at how preoccupied with Sabrina he was becoming. He hadn't experienced anything like it before. The simple little Memphis girl had stolen his attention within the first few seconds of their meeting. For the first time in a long time, Prince Marco found himself unsure of what to do.

As Marco crawled under the covers of the bed and relaxed his head into the over-stuffed pillow, he realized that there wasn't much he could do right in that moment anyway. But he made a goal. He'd figure out how to pursue Sabrina in a way that was more serious, and gentler, than his usual one-night-stand ploys. Surely he could think of something.

*Maybe I'll show her some light flirtation and some generosity and see how she reacts. We could always go to some nice dinners and some fun activities when we're in New York. I'll show her that I'm not just interested in a quick fling. I want to get to know this girl. She's different. So very different,* he thought.

He closed his eyes and drifted into a half-sleep. He began to dream. In his dream, he was home, walking around his elegant room at the palace on Orsino Island. He walked up to the window and looked out into the courtyard, where his father was playing polo with his friends. King Carlo looked happy and healthy in the dream. He was strong, like Marco remembered him being when he was a child. Warm sunlight poured over him as he stepped a little closer to the window. It caused him to squint and look away, back toward his bed.

There was a girl in his bed, but he couldn't tell who it was because she was facing away from him and the covers were pulled up to her shoulders. The only thing he was able to see was her auburn hair. He reached for the covers, curious to see the beauty in his bed. For some reason, this didn't feel like a recent conquest. It felt like this was how it had always been.

It felt safe and warm.

His hand brushed against the blanket and suddenly the image blurred and he woke. He lay in bed, wishing he could have seen the woman's face. Who could it be that would make his dream feel so content and calm?

His dream had felt short, but powerful. It left him with a warm feeling in his chest. He rolled over, hoping to fall back into the dream and find the girl again, but found that he was no longer tired. He lay there, letting his mind drift and his thoughts wander.

The image of the blonde girl in his bed at the Palace, the one from the dream, kept coming back into his mind clear as a photograph. The auburn hair was his only clue as to her identity. Was it a premonition or just his current preoccupation with the new hire? He couldn't be sure.

## CHAPTER 3

Sabrina

SABRINA WAS on cloud nine as she left the conference room and walked toward the lobby of the hotel. There was a beat of exhilaration and energy in her step, now that the interview was over and she had landed the job of a lifetime.

*Things are turning around for me,* she thought. *This opportunity is going to be the new beginning that I've needed for a long time. I can't believe how things are coming together right now.*

She flashed a confident smile toward the young man working at the hotel's front desk, before striding out of the entrance and into the parking lot. She found her old beat up Toyota Corolla sitting lonely at the edge of the parking lot. She hopped in and turned the key.

The engine jerked and then rumbled to a start, causing the worn belts to squeal in agony. While the engine warmed, she pulled out her cell phone and dialed her mother, Anna. It rang four times before she finally picked up.

"Hello?" her mother said. Her tone made it sound like Sabrina had interrupted her, which was highly likely, since she was always busy.

"Hey, Mom," Sabrina said, her smile from the successful interview still plastered across her face. "What are you up to?"

"Hi, honey," she said, her southern accent thick and warm like honey. "I actually just walked in the door and was about to clean up the house a bit."

"Were you teaching today?" Sabrina asked.

"Yes. Ms. Donahue, the first grade teacher over at Belmont, called in sick again today," Anna said. "But it's great, because I'll be able to get a lot more hours in. With your father not working, I need to make as much money as possible. I'm sad that Ms. Donahue is ill, but glad to have the extra hours."

"Are you done for the day?"

"Unfortunately, no," Anna said, with an exaggerated sigh. "I've got an after school meeting after my shift."

"You're a substitute teacher, though," Sabrina said. "I thought you didn't have to attend those meetings."

"Normally that's the case, but I've been putting in so many hours over there that they have asked me to participate anyway. I'm practically a full time teacher with how many shifts I've put in this year," she said. "But it's not a bad thing that they want me to come to the meeting. They're paying me to show up, so I'm not complaining. I'll just grab a cup of coffee on my way there."

"Please take care of yourself, Mom." Sabrina pleaded. "I know we need the income, but it's not worth risking your health. I don't want you to work yourself to death. We'll figure things out, one way or the other. You know that."

"I know, but when the opportunity is here I need to take it. I have to make hay while the sun shines," she said, repeating the phrase that Sabrina had heard a thousand times growing up. "Anyway, what are you up to, honey? How was your day?"

"I just finished my interview. I was wondering if I'd be able to catch you and Dad before you guys leave for work tonight?" Sabrina glanced at the clock on the dashboard as she spoke, surprised to see that the evening was fast approaching. "I'd like to see you guys and fill you in on how it went."

"Oh baby girl, I'm so excited to hear how it went. I hope you have good news. How far away are you?" Anna asked. "Your father has to leave in an hour. I'll be right behind him."

"I'm just downtown right now, about to leave the hotel," Sabrina said, as she put her car into gear and began pulling out of the parking lot. "I can be home in ten or fifteen minutes."

"Okay, that sounds great," Anna said.

"Have you and Dad eaten dinner yet?" Sabrina asked. "Do you want me to stop and grab something on the way home?"

"Yes, good idea. I didn't have time to make anything this evening," her voice trailed off with a faint bit of guilt.

"That's okay, it's no big deal," Sabrina said. "I'll just grab some burgers and be home soon."

Halfway to home, Sabrina pulled up to a little burger stand that was on the side of the road. They had the best burgers in town, though nobody would have ever guessed. The small stand looked like it would have fallen over if a stiff breeze had blown by it. Even so, there was still a line of cars, all filled with locals who knew just how good the food was.

While waiting in the drive-through line, Sabrina replayed the interview over in her head, the images still vivid and alive. More than the series of questions, though, she reran her brief conversation with Marco. The elegant tone of his voice was a song stuck in her head, something she could hear above the hum of the radio and the idling of her car.

After five minutes in line, she bought dinner for her family and pulled away. She rolled her windows down as soon as she hit the highway, allowing the air to whip across her face in celebration. It gave her the feeling of freedom and release, a sensation she hadn't experienced in a long while. Her racing heart, combined with the intensity of the wind, kept the feeling of triumphant excitement alive in her chest all the way home.

When she arrived at her parents' trailer, she parked the Corolla nearby, on a small square of land where the grass had died from years of parked cars. All that was left was a small field of gravel and dust, which had become the official parking lot of the Wise residence. Wedged between Sabrina's Corolla and the trailer that she called home, was her family's Honda Civic. Next to that was a small porcelain fountain. It had collected a small amount of rain water in the bottom, which had turned it into a bird bath. Surrounding the fountain were three garden gnomes and several tacky wind spinners, all things that Sabrina had wanted to throw out for as long as she could remember.

Her family's trailer was as dilapidated as its surroundings. It had once been painted brown, but now the color had faded and chipped, exposing the graying wood underneath.

The small home looked as though it had seen a few too many seasons. And as the light of the setting sun blanketed the trailer's exterior, it only helped to amplify its many faults.

Sabrina got out of her car and skipped toward the trailer. The front door required a jerk and an upward heave to open, but once she had done so, she stepped in.

"Hey, guys. I'm home." She sang the words as she entered. Once inside, she was greeted by a familiar stale and musty scent. It was the kind of smell you could only get used to after several minutes of pretending it wasn't there, or after years of growing up in it. In many ways, the trailer would have been jarring to most people, but for Sabrina it was the smell of home.

Her father, Peter, was seated a few feet from the door on a small couch that doubled as an even smaller pull-out bed. Checkered with a colorful and outdated pattern, it was his favorite spot to sit and rest his ailing back.

"Hey, sweetie," he said, breaking his gaze on the news-paper in front of him to greet her as she came in. When he laid it down Sabrina could make out the word *employment* headlining the top of the page.

"Hey, Dad," Sabrina said, as she closed the front door behind her.

She noticed that her dad was still wearing his grease-stained blue jeans, the one he wore whenever he was working on cars.

"How was your day today?" she asked, glancing down to his dirty clothing.

Before he could respond, Anna emerged from the back half of the trailer.

"You made it," Anna said, pulling and twisting her thick hair into roll behind her head. There were days when people marveled at the striking similarities between her and Sabrina. Sabrina truly looked like a younger version of her mother. The only real difference was that Anna had crows' feet on the outside of her eyes and her hair had gone mostly grey.

Sabrina dropped the paper bags full of fast food burgers onto the small table in the corner of the trailer. Her father rose slowly from his chair, using one hand to push himself up while holding his lower back with the other.

"Dinner time," Sabrina said, looking at her dad. "I got some burgers."

"That was really nice of you," he said, his voice soft and appreciative. "Thank you, honey."

It occurred to Sabrina that had she not stopped and bought dinner, her father probably wouldn't have eaten before going to work that night.

"Happy to do it," Sabrina said, pulling out a wrapped burger and handing it to her father. He smiled gently and slowly sat down at the table.

"Do you still have time for dinner?" she asked her mother, who had dipped back into her bedroom.

"I need five more minutes." Anna called out, after disappearing around the corner.

"So, how was your day today, Dad? You didn't get a chance to answer when I first came in," Sabrina said, as she sat down at the table with her father.

"My day was fine," he replied. He had unwrapped his burger and was preparing for a bite before Sabrina had even dug hers out from the bag.

"You were gone when I left earlier today," Sabrina said, trying to bait more conversation.

Her father swallowed but didn't look up. "Phil from Memphis Mechanic gave me a call, said he could use some help working on an old Mustang they had in the shop. I said I'd give him a hand."

"He pay you?" Sabrina asked, studying her dad over.

Peter nodded. His soft gray eyes were like craters on his lean face, his skin worn from years under the sun. Gray-colored stubble lined his chin and jaw like short and thin blades of grass on a rugged field. "Yeah, he paid me. It was just a few hours' worth of work, though. Nothing steady. But I couldn't turn it down. The hospital called again and we need to pay up."

Sabrina nodded, taking a bite of her burger. The hospital was always calling it seemed.

The bills were always late. The collectors always banging on their door.

They had been getting by until a little over a year ago when Peter was laid off from his job. The halted income was just part of the detrimental effect, though. The psychological blow of the loss was far worse. The whole thing had sent her father into a spiral of depression that Sabrina wasn't sure he'd ever truly recover from. He refused to talk much about it, but his face wore the evidence of his grief and shame, which pained Sabrina just as much as it pained him.

"And it sounds like you were able to find something for tonight, too?" Sabrina asked, trying to get her father to talk to her more.

"Yeah. Dan said the bar's been having some trouble lately," he said, focusing on his burger

"The Blue Star?" Sabrina asked. "Is it about to close down?"

"Nah, not that kind of trouble," he said. "Dan told me they've been getting some especially rowdy guests lately. Something about some local bikers coming in there and acting like they own the place. Said he'd appreciate an extra bouncer for tonight. They're expecting a lot of people there because of some UFC fight. He's hoping extra people will keep the bikers from acting up, *if* they even decide to show up tonight."

"Really?" Sabrina said.

Peter nodded and swallowed another bite of burger. "Yeah, but it's just tonight. This isn't exactly a career move or anything, just a chance to make a few extra bucks."

Her father was tough as nails and could handle himself, but with his bad back, Sabrina wondered how great of an idea it was to take a job like that.

"Is that going to be dangerous?" she asked.

"Shouldn't be. That's what Dan said anyway. He figures just having an extra person at the front door will be good enough."

Sabrina pressed her lips and smiled, knowing that even if it *were* dangerous, her father wouldn't admit to it. Not if it meant extra grocery money and one less collector knocking at their door.

Her mother bounded out from the bedroom a moment later, wearing a white-collared shirt under a blue vest with the Walmart emblem stitched in the top corner. '*How may I help you?*' the shirt read.

"Those burgers smell amazing," Anna said, reaching into the fridge and pulling out a can of diet soda.

"One of them is for you," Sabrina said, as she pulled the third burger from the paper sack.

Her mother nodded and took a quick sip of her soda. Then, without responding, she darted back into her bedroom.

On most normal evenings, Sabrina would watch the chaos without involving herself any more than a helping hand, and even that she did cautiously. She'd learned a while ago that it was best to allow her mother's pre-work tornado to run its course without giving it any fuel or obstacles. But tonight she had some big news and she couldn't wait to share it with everyone.

"Are you going to have to time to sit and eat?" she called to her mother, who reemerged carrying a handful of papers.

"I've got to fill this out," she said, her voice sped up and distant. She dropped the papers onto the table but didn't sit down.

Sabrina's father had finished his burger and sat back with his hands in his lap. She looked at him and smiled, hoping to break through his stoic expression, even just slightly. He returned her gesture with a half-smile that ended at his cheeks, but was genuine all the same.

"Tell me about your interview, sweetie," he said, his soft gray eyes like clouds hiding the sun.

Sabrina's chest inflated with a small flurry of the excitement she'd felt earlier that day. She smiled involuntarily.

"It went really well," she said. All at once everything flooded her mind and she didn't even know where to begin. "I've got some exciting news."

"Did you get the job?" her mom asked. Her eyes widened with excitement as she looked up from her papers.

"I did," Sabrina said and nodded affirmatively. "They offered it to me on the spot."

"Honey, that's amazing," Anna said, smiling with motherly pride. "And this is the one that'll..."

"This is the one that'll get me to college," Sabrina finished her sentence for her.

"That's wonderful," her father said, his lips curling into the largest smile she had seen from him in a long time.

"Thanks, Daddy," she said.

"This is the best news I've heard in weeks," Anna said, practically jumping up and down in excitement. "I'm so proud of you, baby girl. And you're sure this job will be able to put you through school? I'm not trying to question your math skills, but I just don't see how three months of work can possibly add up to enough money for four years of school."

"I'll actually end up making more than I need," Sabrina said. "I'll save enough for tuition and have a bit for grocery money on the side. I'll finally be able to put myself through college."

"You're an incredible young woman, Sabrina," her father said. "Seriously, I'm proud of you."

"My daughter will be going to college, huh?" Anna said, looking dreamily toward the ceiling. "Won't that be something?"

"It almost seems too good to be true, but it's all about to become a reality," Sabrina said. "This is the opportunity I've been waiting for."

"What kind of work is it again?" her mother asked.

"I'm a sort of assistant," Sabrina said. "Among other things." It was the best explanation she could offer.

"Other things?" Peter asked. He raised one bushy eyebrow at her.

"Yes. That actually brings me to another thing that I need to tell you about this job." She trailed off and looked to her parents, who returned her stare without speaking. Sabrina gulped a short breath before starting again. "This job means I'm going to have to travel. I'm going to be gone for a while."

She studied her parent's expression, trying to guess a response before they spoke.

"How long?" her father finally asked. His smile had

faded back to his usual defeated demeanor.

"A few months," Sabrina said softly, her eyes meeting his gentle gaze. His nod spoke a thousand words that she knew her father couldn't say.

"Traveling assistant work?" her mother asked, sounding skeptical.

"It's kind of a unique position." Sabrina directed her gaze toward her mom. "I'll be an assistant for someone while they tour the country."

"*Tour the country?*" her mother said, her eyes going wide.

Sabrina nodded. "That's why the pay is so good, Mom. I wouldn't be able to make a quarter of this amount if I stayed in town."

For a few moments, a heavy energy filled the trailer, shrinking the already small space.

"Are you sure it's safe?" Anna asked.

"Yes, Mom," Sabrina assured her. "I made sure everything is on the up and up after the first phone call. One of their references was the chief of police. It's a real job."

"You spoke with the chief of police?" Peter asked, slightly surprised. "That's a pretty good reference."

Silence filled the trailer for a moment as her parents took in her words.

"I realize that this might be a little shocking, but I honestly didn't know it was a traveling position when I applied," Sabrina said, breaking the silence. "I'll miss you guys so much, but I won't be gone too long. Just a few short months."

"We're going to miss you too," her father said, his words potent and sincere. "But you know, as much as I hate to see you leave, I want you to know that I totally support your decision. If I had an opportunity like this, you can bet your butt that I'd be all over it. I think this is a good thing. I'm proud of you for taking the leap and going for it."

"Baby, your father is right." Anna's tone was the softest it had been all evening. Sabrina even noticed her mother's eyes welling up with tears. "This is a great opportunity. I hope that it's not too good to be true, though."

"It's not, Mom. It's real, I promise you." Sabrina smiled. "Police chief, remember?"

"No matter what happens, we'll be here when you get back," Anna said. "If you don't like it, then come home. Our door is always open, you know that."

"I will," Sabrina said. "I definitely will. But I think this will be great. Not just for me, but for all of us. I'll be able to make money that will end up helping us all in the long run."

*I'll make a ton of money,* Sabrina thought. *And I'll get us the hell out of this trailer park.*

"Speaking of money, your father and I have to run to work. Peter?" her mother glanced at the clock as she bundled up the papers in front of her. "You ready?" She tilted her wrist in an attempt to signal the time on her watch.

Her father nodded and began his long process of standing up.

Sabrina's heart grew heavy, drooping in her chest. Too many emotions were crowding her head all at once and she fought to keep them suppressed. While her mother went to fetch a pair of shoes, her father hovered by the table, realizing what neither of them wanted to say. But time was slipping and it pushed Sabrina to speak up.

"So the last thing I wanted to tell you guys is that I'm leaving the day after tomorrow," she said. "With your work schedules, I'm not sure I'll get to see you again before then."

Her father nodded. Before he could respond, Sabrina

smiled at him and launching into his chest for a full bear hug.

"Have a safe trip, Sabrina," Peter whispered, squeezing her tightly. "We're here if you need anything. Anything at all."

Sabrina released him and looked into his eyes.

"Thanks, Dad. I'll call all the time. I promise."

"Do I get a hug?" Anna asked, coming up behind her husband.

"Of course," Sabrina said and pulled her mother close. She was so frail, especially compared to Sabrina's father, and Sabrina almost felt wary about squeezing her too tightly.

Her mother broke the hug and pressed her palms to Sabrina's cheeks, holding her face a short distance from her own before kissing her daughter's forehead. There was a sort of bittersweet flutter in Sabrina's chest. She was excited for the trip, but knew she was going to miss her parents dearly.

After exchanging hugs and goodbyes, her parents left the trailer. Her mom had a tear streaming down her cheek and even Peter's eyes appeared a little bit watery from the occasion. Sabrina watched from the trailer window as the two climbed into the Honda Civic and backed out of the driveway.

Sabrina's eyes fogged and she blinked away the tears before they escaped down her cheek. After a few seconds, a cloud of dust was all that was left in the driveway. Sabrina stared until it cleared. She could never get used to the forced feeling of her parent's disappearance when work came calling.

*But I'm going to change that,* she thought. *This new job is just the beginning. I'm going to do everything in my power to make it so that, one day, my parents won't have to work anymore. I want to give them, and myself, the freedom that we all deserve.*

Thump-thump, *thump-thump-thump.*

She beat the screen door on the neighbor's trailer with the same rhythmic knock she'd been using since her childhood. It was a pattern that hadn't changed in almost twenty years.

The door hinges squeaked as it opened and Aunt Faye stood in the trailer, smiling wide. She was a stout woman whose weight gave way to a particularly jolly laugh. Like most days, she was wearing a cotton dress and shoes that hugged her tiny feet.

She was clearly happy that her goddaughter had paid a visit. It was written all over her face.

"Hey, Bean," Faye said, her English accent formal and friendly at the same time.

"Hey, Aunty," Sabrina said, pulling the older woman in for a hug. The two embraced each other as if it'd been years since they had spoken, even though it had been less than a day.

"I bet you have some news for me," Faye said as they broke from their hug, her eyebrows arching into her gray wispy bangs.

Sabrina grinned.

"Come inside, love," Faye said, stepping back into her trailer. "What are you waiting for?"

Faye's mobile home was just two down from Sabrina's parent's trailer. It was larger in comparison and significantly newer. Because of that, it was also more elaborate and in much better condition. But the contrast wasn't something Sabrina had ever paid much attention to, especially because the place served as her second home. It was a spot where she'd spent countless days, and even nights, as a child, while her parents were away at work.

All of this time brought the two very close and eventually led to the woman earning the title of 'Aunty Faye.' In fact, the only technical relation between them was that Aunt Faye was Sabrina's godmother.

"Well, I suppose you didn't get all dressed up just to see me," Faye said. "Tell me how the interview went."

"It went really well," Sabrina said, taking a seat on a small couch across from the miniature chair where her aunt Faye often sat.

"I knew it would." Faye's eyes sparkled with excitement. They were a unique shade of lavender that Sabrina had never seen anyone else have. "Tell me everything."

"I got the job. I'll be doing assistant duties similar to what I told you about," Sabrina explained. "I'm kind of a trip assistant."

"Trip?" Faye asked, shifting in her seat and frowning slightly.

"It's a travel position," Sabrina said. "I didn't know all of the details when I applied, but I figured there would be a catch. Traveling will be fun, though, I think."

"That sounds like a ball," Faye said, her tone alive with excitement.

"Yeah, it really does," Sabrina said.

"And so who will you assist?" Faye asked "What's this person like?"

Suddenly the image of Marco in his soft linen shirt and glowing skin filled her head.

"He's incredible." The words spilled out before Sabrina could filter a more appropriate response.

Aunt Faye laughed and leaned forward. "Do tell."

"I mean he seems great, at least from what I can tell so far." Sabrina tried again, this time with a little more control. "His name his Marco and he's from some island in the Mediterranean. He's a *very* wealthy person, which I guess is why he needs an assistant. But he's also super genuine. I could tell after only a few minutes of us talking. He's definitely someone I think I'll absolutely love working for."

"That sounds wonderful," Faye said. "And the pay is what you expected? There's no catch besides having to travel?"

"No catch at all. Nothing so far anyway," Sabrina said. "They outlined everything one last time right before I left, including going over the pay one more time. I'll easily make enough to save for tuition."

"Oh, Bean," Faye said, her face melting into a smile of pure happiness. "Look at you."

Sabrina couldn't help but break into a smile of her own.

"I'm so proud of you," Faye said.

"Thanks, Aunty. That really means a lot," Sabrina said, and for the first time she felt her anxious emotions mellow into something controllable. She took a breath and appreciated the momentary peace.

"When do you start on this grand adventure?" Faye asked, settling into a comfortable chair.

"The day after tomorrow is when we leave," Sabrina told her. "But, I'm meeting with his usual assistant to find out how everything is going to work tomorrow. She's going to teach me how to set up what he needs and exactly what my job requirements are. I think for the most part, I'll be the face on the accounts. I'm fairly sure he's some kind of famous, so they don't want his name on anything or for people to be able to discover he's there."

"I'd say this calls for a celebration." Faye reached for the counter beside her and pushed herself up from her chair. "I have just the thing."

Sabrina had a few decent guesses for what could have meant, one of which was confirmed when her aunt returned from her bedroom. She carried a tray with an antique ornate tea set, which she placed gently onto the coffee table between them.

The porcelain tea cups were painted with delicate blue patterns that danced and twisted around each piece. The tea pot itself had a similar pattern, but not exact. It was clear that these designs were hand painted, not just applied in a factory somewhere. The set was beautiful work of art. Sabrina admired it, thinking that it should have been sitting in a museum somewhere instead of on the fiberboard table in front of her.

"I know you've shown me this before," Sabrina said, as she gently lifted one of the cups to get a closer look. "It's been years since I've seen it, though."

"Yes, I only bring it out for special occasions, which don't happen as nearly as often as I'd like," Faye said.

"Tell me more about this tea set, Aunty," Sabrina said. "I don't really know anything about it."

"This set was once one of my favorite possessions," she said. "It's still special to me, but in a different way. It's hard to explain. The one thing that you should know, though, is that it will get passed down to you one day."

It wasn't exactly the explanation Sabrina was hoping for. It was vague and explained nothing about the actual set. Still, Faye was just too sweet to argue with.

"Aw, Aunt Faye," Sabrina hummed, bowing her head to

look closely at the intricate designs. "That's really nice of you. I'll be sure to take care of it, just like you have."

"Just give me one moment and then we can share a nice cup of tea," said Faye, moving to light a burner in the kitchen.

"You *drink* out of this?" Sabrina asked. It felt wrong to use the beautiful cups for anything other than looking at.

"Only on special occasions, like I said. It's not for the everyday." Faye filled a kettle and placed it on the stove.

"Yeah, definitely not," Sabrina said. "I'd be too scared to break it. Where'd you even get this thing?"

"Oh, long ago," Faye said but trailed off. There was a pause that seemed oddly out of place for the current conversation. She returned to her chair in silence with a gaze that looked distant. "Long ago and far away. A life long before this one."

"It's beautiful," Sabrina told her. "I've never seen another tea set like it."

"There was a time when I thought about donating the set," Faye said. "Many times, actually. But there has always been something of me that told me to me keep it. And at this point I'd rather pass it on to my goddaughter."

"I hope it's a long, long time before it gets passed onto me," Sabrina said. "I don't want to be going over your will anytime soon."

"Oh Bean, stop that," she said. "Your Aunty Faye is still kicking just fine. I'm sixty-five years old and haven't even had my mid-life crisis yet. It'll be decades before you'll be able to get rid of me."

"Thanks for bringing it out, Aunty. It really is beautiful."

Just then the kettle screamed and steam pooled into the air above the stove.

"Oh." Faye jumped and prepared to stand up.

"I got it," Sabrina said and stood to retrieve the kettle. She poured the hot water into the tea pot and tossed a couple of tea bags in with it. After a few minutes of letting it steep, Sabrina distributed the tea into two of the cups and carefully handed one to her godmother.

"Thank you, Bean." Faye nodded her head as she accepted the cup and saucer. "And congratulations about the job."

She held her glass up, as if to "Cheers" the occasion. Sabrina did the same.

"Thank you, Faye," Sabrina said. She blew carefully on her tea before taking a sip. "Without your support and advice, I wouldn't have gotten the position."

"Nonsense," Faye said, after taking a small sip of tea. "You did it on your own."

Sabrina didn't say anything. There was no arguing with Faye about subjects like this.

"So I'll bet your parents were happy for you," Faye said, after a few seconds of pause.

"Yeah," Sabrina said blankly. "I mean, I think they were."

"Oh love, don't kid yourself now," Faye scolded. "I know they are."

"You know how it is, though," Sabrina said. "I told them, but we were only able to talk for about twenty minutes before they both had to leave for work."

"Yes. I know how it is." Faye blew gently at the top of her tea. "But you can't ever think that it's because they don't love and support you."

"I know. I would never think that. But it's just..." Sabrina paused to collect herself. "I don't know. I would have loved to have been able to spend some time with them before I leave tomorrow. Something I can think back to while I'm gone for the next few months. I've never been away and I'm honestly afraid I'm going to get homesick."

Sabrina directed her gaze to the cup and saucer in her hand, not wanting to meet Faye's eyes.

"How about this?" Faye said. "How about in all those upcoming moments when you need something to think back to, think about why it is that you wanted the job in the first place. Think about where it's going to lead you. I know you'll miss home and we'll all miss you too. But now is the time when you should focus on where you're going and not where you're from. What you're doing now might just be the thing that gets you and your parents out of this place, which I know is something you've always wanted. Don't let your emotions get in the way of that."

"You're right," said Sabrina. "There's no bigger motivation in the world than how badly I want to get my parents out of here. Out of their trailer, out of this park, out of this life.."

"And that's what makes you so special," Faye said. "There's not a lot of people around here with the gumption to actually do it."

"But I can't do any of that without college."

"One step at a time, love." Faye's voice was gentle but affirmative. "One step at a time."

"I know," Sabrina said. "And this is the first step."

"Yes, it is." Faye nodded and took another sip of tea. She exhaled and brought the cup back down to the saucer in her lap before speaking again. "Listen to me, Bean. You're a special girl. You were made for bigger and better things that you just can't find around here. Your parents have worked hard to raise you as best they could, and they instilled a lot of great qualities in you. And you *yourself* have many tremendous qualities. I saw it from day one. For people like you, the position you started from is not a handicap, but a tool for motivation. You *will* move on from this place and you *will* go on to succeed, but don't forget, it takes time."

Sabrina nodded as she took it all in. Her godmother had a hypnotic quality, the ability to place everything into its proper perspective. It'd always been that way, so much so that Sabrina now associated Faye's London-style accent with feelings of familiar comfort. When Faye spoke from her heart, Sabrina heard words laced with the melody of a well-known song.

Faye's lips smoothed into a warm smile. "You know I'm going to miss you."

"Oh Aunty, don't start that." Sabrina glared at her over her teacup. "I don't know if I can handle many more good-byes right now."

"You can handle a lot. More than you think," Faye said. "Especially one more goodbye for your Aunty. Besides, you *are* my goddaughter. And sometimes you feel like my real daughter."

"*Sometimes?*" Sabrina said, knowing she'd caught Faye on a slip. They both laughed.

"Not a day has passed where I haven't thought of you as one of my own," Faye said. "How about that?"

"Yeah, that's better." Sabrina grinned and took another sip of tea.

It was after nine and completely dark when they finally got around to bidding their final farewell. The time had been spent talking about anything and everything besides her new job and the fact that she'd be leaving town in a matter of hours. And they hadn't talked about Marco either, although Sabrina had bit her tongue several times in order to keep herself from bringing him up.

Sabrina departed and made her way back to her parent's

trailer. It was a stroll she had made more times than she could count.

*I've got to get home and get packed,* she thought.

Then out of nowhere, her father's words flashed into her mind.

*We'll be here when you get back,* he'd said to her, during their conversation that morning.

*Sure you will, Sabrina thought. But you won't be stuck here forever. Not if I can help it.*

# CHAPTER 4

 arco

MARCO SAT in the back of the rented Lincoln Town-car. He was quickly realizing that he was far too tall to be sitting in the back seat.

"Valetta, I thought we rented the biggest car we could find," he said, attempting to stretch his long legs. "I'm cramped back here."

"This is the biggest car they had," Valetta said, as she looked up into the rear view mirror and smirked. She brought her gaze back to the road as she pulled the car off of the highway and into a suburb near downtown Memphis. "Unless we wanted to rent a limousine, but then that would have defeated our efforts of trying to remain inconspicuous."

"Good point," Marco said. "I'm starting to wonder if that would have been a better option, though. I'm not sure how we're all going to fit."

"Now, now," Valetta said. "Neither of us needs the headache of someone realizing that the Prince of Orsino is in the States. Besides, you were the one who wanted to come with me to pick Sabrina up. I was going to send a car so she could meet us at the airport, but you insisted upon this." He grumbled a response but she continued. "Neither of us needs the headache of someone realizing that the Prince of Orsino is in the States," Valetta reminded him. "You don't want that kind of attention and neither do I. Plus isn't that part of the fun? To have a secret trip here?"

"Yes, definitely," he said, as he rolled down the rear window and hung his arm out of it. "I'm just happy I only have to ride in this car for a little while longer."

"An hour at most," she said. "Once we pick up Sabrina, we'll go straight to the airport. You'll never have to set foot in one of these cars again, I promise."

Marco breathed in the air. It was only mid-morning, but it was already hot and humid. As they rode along the highway, his thoughts were focused on the new maid who would be escorting him throughout the United States over the course of the next three months. He felt more nervous with each passing minute, and with each mile, that they got closer to her home.

"We're just about there," Valetta said, glancing up into the rear view mirror once again.

Marco sat up straight and ran his fingers through his shoulder-length black hair. Then he glanced down, making sure his white dress shirt was spotless and without wrinkles. When he looked back out the window, he was shocked by what he saw.

"Where are we?" he asked.

"Sabrina's neighborhood," Valetta said.

Marco was surprised to find himself being driven

through a trailer park. Old trailer homes were scattered along both sides of the road, with hardly twenty feet of open space between each of them. Most had at least two cars parked in front, all of which looked just as dilapidated as the homes they were near.

It reminded Marco of an area on Orsino Island called Devil's Elbow, sometimes referred to simply as 'The Slums'. It was a small peninsula where the lower class population lived. It also housed the highest crime rate on the island and likely the most hatred for the royal family, or at least that was what Magdalena had often told him as a child.

*This is where Sabrina lives?* he thought.

Marco couldn't believe that the beautiful woman he had interviewed the day before lived in a place as rough-looking as the trailer park. He had imagined her living in a nice high-rise downtown or at least a large house in a suburban cul-de-sac.

*A woman of her beauty can't live here,* he thought. *It just doesn't make any sense.*

"Are you sure we're in the right place?" he asked.

"Yes," Valetta said, now focused as she maneuvered the car down the dilapidated road. "This is the address Sabrina gave us."

She drove all the way to the end of the road and pulled the car up to a small brown trailer on the right. Outside of the home was a beat up old Honda parked out front. The vehicle looked like it used to be white, but now it was more rust-colored than anything else.

Marco frowned as he took in the view.

*This isn't where a girl like Sabrina belongs. She should be soaking up the sun on a beach somewhere. She should be shopping in nice stores, buying fancy purses and shoes, getting her hair done any way she wants. No girl could feel beautiful in a place like this. This doesn't seem fair.*

"Well, this is it," Valetta said.

Marco nodded and reached for the door handle to step outside.

"Hold on." Valetta stopped him. "Let me go get her. We're already conspicuous enough being in this neighborhood in this nice of a vehicle. Someone will surely recognize you if you get out. God knows the neighbors are peeking out of the windows as we speak. Let me run up and get Sabrina. You wait right here."

"Good point," Marco said with a nod. "I'll sit tight."

From the back seat, Marco watched as Valetta walked up to the front door of the trailer home. She looked remarkably out of place in her designer shoes as she walked up the well worn path. She knocked a few times and a moment later, the door opened up. Sabrina stood in the doorway with a smile on her face.

Sabrina followed Valetta out to the car. She carried a large black suitcase in her right hand and had a giant gray duffel bag slung over her left shoulder. She walked with eagerness and had a cute spring to her step that made Marco smile. Valetta took Sabrina's luggage and put it in the trunk, then opened the rear door of the car for her.

"Good morning," Marco said, smiling.

"Good morning, sir," Sabrina replied cheerfully.

"No, no, please, Sabrina. Call me Marco," he said, as he motioned for Sabrina to take a seat. "We're going to be spending a fair amount of time together over the next couple of months. No need for formalities."

"Okay, sounds good," she said, as she scooted onto the seat and buckled her seat belt.

Marco watched as Sabrina fidgeted in her seat, unable to

sit still as they pulled out of her neighborhood. He could tell she was nervous, but he hoped that she'd relax a bit once they were on the plane.

"Are you okay?" he asked. His eyes were locked onto Sabrina as he spoke. The tingling feeling of attraction filled his chest as her face lit up, hanging onto every one of his words.

"Yes, I'm fine," she said, tapping her fingers onto the top of her knees. "Just excited about all of this. I'm really looking forward to seeing New York."

"Have you been before?"

"No, never," she replied. "I've wanted to for so long, but never had the chance."

"Well, that's one thing we have in common," he said. "I've seen pictures, but that's about all."

Sabrina smiled and then brought her gaze out of the car window, watching as the trailer homes passed by. Marco wanted to ask her more about her life, but didn't want to come on too strong. He was curious about her, though, and looked forward to getting to know her.

*I'll have plenty of time to ask more questions on the flight to New York,* he thought.

"THIS IS *YOUR* PLANE?" Sabrina asked, as they boarded the small jet that was parked on a private runway near the airport.

"Kind of," Marco said, as he led the group onto the plane. "I'm able to use it right now, so it's as good as mine."

"I've never even seen a private jet before," she said, looking around the plane with the awe of a young child. "To be honest, I've never actually been on any plane."

The pilot greeted Marco and they shook hands, while Sabrina and Valetta continued on toward the back of the jet.

"The weather is looking excellent today, so it should make for a smooth flight to New York City," the pilot informed him. "Shouldn't take but a few hours."

"Perfect," Marco said. "How long until we take off?"

"Ten minutes. If all of your party is here, we can start taxiing to the runway now."

Marco nodded and turned down the aisle leading away from the cockpit. The cabin of the plane was small to his eyes. He was used to his private jet back home, but he was assured this plane could comfortably sleep ten. He wasn't so sure it would be comfortable, but as this was the best way to keep a low profile, it would work well enough. Besides, the flight would be relatively short.

Valetta had taken her seat in the very back row. She already had her sleeping mask over her eyes and her headphones on. She had been on countless flights with Marco and often used the opportunity to catch up on sleep. Sabrina, however, was still up and moving around. She had just handed off her luggage to the tall, brunette stewardess who worked for Marco's pilot and was standing in the aisle when Marco approached.

"Where should I sit?" she asked.

"Sit next to me," Marco offered, as he plopped down in a chair in the very front row.

Sabrina sat next to him and buckled her seat belt. Marco did the same and a few seconds later, the plane lurched forward, taxiing down the runway. She clutched at the arm rail in surprise.

"I'm really glad you decided to take this job," Marco said in an attempt to distract her so she wouldn't be afraid of flying for the first time.

"I'm so happy you offered it to me," she said, twirling her auburn hair between her fingers. She smiled at him, her blue eyes glowing in the fluorescent lights of the plane. "It's already the coolest job I've ever had. I can't believe I'm on a private jet right now."

Sabrina's expression of innocent wonder said it all. It was utterly clear to Marco that he had just transported her into a world completely different from her own. And he loved it. He took great joy in the fact that he could treat such a beautiful woman to a piece of the life to which he was accustomed.

"So tell me a little bit about yourself," Marco said, eager to learn everything he could about his new hire.

"I don't have anything exciting to tell," she said, with a frown.

"Nonsense. I don't believe that for a second. Tell me where you were raised. Tell me something about your childhood. Anything. If we're going to be spending time together over the next couple of weeks, I want to know who it is that I'm spending time with."

"I'm honestly not sure what to tell you that I didn't say in the interview," Sabrina said.

"Okay, well, why don't you tell me why you wanted to take this job?" Marco asked. "It's an unusual position, no doubt. I can't imagine there are a lot of job openings for a traveling assistant. What about it intrigued you?"

"It seemed like a job that I would be good at and when I saw the pay, I knew that I had to try," she said. "I really didn't think I'd get it. I figured that there would be a line out of the door with people trying to get the position."

"Many did apply, but I knew you were the one," Marco said, with a satisfied smile. "So that's it, though? You just thought it looked like a good job? Nothing else about it called to you?"

"I need to save up as much money as I can before the summer is over," she said, bashfully. "And with the amount you're paying me, I should be able to save enough."

"Enough for what?" Marco asked.

Sabrina's cheeks turned a little red. Marco was beginning to notice her shyness.

"I'm trying to save up for college," she explained. "I know that's what a lot of girls say they are doing, but I really am. I want to go to school and get a degree. You know, make something of myself."

Marco listened intently as she spoke. His eyes lit up when she mentioned college. He had often wondered what a formalized education in the States would be like, since his only experience with it had been through movies and stories from friends. His own education had been completely taken care of in Orsino.

"I think that's wonderful," he said. "Do you know what you want to study?"

"English," she stated, clear as day. "I'd like to teach English to people looking to become United States citizens. I love helping others and if I could get paid doing that, then I'd be happy as a clam."

"I think you'd make a great teacher," Marco said.

"You really think so?" she asked.

"I do," he said. "You're relaxed and you seem patient. I think most other teachers would hear my accent and eat me alive."

Sabrina laughed and brought her hand down onto Marco's knee. As soon as she realized what she had done, she quickly pulled away.

"Sorry," she muttered.

Her touch made Marco smile. There was an obvious connection between them and he could feel it. If Sabrina had been any other girl, he'd have jumped on the opportunity to increase his flirtation with the intention of getting her in the sack. But Sabrina *wasn't* just any girl, and Marco didn't want to treat her as such. So instead, he just relaxed and decided to let things between them play out naturally, without his interference.

After a few moments of silence, Sabrina spoke again. "So what do you do for work, Marco?"

"I'm the..." Marco began, then stopped himself. He'd nearly told her who he was without thinking.

Her brows raised as she awaited his response. He'd nearly let the words "Crown Prince of Orsino Island" slide off his tongue. He'd manage to stop mid-sentence, but Sabrina was still sitting there, waiting for an answer to her question. It had felt so right to just tell her the truth that it was difficult to come up with an answer now. Marco wished that he could tell her who he really was, but he was still a little bit cautious. Sabrina was nearly a stranger to him and for now, the less she knew, the better.

"I'm the... luckiest man alive," he said.

"Lucky?"

"Yes, well, I just happened to be born into a fortunate situation," he said. "I'd call that pretty lucky."

The explanation was vague as hell, but at least he wasn't lying.

"The luckiest man alive." Sabrina repeated the words quietly, her eyes still focused on Marco. She blushed and looked down. "I feel like maybe I pried by asking. I'm sorry, Marco. I was just letting the conversation flow. I didn't mean to offend you. You don't have to tell me what you do."

"You absolutely *did not* offend me." Marco assured her.

"In fact, I'm glad you have an interest in what I do. I wish I could explain more about who I am, but I can't right now. It's kind of a complicated situation."

She nodded in response, but Marco knew that his half-assed explanation would only make her more curious.

*Now she's probably going to think I'm a leader of some drug cartel or something,* he thought.

Once again, he had the urge to just tell her, but he ignored it. There was too much risk in it. For all he knew, Sabrina could be an undercover journalist.

"Anyway," Marco said, trying to shatter the awkward silence. "Tell me more about you. Were you raised in the same area where we picked you up this morning?"

Sabrina blushed and looked straight ahead. She seemed so embarrassed by the question.

"Yes," she said. "My parents have lived there for my entire life. I know that it's a dump. The entire area is pretty bad, but it's all that they can afford. My parents are good people, though. You'll never meet people who work harder or have bigger hearts than they do."

"I'm sure they're great people," Marco said. "They'd have to be, to raise someone like yourself."

"That's nice of you to say," she said with a slight blush.

Marco beamed, pleasantly surprised to see that Sabrina accepted his compliment.

"What do your parents do for work?" Marco asked.

"My dad used to work at a factory, where he assembled air conditioning units for cars," she said. "He got laid off last month, though, so he's looking for a new job right now. My mom is a substitute schoolteacher and works retail for extra money whenever she can. She works all the time now, just to try to make ends meet. There are weeks when she'll put in eighty hours. Dad was in an accident a few years ago, so medical bills tend to eat up most of our money. Finances became even more stressful since my dad lost his job."

Marco frowned as he listened. There was so much history and so much pain behind Sabrina's eyes as she told the story of her parents. He knew that there was no possibility that he could ever relate to such a struggle, so he just listened.

"They sound like they're trying to make your life better," he said. "I can respect that."

"They really would do anything," Sabrina said. "But they're getting older and now it's my turn to try to repay them for everything they've ever done for me. That's why I want to go to college and give myself, and my parents, a life that we've never had."

"And a few minutes ago you said that you didn't have anything interesting to tell me about your life," Marco said. "I think you just told me a fantastically interesting thing."

The sound of the jet engines powering up temporarily filled the plane, interrupting their conversation. Sabrina paled slightly, but put on a brave face for her first flight.

"Good afternoon, everyone. This is your captain speaking. We're all set for takeoff. Please remain seated and buckled until our wonderful stewardess, Alyssa, tells you that it's okay to move around."

Moments later, the plane took off down the runway and lifted into the air. Neither Sabrina nor Marco spoke during takeoff, but it was mostly because Sabrina's gaze was fixated out of the window.

"What are you looking at?" Marco asked.

"Just wanted to catch one last glimpse of my home town before this adventure begins," she said. "I wonder if my dad is looking up right now and seeing us fly off. Wouldn't that be cool?"

"You never know. Maybe he is," Marco said.

A plane that small gained elevation quickly and before they knew it, Alyssa was pushing the steel drink cart down the aisle toward them. "What can I get you two to drink?"

Marco looked to Sabrina. "What would you like?"

"I'll just have a tomato juice," she said.

As Alyssa opened up a can of tomato juice for Sabrina, she brought her gaze to Marco. "And for you, sir?"

"A dirty martini, with extra olive juice and three olives," he replied. It was his usual drink.

She expertly made his drink before taking her cart back into the galley to give them their privacy. Valetta was already snoring softly in her seat.

"Cheers," Marco said, holding up his martini.

The olives swirled in his glass, spiraling clockwise in the center of the drink.

"What are we drinking to?" Sabrina asked.

"To my beautiful new employee, and to the amazing experiences that both of us will have over the next couple of months," Marco said.

"I like that," she said. "Cheers."

Marco clinked his glass against Sabrina's tomato juice can and they both took a sip.

"Go slow with that tomato juice," Marco said. "I don't want you getting too crazy on your first day of work."

Sabrina chuckled and took another sip. "I know, this stuff goes straight to my head. It's more powerful than gin or vodka. One of these and you'd be dancing all over this plane in no time."

They both shared a laugh.

"Just so you know, Sabrina, you're welcome to have an alcoholic drink whenever you like," he said.

"But I'm technically working right now," she said.

"This is true," he said. "But I certainly don't mind it if you feel like cutting loose once in a while. Just want you to know, in case the opportunity arises while we're in New York City."

"I'll keep that in mind," she said. "Thank you, Marco."

Marco took another sip from his martini and then leaned back in his seat. He felt great about how the conversation was going with his beautiful new hire. She was absolutely perfect for the position. She was easy on the eyes, sweet beyond belief and seemed to also carry a sense of humor. There was nothing that Marco didn't adore about her. But that fact concerned him as much as it excited him. He worried that he would have trouble keeping secrets from her, especially knowing that they would likely become closer over the next couple of months.

"Sabrina," he said, in a relaxed voice.

"Yes," she replied, turning to face him.

"I just want to say thank you for taking this job," he said. "I've got a really good feeling about this."

"I've got a good feeling, too," she said. She grinned. "It's already better than I could have imagined."

"I want to apologize again for not being able to be completely open with you about who I am and what I do for a living," he said. "I feel terrible about it."

"No need to feel bad," she said. "I understand. And besides, it doesn't matter what you do. I'm here to make sure your needs are being met that's all. Anything else you wish to share with me is completely up to you."

Marco nodded and relaxed into his seat once more.

"Thank you for your understanding," he said. "Truly, it's appreciated."

*I don't even know her, so why am I having to fight this powerful urge to open up to her? I haven't felt this in a long time, and certainly not for someone who is basically a stranger. There's something special about Sabrina, there's no denying that. I can't tell her everything about who I am, but I'll be as honest as I possibly can without giving away too much personal information. That's the best I can do. I want this girl. I want her bad. I just hope that keeping my royal blood a secret from her doesn't somehow screw things up between us,* he thought.

# CHAPTER 5

*abrina*

SABRINA'S FACE was practically plastered to the small window of the plane. She watched with absolute wonder as they descended into New York. For her, it was as if they were about to land upon a newly discovered city, something reserved for daydreams and fairy tales. The downtown city of Memphis paled in comparison to New York's skyscrapers that reached like modern-day castles into the sky. A fraction of New York could swallow all of Memphis, Sabrina thought, and she had never felt so tiny.

After a smooth descent, Marco's plane landed on a small, private runway at John F. Kennedy International Airport. This put his private jet was out of the way of the big commercial airliners landing nearby. Once the pilot had stopped the aircraft, they all exited directly onto the runway's pavement where their driver would pick them up.

A gust of wind was the first thing to greet Sabrina when

the door opened. It caught her hair and whisked it chaotically as she climbed down the jet's attached staircase. Marco and Valetta were close behind.

"This is where I leave you two," Valetta said, stopping and standing at the foot of the staircase with a hand still rested on its railing. "I believe that's the driver right there." She was forced to shout against the wind, pointing into the distance at a black Cadillac sedan approaching on the runway.

Marco pulled his baseball cap down onto his head and slipped his sunglasses on. It was his attempt to look like an average tourist. He replied to Valetta with a thumbs up and Sabrina felt compelled to give her a hug and offer a sincere thank-you, but Valetta waved quickly before turning and beginning her ascent back into the jet.

The driver pulled up to Marco and Sabrina. He lowered the passenger window and gave a business-like nod. He was a middle-eastern man in a black suit and white dress shirt. His sport coat was buttoned over his crisp black tie and Sabrina could smell his cologne even though she was standing outside of the car.

"Good afternoon," Marco greeted him.

"Good afternoon, sir," the driver said. He hopped out of the car and opened the trunk. Then he took Sabrina and Marco's luggage and placed it gently inside, before returning to the driver's seat.

"Do you want to take shotgun, Marco?" Sabrina asked.

"Shotgun?" he replied, with a confused expression.

Sabrina giggled. "Yeah, sorry. I hadn't considered the fact that you've probably never heard that phrase. It means the front seat of the car. Do you want to ride in front?"

"No, no," Marco said, as he opened the real door for Sabrina. "I'm happy to ride in the back with you."

Sabrina nodded and climbed inside, followed closely by Marco.

"We appreciate the ride," Sabrina told the driver as she buckled up. "Do you know where you're headed? I really hope so because this is our first time here. I wouldn't even know where to start."

"Yes, ma'am," the driver replied, as he brought his gaze up to the rear view mirror. He looked at Sabrina. "Your travel agent, Valetta, told me where you were staying when she called this morning. I know this city like the back of my hand. I'll get you there, no problem."

"But sir, before we go to the hotel, can you take us somewhere nice to eat?" Marco asked. He tucked his sunglasses into his pocket and put his hat in his lap.

"Of course, sir," he said. "Where would you like to go?"

"I'm afraid I don't know the city," Marco admitted." Any recommendations?"

"Do you like Italian food?" the driver asked, as he pulled onto the main street that led into the heart of the city.

"I love Italian food," Marco said, turning to face Sabrina. "How does that sound to you, Sabrina?"

She'd been too excited and overwhelmed to even think about how hungry she was. But since he'd mentioned it, she noticed a rumbling in her belly. To be honest, she couldn't remember the last time she'd eaten other than her tomato juice, which didn't really count as a meal.

"Italian sounds perfect," she said with a smile.

"I know a great little spot," the driver said. "I'll take you two there. It's just a few minutes away."

The driver stepped on the gas. He zipped through the city with a controlled urgency that impressed Sabrina at every turn. The way the driver wove in and out of lanes and between cars made her think he was avoiding a hundred invisible obstacles between every block. Her gaze darted between his hand viciously jerking the stick shift and the passing scenery out the window, sights that Sabrina had only ever seen in movies.

*I can't believe I'm actually in New York City,* she thought.

She rolled down the window and stuck her head out, looking straight up to try to see the tops of the high rise towers. She'd of course seen pictures, but being there was completely different. When she brought her gaze back down, she noticed the crowds of people on the sidewalks, all busily moving forward, as though every one of them was about to be late for something very important.

*I don't think anybody walks that fast where I'm from,* she thought. *I wonder where they're all going. Probably someplace fashionable and incredibly New York.*

But it wasn't just the people who were looking busy. The traffic on the street was just as chaotic and everyone drove with an aggressive sense of urgency that she wasn't used to. Still, though, the intense energy excited her. She could feel it buzzing throughout everything, like electricity. She could understand now why it was called the city that never sleeps. It felt new and different. And even though she had only been there a few minutes, she was positive that she was going to have a great time over the next couple of weeks.

While she took in the city's features, Marco made casual conversation with the driver, their accents intertwining into a musical conversation. At first, Sabrina listened in on bits and pieces, but as it didn't pertain to her, she began to tune out and just enjoy the scenery.

*This is going to be the best trip ever,* she thought. *I wish my parents could see what I'm seeing right now.*

They drove for fifteen minutes before the driver pulled the car out from the heavy traffic and pulled to an abrupt stop beside the curb. Without a word, the driver flung open his door and walked around to the right side of the car to open Marco's door. Marco stepped out and then turned and offered his hand to Sabrina. His touch made her heart speed up for a moment.

"Thank you, Marco," she said. "But isn't helping you *my* job?"

He chuckled. "We can take turns being the gentleman," he said and shot a sideways grin back at her.

She squeezed his hand as he helped her out of the car. She couldn't believe how wonderful Marco was. She didn't feel like an employee when she was with him. Even as her boss, he still treated her more like a princess than anybody ever had.

Once Sabrina was standing, Marco released her hand and then pulled out some cash to give the driver. Meanwhile, Sabrina smiled and soaked up the experience surrounding her. There were horns honking, people talking and the sound of feet scurrying against the concrete. She drew in a breath, letting the smell of at least five different kinds of food enter her nose. She was overwhelmed, but in a good way. It made her feel alive.

"Shall we go see if we can get ourselves a table?" Marco asked, as he gestured toward the building in front of where they'd stopped.

It was a quaint little yellow building, with a small sign over the top that read *Voir*. On either side of it were massive high-rise towers. It looked like the kind of place that had been there forever and had refused to leave, even when the major construction came along.

Sabrina took a step before saying, "Wait, should we get our bags out of the car before we go in?"

"Oh, no. I asked the driver to wait for us while we eat,"

Marco said, as he slipped on his hat and sunglasses back on to try to disguise himself. "Don't worry. Our luggage will be safe."

Sabrina walked into the restaurant, with Marco right behind her. She greeted the hostess and requested a table for two, preferably something near the back. They were seated at a small table in the far corner. It was the perfect spot, with enough privacy so that Marco could comfortably remove his sunglasses without having to worry about being recognized.

While the waitress ran through the lunch specials, Sabrina's eyes wandered about the restaurant's breathtaking interior. Colorful modern art was hung on every wall, and standing randomly throughout the restaurant were welded metal sculptures of different animals. She raised her eyes, admiring the details of the ceiling. Everything was painted white, reflecting the shine from the lights on the wall and illuminating the restaurant under one glow.

"This place is incredible," Sabrina said. "The outside of this building doesn't do the inside any justice at all."

The waitress chuckled. "I hear that a lot. It's kind of surprising for people when they walk inside. The owner has talked about remodeling the exterior, but somehow he always gets talked out of it."

"It's beautiful," Sabrina whispered, finally bringing her attention back.

For the first time since landing in New York, Marco removed the hat and sunglasses he'd been wearing. He'd looked cute in his attempted costume, Sabrina thought, with his tightly fitted cap and reflective blue Ray-Bans. Still, she couldn't deny it was refreshing to see his undisguised face again, especially with the way the restaurant's lighting seemed to highlight his every feature.

"I'll give you two a chance to look over the menu while I go get some water. I'll be back shortly," said the waitress, her voice high-pitched but pleasant.

"Perfect," Marco said, running his hand through his hair to tousle it out of the matted appearance leftover from his hat. The gesture made Sabrina's heart skip and she quickly glanced away.

"Thank you for joining me for lunch." He leaned in as he spoke and Sabrina felt the room shrink around her until it was just the two of them.

"I've gotta say, you have an odd way of speaking to your employees," Sabrina said. "I imagined much more of a, *fetch me a table for lunch, and be quick with it,*' kind of deal."

"What would be the fun in that?" Marco said. "This is much more pleasant."

Sabrina's heart skipped again and stuck high in her chest.

"I didn't know I was getting paid to be your company, though," Sabrina said, playfully. "I must have missed that in the job description."

"You must have. You should read a little more closely next time." Marco smirked at her, his dark eyes were lit up and gleaming.

"I'll make sure to study the fine print moving forward," Sabrina said, giggling. "Per Valetta's instructions, I am going to check us in under my name using the credit card Valetta gave me earlier. Everything is set up and ready to go."

"What about housekeeping?" Marco asked.

"I'm going to take care of everything," Sabrina said. "I'll be the one cleaning the room so that the housekeeping staff won't have access. Valetta said the last time hotel staff cleaned your room, the maids auctioned off some of your clothing, so I won't let that happen."

It wasn't the first time that Sabrina wondered exactly who her employer was, but she was determined to hold up her contract. She wouldn't look him up and she wouldn't pry. Her payment depended on it. When this was all over, she would find out everything and be amazed. Until then, she was keeping her curiosity in check as best as she could and purposefully staying away from the search feature on her phone.

"Sounds like you're on top of everything," Marco said. His smile lit up his face and she felt her heart skip a beat when he looked at her. "Thank you for doing such a good job. Out of curiosity, are you staying in a different room or are there two beds in mine? Just wondering how you arranged your own stay."

"I'll be in the adjacent room," she said. She hoped he didn't notice the blush starting to heat her cheeks.

While she spoke, Sabrina pulled a small notebook out of her purse. Valetta had made her a list of tasks for each day, and for the entire week. Everything was organized, including check-in times on hotels and pick-up times for transportation.

Marco laughed when he saw the notepad. "What do you need notes for? Did you forget to tell me that you're really just an undercover journalist or something?"

"You caught me." Sabrina shrugged dramatically. "They're actually from Valetta. She says the most interesting things about how you want your socks folded." She tried to replicate the smirk he'd shot at her.

Again he chuckled. "I bet there's nothing in there about that."

She flipped through the book and held open a page. "Client prefers socks to be folded lengthwise with minimal wrinkling before being paired," she read aloud. "Valetta was incredibly thorough. You should see what she says I should do for meals."

Marco laughed again. It made Sabrina smile without even thinking and she found herself hoping he'd do it again.

"How about instead of worrying about all that, you try to enjoy yourself? I want you to have some fun on this trip as well," Marco said, as he unfolded a cloth napkin and placed it in his lap. "If you do that, I'm sure your other duties will fit in naturally."

"I *am* enjoying myself," Sabrina said.

"Good. Then what would you be interested in doing tonight?" he asked.

"What do *you* think we should do tonight?" Sabrina said. "It's your vacation, Marco. I'm just here to make sure it goes smoothly."

"What if I'd like to take you out to see the city?" He crossed his arms and leaned back. "It's more fun to explore a city with someone than by myself."

"Are you sure?" Sabrina asked, hesitant. "I'm just your employee."

"Yes," he agreed. "But right now, you are the only person I know in this city. I'm supposed to meet some friends here later this week, but they aren't here yet. I'm enjoying your company, but if you'd rather stay in the hotel alone all night, that's fine too."

Sabrina wasn't quite sure what to say. She was definitely enjoying her time with Marco, but she didn't want to intrude upon his vacation. His flirting on the plane was charming, but she'd assumed it to be in-flight boredom, nothing to read into. Though now that they'd landed nothing in his tone had changed.

"You're sure?" she asked. "This is your vacation, not mine."

"I'm sure," he assured her. "I enjoy your company."

"I'm up for anything, I think," she said, scrambling for a response. His charisma had taken her somewhat out of her comfort zone. It would have been easier to reply with, 'yes sir,' 'no sir,' but this was some sort of gray area between flirting and working. It was uncharted territory and Sabrina was still learning exactly how to navigate. But, he was the boss, so she would adapt.

"Would it make you feel better if I officially added it to your job description?" he asked. His dark eyes sparkled as he grinned at her.

"Add what, specifically?" she asked confused.

"From now on you're my assistant/maid/tour guide/company for the trip." He extended his hand for a shake. "Do you accept the position?"

Sabrina laughed. "Only if it's official."

"Of course," Marco assured her. "I'll have the paperwork drawn up right away. You are to be my company when agreeable."

"That does lead me to ask one question. Since it's official and all now." She grinned at him. "Does that mean I get a raise?"

Marco threw back his head and laughed.

# CHAPTER 6

"Reservation for Sabrina Wise." It was her first time ever checking into a hotel, but Valetta had instructed her exactly what to say. Still, Sabrina felt nervous, but she was determined not to show it.

"Certainly, Ms. Wise." The hotel receptionist's fingers tapped rapidly on the keyboard in front of her. "I see here that you have reserved our suite, as well as an adjoining room. Is that correct?"

"Yes, that's right," Sabrina replied.

There was another flurry of keyboard tapping behind the desk. "How many room keys would you like?"

"Just two will be fine," Sabrina said, stumbling slightly. "Or, one for each room, I guess."

The girl behind the table nodded.

After paying with the credit card Valetta had given her, Sabrina turned around to admire the rest of the lobby. It was immensely grand and spectacular, looking more like the inside of a castle than a hotel. From the ceiling hung an elaborate chandelier that reflected brilliantly off the marble floors. At one end was a massive staircase, covered in red velvet carpet. On the opposite side, was a fifteen-foot-tall fountain. It was made of white stone that spiraled upward toward the ceiling. Next to it were three large windows, covered by heavy drapes. Beneath those windows was a lounge area with plush chairs and a few glass tables. That was where Marco was seated. His sunglasses were on and he looked as relaxed as could be. His legs were crossed and his head was leaning back into the cushion behind him.

"All set?" he asked, as Sabrina closed in.

"Yep. Everything's ready to go."

The two of them made their way to the elevator. Their luggage was being brought in from the car and would be brought up by the bellhop. Sabrina had the cash in her pocket ready to tip him so that he would never see Marco.

"We're on the fifteenth floor," Sabrina said, as the elevator doors opened.

They rode up in silence. Sabrina stared forward, but she could have sworn that Marco was looking at her. She liked it, but she didn't want to acknowledge it. Instead, she just kept her gaze straight ahead on the ascending elevator numbers.

"After you," Marco said when the doors opened once again and the elevator chimed to signal the fifteenth floor. "Seriously, though, Sabrina. I wasn't joking at lunch when I said I needed your help. I need you to brainstorm something fun for us to do this evening."

"Can you give me an idea of what you'd enjoy?" Sabrina asked. She checked the numbers above the hotel doors and pointed down the hallway.

"I'd be interested in anything that involves relaxation, good alcohol and proper entertainment. The one thing that is not an option tonight is staying in and doing nothing." His eyebrows playfully arched when Sabrina didn't respond.

Sabrina wanted a chance to exhale, settle in and unpack, but it was her job to cater to Marco and escort him wherever he wanted to go.

"I'll try my best to think of something," she promised. She pointed to a door. "This one is your room."

She held out a key card which Marco snatched from her hand as if he were stealing candy from a sibling. He slid it into the door before pushing it open.

"Start thinking," he advised and opened the door to his suite and went inside.

Sabrina shook her head and went to the next door and slid her key card in just as she'd seen Marco do for his. Inside, the room was cool and comfortable with a soft light coming from the window.

The windows were draped with pale curtains that let in a comfortable light. She stepped in and let the heavy door swing shut behind her.

*Oh, my God,* she thought, as she looked around.

The lights revealed a hotel suite that was twice the size of the trailer she'd grown up in. She gasped and walked straight to the curtains at the far end, letting her fingers dance over the expensive-looking furniture as she moved. Everything looked brand new. Even the carpet, though light in color, was plush and looked as if it had never been walked on.

Sabrina pulled back the thin curtains to the heavier ones on the side to look out the window. Never before had she been so high up in a building and it took a moment for her to convince herself that it was all real and not one big daydream. Her eyes perused the landscape and stopped when they came upon the Statue of Liberty standing tall in the bay.

*Unbelievable,* she thought, shaking her head in wonder. It was like something out of a movie.

Sabrina stared out the window for another several minutes before finally drifting to the bed. She collapsed face first into the comforter, enjoying the delightful fluffiness before immediately standing back up.

*No time to relax. I should get unpacked and start trying to figure out something fun to do tonight,* she thought.

She wondered when the bellhop would arrive when the phone on the nightstand rang. It was loud as could be and caused her to jump.

*Who could that be?* She thought, picking up the receiver.

"Hello?"

"Hello, Ms. Wise," a man said theatrically.

Sabrina quickly recognized the voice. It was Marco.

"Are you finding all of your amenities to be in order?" he asked, mocking an overly formal tone.

"Everything is incredible," Sabrina replied, sounding a bit more awestruck than she'd intended.

"I'm very glad to hear it, love," Marco said, his voice dropping back to its normal pitch. "I don't know if you've had the television on at all, but I just saw my third commercial for the Yankees / Red Sox game this evening."

Sabrina hadn't even thought about turning on the TV yet. She'd been much too captivated by the show on display out her window.

"I'd like to attend this event," Marco said after a short beat.

"You want to go to the game?" Sabrina asked.

"Yes. This evening, I'd like us to attend." he said. "It

appears that it must be a rather important game. Or at least that's how it has been advertised. It's certainly something for us to do."

"I think there's a pretty big rivalry between those two teams," Sabrina said. "Are you a baseball fan?"

"No, not exactly," he admitted. "Are you?"

"My dad is. We root for the Atlanta Braves, and he watches the games on TV on his days off," Sabrina replied. "Do you have a favorite team?"

"We don't have professional baseball where I'm from," he explained. "But everyone knows about the Yankees. And we're in New York. Let's go to a game together."

"The only problem, is that if the game is tonight there's a good chance they might be sold out of tickets already," Sabrina said. "It's probably been sold out for months."

"It won't be a problem for Valetta," he assured her as if it were the most casual thing in the world to get last minute tickets to a sold-out game. "Will you go with me?"

"I'd love to." The words seemed to fly out from her chest instead of her mouth.

"Good, I'm delighted to hear it. It makes me happy that my maid/assistant/tour guide/*company* for the trip will join me on this little adventure," Marco said and Sabrina loved the way he'd stressed the last title in the list.

MARCO'S personal driver pulled up and stopped the vehicle in front of the stadium. As soon as the car stopped, Sabrina and Marco hopped out quickly, as if their exit were being timed. Marco pulled the brim of his plain cap down and put on his sunglasses.

Their ride drove off, and the two of them joined one of

many lines of people being filtered into the stadium. The massive crowds reminded Sabrina of ants funneling into a colony. She felt glad to have Marco by her side and never allowed herself to get beyond an arm's reach away.

Valetta had secured two club-level seats just to the right of home plate. From what she could figure, these were very good seats.

*I guess a lot of money makes most things possible,* she thought.

When the elevator opened on the club level, Marco stepped out and began walking as if he'd been there a thousand times. His type of confidence wasn't conceited, but more of a levelheaded certainty, something that Sabrina found especially alluring.

Without warning he stopped abruptly and Sabrina nearly crashed into him from behind.

"I should buy a hat." He turned to face her as the two stood to the side of a merchandise concession stand. "I'd like to wear a proper Yankees hat instead of this thing." He removed the Polo hat he'd worn since their arrival in New York and Sabrina got another much appreciated sight of his hair ruffled into a perfect tangle.

"Which one do you like?" Sabrina asked, looking up and down at the various ball caps and other baseball paraphernalia.

"That black one," he said, pointing to a cap in the top corner of the stand. Sabrina nodded and marched up to the stand.

"Excuse me," she said, more assertively than she'd ever sounded before. "I'd like to purchase that hat."

The man behind the counter grabbed it for her and she paid using her company credit card. The man cut off the tags for her before going to the next customer. It was a good thing Marco was rich because this stuff was expensive.

She turned around to see that Marco's grinning at her. She handed him the hat.

"Thank you," he said, and fixed the hat firmly on his head. "How does it look?"

"Looking a little more American," Sabrina replied with a grin.

*But still just as handsome*, she thought to herself.

Marco bowed his head and laughed. "I'll take what I can get," he said.

"All you need now is an American Flag t-shirt and you'll be good to go," Sabrina said, jokingly. "Or maybe one of those 'I Heart New York' ones.

Marco laughed and led them into the box where their seats were located. As soon as they stepped inside, her jaw hit the floor. It was better than anything she'd ever seen on TV. The view of the field was even more incredible than she could have ever imagined. It was breathtaking and caused her to simply stare out across the stadium without saying a word.

After a minute of silence, Sabrina looked up and realized that Marco was also lost in a trance.

"This is crazy," she said. For a moment, she felt like she should pinch herself to make sure she wasn't dreaming.

Marco lifted his stare from the field and looked over to Sabrina.

"Do you like it?" he asked.

"I think it's beautiful," she whispered. She wished her dad could see this. It would be a dream come true for him, even if it was a Yankees' game and not his beloved Braves. No baseball fan could sit in this spot and not be awed.

Their seats were behind a thin table at the front of the

club box, which opened into the evening air. The grass below them was so green and vibrantly alive that it looked almost neon. It was gleaming from the stadium lights that were bright stars against the dimming sky.

"I've never seen anything quite like this," Sabrina said, after a moment. Her eyes were still scanning the view in front of them as she spoke.

"You've never attended a baseball game?" Marco asked, seeming quite surprised.

"Never," Sabrina said.

She thought back to the games that her dad used to watch late at night on their miniature TV. Occasionally as a kid, Sabrina would join him and watch until she faded into boredom. *They're better in person,* her father would always say, and he was right.

"Another first-time experience for both of us," Marco said, using his elbow to gently nudge her arm.

Sabrina smiled. "I guess so."

Just then came a voice from around her shoulder. "May I bring you some drinks?" A young man stood in the aisle staring down at them. Sabrina wanted to reach up and fix the hat that looked unintentionally slanted diagonally on his head.

"Do you happen to have a menu?" Marco asked.

The man reached into his back pocket, removed a laminated drink menu and handed it to Marco as if the action annoyed him. "There's also one right there." He bobbed his head toward a menu sitting on the table a few seats down.

Sabrina continued to survey the stadium while Marco skimmed the menu.

"Two Malibu Dreamsicles," he said, handing the menu back to the man standing in the aisle.

Sabrina's head spun to face Marco and she looked at him, waiting to speak until the attendant left.

"What did you just order?" she asked.

"Something called a Malibu Dreamsicle." He shrugged and grinned. "I've never tasted one before, but it sounded interesting. Have you ever had one?"

"Can't say that I have," Sabrina said. "But I won't be starting now! I hope you planned on drinking both of those."

"What? Why?" Marco seemed genuinely surprised.

"Because I'm on the job," Sabrina explained. "It would be unprofessional."

"No, it would not," Marco corrected her. "We have already talked at length about this. I gave you a new list of responsibilities."

"So?" Sabrina crossed her arms.

"*So*, as part of those responsibilities, you agreed to be my company on the trip," he said. "What kind of company makes their friend drink alone?"

"A friend who doubles as an employee," said Sabrina.

"Fair enough. But right now, your boss is ordering you to join him with a drink," Marco said, and right on cue the attendant returned carrying two glasses with bright orange liquid. He picked them both up and held one out for her to take.

Sabrina took the glass with two hands as if it were some sort of chalice used exclusively for royalty. She sighed.

"What is this thing?" Sabrina asked, watching Marco stir the orange concoction around with a straw.

"A Malibu Dreamsicle," he said matter-of-factly, and sipped from his glass. "Remember?"

"Right, but *what is it*?" Sabrina studied the drink in her hand, still hesitant to give it a try.

Marco sipped again and reached for the laminated menu in front of him. "It says its Malibu Orange Float Rum, Whipped Vodka, fresh orange juice and club soda."

"Sounds intense," she said. She looked doubtfully at the drink. She wasn't much of a drinker, but then again, she'd never really been offered much beyond cheap beer and an occasional pull of whiskey from her father's flask. She'd certainly never had a drink prepared the way this one was.

"Give it a try," Marco urged, taking a sip. "It's actually quite good."

"What's it taste like?" Sabrina hesitated. If this was anything like whiskey, there was no way she'd be able to drink it.

"Just try it," he said. "It tastes even more magnificent than it looks."

Sabrina sipped her glass, feeling the cold ice against her lips and the liquid pool in her mouth. With her tongue she pushed it into a stream down her throat and paused, waiting for the burn.

But it never came. The drink was sweet and pleasant.

"Do you like it?" Marco asked.

"It's actually pretty good," Sabrina admitted, taking another sip. "I've never had a drink like this."

"But you do like it, right?" Marco asked. "I can order something else that's not fruit-flavored if you'd prefer."

"Oh, no. I like it a lot," Sabrina said. She took an even bigger sip this time.

"Good." Marco grinned, pleased with himself.

Sabrina watched him. She liked the way his lips curved as he smiled. Everything he did was elegantly refined and graceful in its own way, as if he were a painting constantly reworking itself.

There was a sudden roar in from the stands below, and

Sabrina turned toward the field. She was no analyst but even she could tell the makings of a good play. She quickly spotted the ball rolling in the outfield. By the time an outfielder scooped the ball and rocketed it back, the runner was already rounding third base. Even if she couldn't have seen his uniform, it was obviously a Yankees' player given the howl of celebration coming from the crowd.

Sabrina looked over to see Marco straining his neck to watch the play unfolding in front of them. He watched it with rapt interest, his dark eyes taking in every motion on the field.

Suddenly, the roar of the fans reached its loudest decibel yet, and Sabrina looked away from Marco to see the runner touching home base. She felt a flurry of energy around her as people in the suite stood and cheered. Marco stood too, feeding off the energy.

He reached down and offered his hand. Sabrina humored his request and stood beside him.

"I think we just scored a goal," Marco said and Sabrina couldn't help but notice how he'd chosen to say '*we.*'

"He hit a home run," Sabrina corrected gently. She shook her head in amazement. "An inside-the-park home run."

Marco turned to her wearing a look that said he was confused, but enjoying himself all the same.

"He hit the ball in the outfield and they couldn't throw it back in time, so he ran all the way home and scored," she explained. "It's pretty hard to do."

When they finally sat back down, Sabrina reached for her drink in the cup holder and realized it was less than half full. She'd drunk the thing like it was juice. Marco reached for his drink and she was relieved to see that his was also less than full, though not quite as empty as hers.

It wasn't more than a few minutes, though, before Marco ordered another two drinks from the attendant working the suite. They finished their first drinks right as the fresh ones were delivered.

Already Sabrina could feel the alcohol setting in. It'd been awhile since she'd drank, but still the buzz felt different than she was used to. Instead of the lift she felt from a few beers, her body was warm and heavy. It sank into her chair while the outside breeze was fuzzy on her face and fingers.

The next drink went quickly also. Too quickly.

Before she knew it, the attendant was circling back with yet another full Malibu Dreamsicle that he placed on the thin table in front of them. Sabrina's eyes moved slowly as she focused on the third drink, her vision cushioned by a frame that shrank the size of the room around her. Her sips had turned into gulps and she took another drink before looking up at Marco.

Sabrina wanted to laugh, not *at* something but out of pure joy. She wanted to throw an arm around Marco and pull him close to her, but resisted the urge. Even though the alcohol was blurring the lines of her judgment, she felt like she shouldn't do that just yet.

"Enjoying yourself?" Marco asked, noticing her gaze fixed on him.

"I'm having a great time," Sabrina said, her words lazy but still full of delight.

"Glad to hear it." Marco beamed at her and she smiled back. It felt like the short distance between them was filled with a blissful connection that only alcohol could elicit, the sort of thing that felt tangible and fervently comforting.

The game itself had faded into Sabrina's secondary focus. In the foreground was Marco, his firm stature and glowing skin, and the fuzzy sensation that had become as much a part of the setting as the stadium in front of them.

By the time the seventh inning stretch came along, Sabrina was feeling amazing. The alcohol had seeped into her veins and slapped a big goofy smile on her face. The best part, though, was that Marco was enjoying himself just as thoroughly. Almost too thoroughly. When the attendant came back with another round of drinks, Marco stopped him and forced him to sing along with him to "Take Me Out To The Ballgame."

*This is more entertaining than the actual game,* she thought, as she watched Marco wrap his arm over the attendant's shoulder, forcing him to sway to the music.

The young attendant played along, though, and sang the lyrics at full volume. Sabrina decided to join in as well. She started singing quietly at first, but within a few verses, she was shouting the lyrics louder than anyone else in the suite.

*This is so fun,* she thought while trying to curb her giggles.

Sabrina reached for another sip from her drink. She couldn't remember how many she'd had at this point. All she knew was that she was on cloud nine. Or cloud ten.

*Is there a cloud eleven?* she thought, as a small wave of dizziness swept through her.

Everything was clouds.

Everything was fuzzy.

Everything happened all at once, yet at a pace so slow she could watch it unfold in amusement.

The surrounding stadium faded out of Sabrina's perception and Marco was the only one left. He might as well have been the only person in attendance at the game. His every move was personified into a movie that Sabrina watched with a concentrated affection. She wanted him and didn't even feel bad for it, thanks to the alcohol. The Malibu Dreamsicles had stirred a flurry of energy in her, a fire in her belly, a fire that wanted nothing more than to absorb Marco into a single blaze.

Sabrina could have sat there and stared at Marco forever, but there wasn't time. Because the next thing she knew, the game was over. Time had sped up and she had no idea what happened to it. One minute she was watching Marco trying to sing along to a classic American song and the next, she was stumbling behind him as he led her through a crowd of people. She was a fish in a stream, and the alcohol had made it so that the people around her were more like rushing water than actual bodies.

Marco looked back and must've taken notice of her crooked and clumsy steps, because he extended an arm that she gladly took. Linked together, the two ambled out of the stadium onto the street and into the blurred lights of the surrounding traffic.

Sabrina no longer felt the night air on her skin, like she was in a bubble of her own incoherent haze. Everything was moving fast and she had given up on trying to fight off the lens of fog in front of her eyes. She held onto Marco's arm with both hands as the two waited for his driver. There was something about feeling him in her grasp that was both soothing and exciting at the same time.

After pulling up, the driver stepped out from the car, nodded at Marco and opened a back door.

Marco politely motioned for Sabrina to get in first. She fell into the car before wildly scooting to the opposite side to make room for him to follow.

Sitting down had brought on a woozy sort of feeling that was intensified by the tight space of the car.

*My god, I'm drunk,* Sabrina thought as she reached

toward her face. She barely recognized the feel of her skin, like the alcohol had severed the connection between her hands and the rest of her body.

Every jerk and jolt of the car was exaggerated to the point that Sabrina closed her eyes and felt herself spinning with the motion of their drive.

"Would you please open a window back here, sir?" she heard Marco say, and opened her eyes in time to feel the rush of the outside air brush against her face.

"I'm okay," Sabrina murmured, though she wished she hadn't felt the need to defend herself. She could barely make out the contours of his face now, but she felt his grip come down on her hand and squeeze.

The gesture sent a burst of butterflies into Sabrina's chest that was almost too much to handle in conjunction with the heavy alcohol sloshing in her stomach. The air from the window to her left was the only thing that grounded Sabrina on the drive back. It didn't make her feel a hundred percent, but at least it was enough to keep her from throwing up.

She couldn't remember disembarking from the car and into the hotel. The familiarity of the elevator was the only thing that stood out among the jumble of soft and blurry objects around her. When the elevator door opened it gave way to a hall that spun and twisted side to side.

*Crap,* Sabrina thought. *What have I done to myself?*

She'd rarely gotten drunk before and although she recognized the feeling, *this* was a new level.

When Marco reached his hand back, Sabrina realized she'd been standing in the elevator without moving, trying to regain her senses. The doors began to close and Sabrina jumped out of the elevator and into Marco's chest theatrically.

"Whoa," he said, laughing and holding her in a hug.

"The doors were about to close on me," Sabrina said. She was glad he was holding onto her.

"You made it," Marco said, playing along. "You're right though, that was a close one."

They both laughed and Marco released her and offered his arm for her to link like they had at the stadium. In that position, he led them slowly down the hall.

"I'm sorry," Sabrina said, trying her best to sound composed.

"Sorry for what?" he asked. "You've nothing to apologize for."

"I'm drunk," she said while subconsciously gripping his arm tighter.

"Not even remotely," Marco said, and even in her intoxicated state Sabrina picked up on his sarcasm.

She looked up and smiled.

"I really am sorry, though," she said. "I don't like you seeing me like this. I'm supposed to be watching out for you, not the other way around. It's my second day and I'm already a terrible employee."

"Did you have fun tonight, though?" Marco asked, ignoring her comment altogether.

"I had a ton of fun," Sabrina said, her voice high and jolly. "But I didn't mean to get myself into this state. Apparently, I'm kind of a lightweight when it comes to alcohol."

Just then they reached rooms 1505 and 1506 and Marco stopped, pulling her into a hug.

"You don't have to apologize," he said. "I'm just delighted that you had fun."

"This is why I didn't want to drink," Sabrina said, feeling her cheek against the firm wall of his chest.

"Stop," he said. "Don't worry about it. We had a proper good time tonight and that's all that matters. Thank you."

"So you had fun too?" Sabrina asked. Her world now was composed of a single blur that revolved around Marco's body. The way he was wrapped around her made for a cocoon and Sabrina wanted to concede to her intoxication and dissolve into his chest right then and there.

"Of course. I had a great time," Marco squeezed her as he spoke.

That was all she needed. He'd popped her balloon of exhilaration and pent up temptation.

She hardly had any control of her movements left, but in one motion Sabrina tilted her head and went in for a kiss. Her push was sudden and steady and was met with a single finger. When she realized that the kiss wasn't happening, Sabrina opened her eyes.

Marco had stopped her lips with his index finger and was staring gently back at her.

She started to speak, started to voice her most heartfelt apology yet, but Marco hushed her and pressed his finger more firmly to her lips.

"Shh," he said, smiling and shaking his head. "I'd love nothing more than a kiss from you, but not tonight."

He lifted his finger and the words leaked from Sabrina mouth uncontrollably.

"I'm so sorry," she said. "I thought..."

"You thought correctly," he said. "But not tonight. Not when we're both drunk. Do you have your room key?"

Sabrina nodded and fished the key from her purse.

Marco opened her door and laid his hand against the small of her back as they entered. He led Sabrina all the way to her bed and took both her hands as she sat down.

"Our moment deserves to be remembered more than

this. More than a drunk night out." He leaned in to kiss her forehead. "I want our kiss to make a moment. Not just be part of one."

"Okay," Sabrina whispered and smiled up at him.

"Besides, I'd prefer if the climax of the trip didn't occur on the first night," Marco said, smiling from ear to ear.

Sabrina couldn't do more than beam up at him, her smile coming out from her chest.

She remained seated as Marco bid her goodnight and kissed her cheek.

After he left Sabrina fell into the pillows of her bed, her eyes clamped shut into spinning darkness. There'd been no kiss that night, but it didn't even matter. His gesture was almost worth more. The way he'd soothed her and assured her, with only a few words and a smile, was more potent than any physical action could've ever been.

Sabrina thought of him in the next room over, recreating the sensation of his soft lips on her forehead. She'd felt it above her drunken haze more than she'd been able to feel anything else that evening.

*She was fading quickly, the room spiraling around her. Everything was fuzzy and nothing was clear, nothing except Marco's image looming and lulling her to sleep.*

# CHAPTER 7

arco

WHEN MARCO WOKE up the following morning, he was surprised by the mess in his hotel room. It looked like a clothes bomb had gone off. In his drunken state the night before, he had carelessly kicked off his shirt, pants and socks. His pants were hanging off of the TV stand, with one of the legs dropping over the edge. A black sock had landed over the lamp shade on the corner desk. His favorite white dress shirt was crumpled up and stuffed into the top drawer of the dresser.

Clearly, Sabrina hadn't been the only one to enjoy a few too many drinks the previous night.

*Wow,* he thought, as he sat up in his bed. *What in the hell happened?*

The change of position caused blood to rush to his brain and a thumping headache filled his skull.

"I probably shouldn't have had that last drink," he whispered to himself. "Or even the last *three* drinks."

Wearing only his underwear, he walked over to the mini-fridge and grabbed a bottle of water. The cool liquid soothed his dry throat and made him feel better almost immediately. Which was good, because he needed to recover quickly. He wanted to make the most of his time in New York and he refused to waste any of it to a nasty hangover.

As he walked back toward his bed, he noticed that the light on his cell phone was blinking. When he picked it up, he saw that he had a missed call from Orsino Palace.

*Father,* he thought, as he clicked on the number to return the call. He waited anxiously to hear his father's voice.

"Marco," a female voice answered his father's cell phone. "How nice of you to call."

Marco winced at the familiar voice. It was his stepmother. Despite marrying his father when he was a young teen, the two of them had never gotten along well.

"Good morning, Magdalena," he greeted her. "I'd like to speak to my father."

"Your father is lying down," she said, crisply. "He's trying to relax right now, which isn't easy since his only son decided to leave town during one of the hardest times of his life."

"He and I have talked about this," Marco replied, doing his best to stay calm. "Father was the one who encouraged me to continue this trip. I had offered to come home."

"I don't recall him mentioning anything of the sort," she said, her snide tone causing the anger inside Marco to flare. "But tell me, Marco. Has it been worth it? Has the trip to the United States been worthy of leaving your family at such an inconvenient time? I hope you're enjoying yourself and not getting into too much trouble."

"The States have been amazing and my days without trouble," he assured her. "But to be honest, my dear Magdalena, I didn't call to get an earful from you or to chat about my vacation. In fact, I called my father's phone in order to speak with him."

"As I said, he's resting at the moment and I won't allow him to exert any extra energy that he doesn't need to. That includes talking to you," she said.

Marco began pacing the room again. He clenched and unclenched his fists before speaking. There were many words that he wanted to say to her, but none of them would be considered polite.

"I would like to speak to him, Magdalena," he said, as he walked swiftly back and forth across the carpet in front of the bed. "If you aren't going to let me speak with him, can you at least tell me what is going on with his health? I've been worried sick about it."

"So worried sick you couldn't take his call earlier?" Magdalena asked. "He had so wanted to speak to his only son."

"That's why I'm calling now," Marco replied testily. "Now, I'd like to know how the follow up appointment went with the doctors."

"Since you couldn't be bothered to speak to him yourself, I will tell you. Based on the size and location of the tumor in his lungs, the doctors said that the best possible plan of action will be surgery," she said. "It's not a simple procedure, but if it's successful then there's a chance that he won't have to go through chemo and radiation."

Marco stopped in his tracks and stared out of the window of his hotel room. He heard the words that came out of the Queen's mouth, but it took a moment for them to fully soak in.

"So the surgery is going to happen?" Marco wished he could speak to his father instead of his stepmother. He had so many questions and he wanted to hear his father's thoughts.

Marco knew that the surgery was the best option for his father, so in a way he was happy to hear the news. But it still meant that King Carlo would have to go under the knife and would be forced to deal with all of the pain that would entail. He also realized that the recovery from such an invasive surgery would likely come with its own host of complications. So, although it was the best possible option, the thought of it still scared Marco half to death.

"What did my father say about all of this?" he asked, as his heart fluttered with worry.

"He said that he's ready and willing to move forward with the operation as soon as possible," she said. "The sooner the better, if you ask me. The quicker that tumor is gone, the less likely it will spread."

"How soon is *soon*?" Marco asked, desperate for more information. "Did Father schedule a date yet?"

"*I* scheduled one for him," she said, her tone as condescending as ever.

Marco let out a frustrated sigh. *What is this woman's problem? Why does she feel the need to control every aspect of everything?*

"Can you please tell me when the surgery is scheduled?" he asked, his words slow and paced.

"July fifteenth."

"*July*? That's next month," Marco nearly shouted.

"Oh is it? Thank you for that wonderful bit of information, Marco. Anything else you'd like to share?"

"Don't be like that, Magdalena. There's no need for sarcasm at this time. It's not going to get us anywhere."

"Well, I'm just a little bit confused why you sound so upset about your father's surgery being scheduled in July," she said. "Does it not suit your vacation schedule?"

"I just didn't expect it to be so soon," Marco replied. "I'll be forced to cut this vacation short."

"No need to do that." Magdalena was abrupt as she spoke. "Please, enjoy your trip, Marco. We'll see you when you get back at the beginning of September. As you said, you and your father already discussed it."

"What are you talking about? I'm going to come home to see my father. We didn't discuss me being away for his surgery," he growled into the phone. The woman enjoyed pressing his buttons. "I won't let him go into surgery without me being there."

"Well, if you're planning on coming home early, then I suppose I should tell you what else is currently being organized for that same week in July," she said.

The vein on Marco's forehead started to pulse as his blood pressure rose. He couldn't understand why Magdalena had to play these games with him, leaking one tiny bit of information at a time. It was as though she liked to see Marco squirm. He knew she had control issues, but now he began to fully understand just how bad it actually was.

"What is it, Magdalena?" Marco asked after waiting a moment. "What else do you have planned?"

"I've decided to hold a ball at the Palace," she said, her excitement becoming obvious in the way she spoke. "It will be in your father's honor."

*A ball? For my father? Why would she schedule it so close to the date of his surgery?* Marco thought.

"He's about to have lung surgery. How can you hold a ball for him if he's going to be recovering?"

"Such a smart boy," she said. "This is why I've decided to hold the ball on the night *before* his surgery. Your father will be in tip top shape that evening, as he will have been resting all of the days before it. The ball will be a celebration of his health and will give him positive energy for his surgery that is scheduled for the following morning."

Marco stopped midstep and stared at his phone. "Do you really think that my father would want to have a ball during a time like this?" he asked.

"I think that it would be good for King Carlo to have one last formal appearance before his retirement," she said.

Marco thought it over some more. It was as though the Queen feared that Carlo wouldn't make it through the surgery, so she wanted to have one last party. It made Marco's stomach turn.

"Is that what this is *really* about, though, Magdalena?" His voice had become a low growl. "Are you *really* doing this for the king, or is this ball more for you? We all know how you enjoy a good party."

"How *dare you*, Marco. You bite your tongue right now before it gets you into trouble."

"I'll do nothing of the sort, Magdalena. Besides, I've said nothing wrong. I've only asked a simple question. I don't understand why you've chosen such an elaborate celebration for a man who is about to go into surgery. I've known my father for longer than you have, and I can tell you that he loathes formal public appearances."

"I've already told you, Marco. It's for the good of the island. The citizens need to see your father healthy and well. It's important for the country's morale to see that their leader is strong and ready. It's the least we can do for the people of Orsino."

"I care as much about the citizens of the island as you do," he said. "But right now, I'm more concerned about my father. The people of Orsino will understand if you cancel the ball for the sake of their King's health."

Magdalena scoffed. "*Cancel the ball*? Have you been drinking today, Marco? Because you're not making any sense. There's not a chance on this green earth that I'll cancel the ball. Arrangements are already being made. The party will be held at the Palace on July fourteenth and that's final."

"And my father is actually okay with this?" Marco asked.

"Of course he is," she said. "He's agreed that this is a good opportunity."

Marco rolled his eyes. He could see straight through her lies. He knew his father, and there was no way that he was looking forward to his palace being filled with strangers. But until he had a chance to actually speak to his father himself, he'd have to take Magdalena's word for it.

"I'd love to hear him say that on his own," Marco said. "But something tells me that you're not going to let that happen."

"Marco, I'm warning you one more time, you *bite your tongue*." Magdalena sounded even more upset than usual. "You've already caused enough trouble by abandoning your family for some silly meandering around a foreign country, and now you think you can just speak to me however you wish? You had better show me some respect, my son, or else I will make your life a living hell."

"I *didn't* abandon my family," Marco said, defensively. "I simply took a little bit of time off to spread my wings. That's all. I don't deserve to be chastised for it, especially since I had my father's blessing to take this trip. He's the only one whose opinion I respect anyway, for your future reference."

Magdalena was silent for a moment and Marco knew that he had managed to strike a chord with the last comment. It satisfied him in one way, but also made him feel uneasy. For every point he scored, Magdalena seemed to find ways to even it.

"I'm curious what your father will say when I tell him the things you've said in this conversation." She threatened him as though he was still ten years old. "Then maybe you'll learn a lesson in respect."

"Please, save your threats for the dirty politicians at the party," Marco said. "I've got more important things to worry about."

He couldn't believe the words that were coming out of his own mouth. Normally, he'd have been able to hide his real feelings a little better. But something about that morning, with the news of his father's surgery, had given him distinct confidence in the face of Magdalena. He wanted to get her riled up. He wanted to make her squirm, like she had been doing to him for years and years.

"When you say things like that, you sound more like a commoner than you do royalty," she said. "You're brash and unrefined. Not fit to be a prince."

Marco refused to fall into her trap. She was baiting him, trying to turn the tables. He wouldn't fall for it.

"I, for one, happen to *enjoy* the presence of commoners. They have this really amazing ability that you seem to have never learned. They know how to smile," he said, smirking at his own comment. "So I take your comment as a compliment. Thank you, stepmother."

"I'm done with this conversation," she said, obviously annoyed by her stepson. "I've things to do. This country isn't going to run itself. You've already wasted enough of my time."

Marco smirked, knowing that the only reason Magdalena was getting off of the phone was because she had run out of rude things to say to him. He'd won the argument, at least for the time being. It was a small feat, but a rare one, especially with Magdalena.

"Give my father my best," he said. "And tell him that I'll be coming home early. I'll see him in a few weeks."

"Good day, Marco," Magdalena said, before hanging up the phone.

Marco tossed his cell onto the bed and collapsed onto the brown leather chair in the corner of the bedroom. He ran his fingers through his hair, pulling it back over the top of his head. He was shocked by the conversation he had just had with his stepmother, but happy he had at least gotten *some* information out of her.

His head hurt, his belly ached and he was already anxious over his father's health. Then Magdalena had to go and drop the news of a celebratory ball, making the situation even more stressful than it already was. His heart ached with worry. King Carlo would be having surgery in just four weeks and Magdalena was playing gatekeeper, making it so that he couldn't even speak with him. He suddenly felt a deep regret about deciding to go on this vacation in the first place.

*If I had stayed home, then I'd be on Orsino right now,* he thought. *Magdalena wouldn't have this kind of control and there sure as hell wouldn't be some stupid ball being held in my father's honor.*

Marco continued to kick himself for leaving the island, but the self-punishment was really just a distraction. The truth was that he was simply scared for his dad. Surgery to remove the tumor was said to be the best option, but that didn't mean it was a definite cure. Lung cancer had a horrible prognosis, as Marco had found out through his research on the Internet.

A wave of dizziness washed over him and he sat back down on the lounge chair, fearing that he might pass out. Tears welled in his eyes, but he choked them back.

*What am I supposed to do?* Marco thought.

He needed to talk to someone, but his father was the one who he usually leaned on in times of stress. And of course, that was also the one person that Magdalena had cut him off from. He feared that if he didn't get this off of his chest he would explode. He'd be a total mess for the remainder of the vacation and everybody that worked for him would end up as miserable as he was.

For some reason, and he wasn't sure why, Sabrina flashed into his mind. The image of her pretty face temporarily eased the torment that was going on inside of him. For a moment, he thought about confiding in her about his feelings.

*I shouldn't, though,* he thought. *I didn't hire her to be a therapist. It isn't fair to her.*

He got up and walked straight to the shower. While the water heated, he stripped naked and stood in front of the mirror. His dream vacation had just turned from a three-month extravaganza into a four week trip.

He thought of simply returning home tomorrow, but he knew his father wouldn't want that. His father had said as much during their last conversation. Besides, there was nothing for him to do at the palace but fight with Magdalena and worry.

His father wanted him to stay. Marco sighed and ran his hands through his hair again. He wanted to enjoy himself, but he knew it would be difficult. Without anyone to talk to about his troubles, he'd be forced to shove them deep down inside.

*It's better that way, though,* he thought. *It's better for me to bear these burdens on my own. I'd rather do that, than risk infecting everyone else with my problems.*

# CHAPTER 8

abrina

THE MORNING SUN pierced Sabrina's eyelids, sending an electric shock of pain all the way to the back of her skull. Her mouth was as dry as a cotton ball and her throat felt scratchy. She ran her tongue against the roof of her mouth, but even that didn't help to ease the dryness.

*Oh, my God. What happened last night?* She thought, as she hesitantly opened her eyes.

The sun, though it was barely coming in between the drapes of her hotel room, felt so bright that she had to look away. Slowly, she sat up and swung her legs over the edge of the bed, making sure her back was toward the window. When she glanced down, she noticed that she was still wearing the same outfit that she had had on during the baseball game the night before.

"The game," she whispered, her words sounding hoarse. "What happened?"

She hardly remembered anything after the third cocktail. The last thing she remembered was being at the game, watching Marco attempt to sing the national anthem. After that, the evening was just a colorful blur with a handful of snapshots. One of which was a brief memory of Marco leading her out of the stadium.

*But then what? How did I end up back here?* She thought.

Sabrina got up from the bed and stood there for a moment, waiting to take a step until the woozy feeling passed. Once the room stopped moving, she walked over to the sink and filled a glass with water. The first sip didn't even make it to her throat, because it was absorbed by her bone-dry mouth. She continued drinking, though, knowing that hydration was the only thing that could rescue her from the of hangover. As she drank, she racked her brain, trying to piece together the puzzle of her memory from the previous cocktail-filled evening.

*Okay, we obviously left the stadium. I remember that. But was it at the end of the game or did we leave early? God, I hope we didn't have to leave because I was too drunk. Then we came back to the hotel, of course, because I'm here. But why can't I remember anything between the stadium and here?* She bombarded herself with questions, trying to put it all into place.

Suddenly, another snap shot memory flashed into her mind. She nearly dropped the glass into the sink but managed to save it.

"Oh, no," she whispered, recalling what had happened between Marco and herself in the hallway outside of her room. "I tried to kiss him."

Sabrina brought her hands up and ran her fingers through her hair as she paced the room. She remembered leaning in and Marco stopping her from kissing him. She remembered how he pressed his index finger into her lips to stop her and how he had said that it wasn't the right time.

Her face became hot and a wave of embarrassment filled her from head to toe. She was of course attracted to Marco, but never would she have consciously let herself try something so stupid.

"What if he fires me?" she said, still pacing frantically around the room. "I can't believe I did that. What in the hell was I thinking?"

Every possible worst-case scenario filled her mind. She feared she'd lose her job or that Marco would distance himself from her, making things between them awkward. She wanted to run over to his room and apologize, but then she also didn't want to bring it up.

*What am I supposed to do?* She thought. *Maybe I'll just pretend I don't remember, and I won't even mention it. There's always the possibility that Marco won't recall what happened anyway. He was drunk too, right?*

Sabrina slipped off her clothes, noticing a stain on the right leg of her jeans. She didn't remember spilling any of the orange concoction on herself, but then, she didn't remember much of anything from that night.

Once naked, she walked into the bathroom and took a quick shower. The heat and steam did a lot to ease the headache she had, and by the time she was finished, she felt substantially better. The shower did a lot, but it didn't help her cope with the embarrassment she had from trying to kiss Marco.

"I'll just pretend it didn't happen," she said, matter-of-factly, stepping out of the shower. "That's the best option."

After drying off, Sabrina got dressed. She had no idea what was on the itinerary for the day, but planned on doing the maid part of her job and cleaning Marco's hotel room for him. So she rummaged through her suitcase and pulled out a simple black t-shirt and some worn jeans, all clothes that she didn't care if she got dirty. After that, she slipped into her tennis shoes. Before walking out the door, she brushed her hair and pulled it back into a ponytail. One last look in the mirror revealed dark bags under her eyes from lack of sleep. She sighed and shrugged.

"Hopefully, I'll get some better sleep tonight," she said, as she stepped out of her room and into the hallway.

She immediately took the three steps down the hall to Marco's door. After a few knocks, Marco opened the door. He was dressed in a white v-neck undershirt and white-washed jeans. His hair was still wet from a shower.

"Good morning. Please, come in," he said, as he held the door open for Sabrina. "I just need to put on some socks and shoes, then we can go get breakfast."

Sabrina followed him inside and took a seat on the chair next to his bed. She nearly told him that he could get breakfast and she would stay here and clean, like a good employee. But, she knew he would just insist on her coming with him anyway.

"How are you feeling?" Marco asked, as he dug through his suitcase for some socks.

"Better than I probably should be, given how drunk I was," she said, as she rubbed her eyes with the back of her hands. "Those orange drinks went straight to my head last night. I'm surprised I'm not sick right now. I'm definitely tired and thirsty, but other than that I think I'm okay."

Marco chuckled, as he pulled some black socks from his bag and took a seat on the edge of his bed. "Yes, those drinks were a little stronger than I thought."

"I don't remember much about what happened,"

Sabrina said, hoping and praying that he'd believe her and not bring up their almost-kiss.

He gazed at her, and his lips curled up into a smirk. "You don't remember anything?"

"I remember orange drinks and the national anthem and..." Sabrina paused, as if she were deep in thought. "That's about it, I think. Thanks for getting me home safely."

"You're very welcome," Marco said, his voice flat. "I hope you have an appetite this morning."

Sabrina placed her hand over her stomach. She had a tinge of nausea, but food sounded like it might actually help with that.

"I could eat," she said. "But I also have a lot to do. I need to get your room cleaned and your bed made."

"Let's get breakfast and then you can take care of the chores," Marco said. "And don't argue with me that breakfast isn't a part of your job."

It was already almost ten in the morning and Sabrina felt like a total slacker for having done nothing productive up to that point, with the exception of taking a few sips of water and getting a shower. But if she were to make anything of the day, she knew that food would be required.

"Okay," she said, with a sigh. "What are you hungry for?"

"There's a coffee shop right around the corner," he said. "Why don't we go there?"

Sabrina nodded in agreement, but didn't say a word. It felt like Marco was being kind of short with her. He was acting more business-like than he had been the day before. She could sense that something was going on him. He wasn't acting himself. He seemed quieter and less than excited about the upcoming day. It almost felt like he was distancing himself from her.

*Maybe it's my imagination, though,* she thought. *Or maybe he remembers how his stupid maid tried to kiss him last night and he's pissed off about it.*

He threw on his hat and sunglasses and walked quickly to the elevator. As they rode down in silence, Sabrina went over everything in her mind. She started to think that maybe during breakfast she should bring up what happened, just to get it out in the open. She figured she could at least apologize for it and blame her actions on the alcohol. The thought of mentioning it made her stomach churn with anxiety, but it was starting to seem like the best option.

They got off the elevator and were greeted as they walked through the hotel lobby.

"Good morning!" the attendant behind the front desk said, waving her hand with way too much excitement. It made her hangover hurt.

Marco didn't say a word, though. He just kept walking.

"Morning," Sabrina said, giving the attendant a nod.

*What is going on with him?* she asked herself, as the two stepped out of the hotel and into the sunlight.

They walked down the sidewalk and around the corner, where a cute little coffee shop was located. The inside of the shop was busy, but nobody was seated in the outdoor patio area.

"Marco, why don't you just wait out here and I'll go in and order," she said. "This place is busy and I'd like to lessen the possibility of you getting recognized."

"That will do just fine," he said, taking a seat in a plastic chair on the patio.

He gazed off into space as he crossed his arms. Sabrina's stomach dropped, thinking she had ruined everything by her actions the previous night.

"What would you like from the shop?" she asked.

Marco focused on Sabrina just long enough to respond. "A large coffee, French pressed if they have it. No sugar, but two teaspoons of cream."

"Okay," she said. "What about food?"

"I'll have whatever you're having," he replied, his arms still crossed.

Sabrina turned and stepped into the coffee shop. After standing in line for five minutes, she ordered two large coffees and two orders of beignets with extra powdered sugar on top. She carefully balanced the overloaded tray of food and went back outside to where Marco was seated.

"Okay, here's breakfast," she said, placing the food onto the table.

She sat across from Marco and fidgeted quietly, while taking an occasional sip from her coffee. The mood between them was heavy and it weighed on her like a grand piano, pressing down into her shoulders.

"Marco, is everything okay?" she asked, blurting out the question without much thought.

She needed to clear the air and figured talking about what happened would be the only way.

"Yes, things are fine," he said, as he stirred his coffee.

"Are you sure? Because you're not acting like you usually do," she said.

Marco sighed and leaned back into his chair. He readjusted the brim of his cap. "I know. I'm dreadfully sorry about that."

"Look, Marco. I'm the one who should apologize. I'm sorry about last night," Sabrina said. "I know you're probably mad about what happened and I just want you to know that it wasn't what I intended. I didn't mean to get that drunk and I didn't mean to try to-"

She wasn't able to finish her sentence before Marco

interrupted her. "Last night? What? You have nothing be sorry for, Sabrina."

"I just thought you were mad at me," she said, looking down toward her plate of food. "I can tell you're upset about something and I assumed it was about me."

Marco reached forward, taking Sabrina's hands in his. She looked back up, feeling the intensity of his stare. "You've got it all wrong. I mean you're correct about me being upset about something, but it has nothing to do with you. I promise."

Sabrina felt a wave of relief.

"Is there anything I can do to help?" she asked.

"I do appreciate the offer, but I'm afraid that what I'm dealing with is my own burden to bear," he said, releasing her hands and picking up his coffee. "It's a family issue."

Sabrina's eyes widened. "I'm happy to listen to whatever is going on. Even if there's nothing I can actually do to help the situation, sometimes it can feel good just to get things off of your chest."

Marco took a bite of food and a little bit of powdered sugar managed to find its way to his chin.

"You have some sugar on your face," Sabrina said, giggling. "It kind of looks like a white goatee."

For the first time that morning, Marco smiled. He brought his napkin up and cleaned up his chin.

"Thanks for looking out for me," he said.

"Any time," Sabrina replied. "But seriously, Marco. I'm here if you need to chat. I can tell something is eating you up and I'd hate to see you struggling like this for your whole vacation."

She wasn't sure if she was overstepping the lines again by offering to be a shoulder to cry on, but it was how she felt. She wanted to help him. This Marco, the one sitting across from her, the one with a forlorn and sad look on his face, was not the same Marco she had landed in New York with.

Marco sighed and slowly nodded. "I guess it might feel good to get it off of my chest."

Sabrina didn't want to push the topic too hard, but she was eager to hear what was going on that had him so upset.

"I'm all ears," she said.

Marco set his fork down and then drew in a long breath. "I received some news today and I'm not sure how I should feel about it."

Sabrina leaned in, bringing her elbows to the table. She wanted to give Marco her undivided attention. "What kind of news?"

"I found out this morning that my father will be getting surgery next month," he said.

"Oh, my gosh, Marco," she said, reached out to touch his hands. "Tell me what's going on with him."

"He has cancer," he said simply.

"I'm sorry, Marco." She didn't know what else to say.

"I appreciate that. But I've known about his cancer for a while now. He has a tumor in his lung. They discovered it a few months ago, but it wasn't until recently that the doctor's decided on the best plan for treatment. I found out this morning that he's a good candidate for surgery and so he's going to go through with it. It's a good thing in some ways, because it means he might not have to get chemo and radiation. But it also means he's having to go through an extremely invasive surgery. I'm worried about him."

"I can't imagine," Sabrina said, rubbing the tops of his hands affectionately. "I wish there was something I could do."

"Me too," he said, gazing into her eyes. A flicker of a

smile touched his lips. "But getting it off of my chest actually made me feel a tiny bit better."

"Are you and your dad close?" she asked.

Marco nodded, as a tear slid down his cheek. "Yes. Very close. I look up to him for everything. He's the one person in my life that I know would have my back no matter what."

"He sounds like a great guy," Sabrina said, still touching the top of Marco's hands.

Even though the news was terrible, she enjoyed the fact that Marco was opening up to her. His vulnerability made him even more attractive to Sabrina. Marco was man enough to cry.

"My father is an amazing human being," Marco said, blinking away a few more tears as they filled his eyes. "I pray that everything turns out okay for him."

Sabrina nodded and then sat back in her chair, breaking her touch from Marco. She wanted to hug him and hold him in his time of need, but was still unsure where the line was with their professional relationship.

"You said his surgery is next month?" Sabrina asked.

"Yes," Marco said, as he aimlessly pushed his food around the plate in front of him. "Only a few weeks away."

"I'm assuming that changes things regarding your vacation," she said, feeling her heart sink at the thought.

It was selfish, but this job was her one shot at making enough money to go to college. If it was cut short, there's no way she'd make enough. She'd be stuck back in Memphis, getting a waitress job. Her dreams of freedom would vanish.

"I hate to say it, but yes, my vacation plans have changed," he said. "It's getting cut short. I'd still like to travel to Hawaii, but after a week there I'm afraid I'll have to head home. I need to be there when my father goes to surgery."

Sabrina nodded understandingly, but didn't know what

to say. She felt horrible for Marco, but was devastated for her own reasons at the same time.

"I'll be here to help until you leave," she said, with an assuring smile.

"You're so sweet," Marco said. "I understand that you need the money from this job and I'm not going to let my father's illness affect us both. So even though you won't be working the full length of time that we had agreed upon, I want you to know that I'm going to pay you in full regardless."

Sabrina's jaw dropped so hard that it practically hit the top of the table. It was the most generous offer anyone had ever extended her.

"Are you serious?" she asked. "You're going to pay me for the whole summer, even though I'll only be helping you for a few weeks?"

Marco nodded. "I'm a man of my word, Sabrina. And like I said, I won't let my problems have an ill effect on your life as well. It's not your fault that I must return home early."

Sabrina teared up, overwhelmed with gratitude.

"Thank you so much, Marco," she said. "Seriously, thank you."

"It is I who should be thanking you," he replied. "I feel like a ton of stones has been lifted from my shoulders. I appreciate you listening."

"I appreciate you telling me what's going on," she said. "I want you to know how sorry I am to hear about your dad, but if he's anything like you, I'm positive that he'll be fine. He sounds like a strong person."

Marco took a sip from his coffee. "Yes, I think you're right. He'll be fine. In fact, I'm probably more upset about this whole thing than he is. He's probably sitting back, reading a book and not even worried about it. Meanwhile, I'm over here in the States losing my mind."

Sabrina chuckled, relieved that the mood between them had lifted some. Still, though, there were so many emotions inside of her. She was happy that the money situation wouldn't change for her, but also saddened that the trip would be ending much sooner than expected. She was really enjoying getting to know Marco, and had been looking forward to a long summer with him. Now all she had was a few rushed weeks.

*Maybe it's for the best,* she thought. *Maybe a short trip will keep me from getting into trouble with Marco. God knows it would only be a matter of time before I fell for him. I mean, my first night drinking with him and I try to kiss him. Who know what three months could have brought.*

The two ate in silence for a few minutes. They only got about halfway through their beignets before looking up at each other.

"I might have to save the rest of this for later," Sabrina said. "My stomach still isn't one hundred perfect from the alcohol last night."

"My thoughts exactly," Marco said. "Next time we'll get drinks that don't have so much sugar in them. I'd wager a guess that it's part of the reason we're not feeling so well this morning."

They stood up from the table and Sabrina ran inside to get a couple of to-go containers. She came back out and boxed up their food and then faced Marco. His dark eyes were sad and her heart swelled as she looked at him.

*He's a rich, Mediterranean playboy. But underneath all of that, he's just an amazingly sensitive guy,* she thought.

She couldn't help herself. The pain on his face made her do it. She wrapped her arms around him and pulled him in for a deep hug, squeezing him as tightly as she could. He responded well, embracing her affectionately.

"I'm sorry you're struggling, Marco," she said. "Truly."

Sabrina realized that she had nothing in common with Marco. He was rich, she was poor. He was worldly, she was sheltered. He was everything she was not. And yet, something inside of him felt familiar to her. Something about him felt like home. It was safe and comfortable, and resonated with the most passionate parts of her being. Maybe they weren't so different after all.

They held each other in embrace for only a few moments, before a bright flash filled Sabrina's vision. At first, she thought it must have been the sun's reflection off of a car's windshield. But when she looked over and focused her eyes, she saw a man in a flannel shirt standing near the edge of the patio. He was holding a giant, expensive-looking camera. It was in front of his face as he pressed the button on top, causing it to flash again. Immediately after, he glanced over to a nearby woman, who was holding a similar type of camera.

"Hey, it really is him!" the man shouted, clicking his camera furiously.

Within seconds, the woman had joined him. They were blatantly taking pictures of Sabrina and Marco. They seemed to have no shame at all.

"We need to get out of here," Marco said, grabbing Sabrina's hand. "Come on, let's hurry."

Marco pulled Sabrina away from the patio before she fully realized what was happening. Her hip hit the table, causing the to-go boxes to spill onto the concrete. The extra powdered sugar on their beignets exploded into a dust cloud.

*Good thing I'm wearing tennis shoes,* she thought, as she

squeezed Marco's hand and quickened her pace, leaving the beignets behind.

The two ran as fast as they could down the sidewalk, away from the cameras. Sabrina had no clue where the people had come from or how they had found out that Marco was at the coffee shop. He'd been wearing his hat and sunglasses, but apparently it hadn't been enough to disguise him from the invasive eyes of the paparazzi. She wondered yet again who he was that other people knew who he was. She wished she could just look him up rather than staying true to her contract, but that wasn't her.

Her adrenaline was pumping. It wasn't like they were in physical danger. But regardless, they were most certainly being chased and that was enough to set off her survival instincts. Her chest burned and her pupils became pinpoints.

"Marco, our hotel is right here," Sabrina panted, still running. "Should we go in?"

"No, no," he said. "That won't work. We can't let them know where I'm staying. Just keep running."

Sabrina glanced over her shoulder to find that the strangers were gaining on them. She couldn't believe how fast they could run, especially considering the cameras they carried.

*Valetta wasn't joking when she said the paparazzi was seri-ous,* she thought. *I had no idea.*

"Marco, we have to hurry," she said, speeding up her pace even further. "They're catching up"

Marco dropped Sabrina's hand. Then the two of them turned their run into an all-out sprint, giving it everything they had to get away from the camera-carrying strangers that followed them. They got to the end of the block and then turned the corner. Halfway down was an alley way.

"Come on," he said. "Follow me."

They made their way down the sidewalk and to the entrance of the alley. Once there, Marco grabbed Sabrina's hand and pulled her into it.

"We can lose them in here," he said, his words broken up by his panting. "We need to hide for a moment."

Sabrina glanced behind her as she followed Marco into the alleyway. The paparazzi hadn't turned the corner yet, so if they could get hidden in the alley, there was a chance that they wouldn't be found. The only problem was that there didn't seem to be any great placed to hide, with the exception of a lonely green dumpster.

"Where do we go?" Sabrina asked, panic stricken.

Marco walked quickly, leading Sabrina down the dimly lit alley. On either side of them were towering high-rises, which shaded the area. It had probably been years since that concrete had seen actual sunlight.

"Over here," Marco said.

There was a doorway into one of the buildings. He tried the door, but it was locked. It didn't matter, though. The doorway was indented a foot or so into the wall of the building, just enough space for the two of them to step into. It was tight, but they didn't have much of a choice.

"Come here," he said, pulling Sabrina toward him.

She scooted as closely as possible, shrinking up so as to limit the possibility of being seen from the street. Her face was pressed against Marco's muscular chest, which rose and fell in cadence with his breathing. She could hear his heartbeat as it pounded against his rib cage. The sweet smell of his sweat mixed with his cologne filled her nose.

Outside of the alley, they heard the footsteps of the paparazzi approach and then slow down to a stop.

"Where in the hell did they go?" the man asked, his

voice echoing down the quiet alleyway to where Sabrina and Marco were huddled.

"I don't know," the woman responded. "I don't see them down here. They must have gone further down the road. We'll catch them, we just need to hurry."

Sabrina held her breath until the footsteps of their pursuers faded away. Then she looked up at Marco, who was still holding her close. He looked back, flashing a playful smile of relief.

"That was close," he whispered. "I believe they're gone now, though. Hopefully anyway."

Sabrina took a moment to catch her breath. She didn't release Marco, though. She didn't want to. Standing there next to him made her feel safe.

"Are you sure they're gone?" she asked.

Marco poked his head out into the alley and looked both ways. "I don't see them."

"I never thought I'd say something like this, but thank God for this sketchy alleyway," Sabrina said, still speaking quietly out of fear that the paparazzi might be nearby.

Marco laughed softly and nodded in agreement. His hands were still clamped firmly onto the top of Sabrina's hips. It was as though neither of them really wanted to leave that spot. Their eyes were locked and they were embraced like a loving couple.

"I have no idea how they found out we were at that coffee shop," she said, lifting a hand and pushed her hair back over her ear. "I need to be more careful."

"It's not your fault," Marco said. "These things happen. Besides, I had intended on going for a morning jog anyway. It appears that I just got that chore out of the way."

Sabrina smiled, her eyes fixated on Marco. They were

silent for a moment. The only sound in the alley was their breathing, which was slowly dropping to a normal rate.

What happened next was something that Sabrina couldn't have predicted. Marco, with his hands still on her sides, leaned in and brought his lips to hers. She froze, as the entire world faded into oblivion and the only thing left was the two of them. Her lips were stiff at first, as she was not expecting the kiss. But Marco didn't break away and within a second, Sabrina relaxed.

His soft lips were pressed against hers in the most passionate embrace she had ever felt. Maybe it was the excitement of the paparazzi escape or maybe it was just the fact that this kiss was the expression of all of the feelings that had been repressed between them. Sabrina didn't know. All she knew, was that it felt incredible. Every cell in her body exploded with a tingling sensation that made her weak at the knees.

Marco slowly pulled away and looked into Sabrina's eyes, but just for a moment. Then he resumed the kiss. Their hands drifted all over each others' bodies as passion filled the air. Sabrina parted her lips and Marco's tongue darted into her mouth. The sugar from the beignets was still on his breath.

Sabrina pressed her body into Marco's, pressing her hips toward him. They made out deeply and passionately for a while, as though they were long lost lovers, finally in each others' arms again. The truth, though, was that they were just two people making out in an alleyway behind a hotel in New York City. But Sabrina was quickly realizing that love can find someone in the most unusual of places.

After a few minutes, Marco slowly pulled away. He gazed into Sabrina's eyes.

"You're incredible," he whispered, as he brought his hand up to cradle her chin.

She was about to respond, but Marco gave her a peck on the lips before she could. When he pulled away, he was smiling.

"What do you say we get out of this alleyway and go find something fun to do today?" he asked, as he poked his head out to make sure the coast was clear.

"Okay, that sounds good," Sabrina said. "What are you thinking?"

Her words came out slowly. She was still in shock over the kiss they had just had and organized thought was evading her.

"I'm not entirely sure," Marco said. "I'll investigate the options and figure something out."

He took a step into the alley and offered Sabrina his hand, which she happily took. They exited the alleyway at the opposite end from where they had entered. Luckily, there weren't any camera-clicking crazy people in sight. But they didn't dilly dally. They went straight back to the hotel. Marco went to his room and Sabrina went to hers.

As soon as her door closed and she was alone, she jumped up and down in excitement. She felt like a school girl who had just kissed the star quarterback of the football team. She danced around her room, spinning in circles and humming to herself.

*I can't believe that we kissed,* she thought. *It felt so natural. It was like we had both been waiting for that perfect moment and it finally came.*

She was fascinated by the natural chemistry between them. Her lips still tingled from the kiss and she savored it as long as possible, not wanting the sensation to ever go away.

*That was amazing. I want more,* she thought. *I just hope that this guy isn't messing with me, though. I hope that this isn't something he does with all the girls he meets. Or hires.*

In the very back of her mind, there was still a tiny bit of hesitation about getting too close to Marco. Partly, because she feared how it would look on a professional level. But mostly because she didn't want to get hurt.

Sabrina danced around for a little longer, giddy as could be. But when she calmed down, she remembered that she still had a job to do. Marco's room needed cleaning and there was laundry to be done. She decided to take care of the chores while Marco figured out what he wanted to do later that day. And she did it with a smile on her face. Which wasn't that difficult, being that the most amazing kiss she'd ever experienced was still fresh on her mind.

# CHAPTER 9

M<sub></sub>arco

MARCO AND SABRINA sat in the back of the car as their driver chauffeured them across the city. After the fiasco that morning with the paparazzi, Marco was ready to do something fun and relaxing. So while Sabrina cleaned up the hotel room and folded his laundry, he sifted through New York traveling pamphlets and researched online.

Finding his own itinerary wasn't something he usually did. Valetta took care of these sort of things. She usually got him the best of everything, but today, he wanted to do it. He wanted to choose something for him and Sabrina to do without Valetta's help.

It took the better part of an hour, but he finally found something that he thought would be enjoyable, not only for him, but also for Sabrina. Even though he was excited about it, though, he didn't tell her what he had in mind. He considered surprises to be much more fun than a boring schedule of events.

"Sir, we're here," the driver said, as he pulled out of traffic and parked next to the curb. "Just send me a text or give me a call when you're done and I'll pick you up right here."

"We're in Greenwich Village?" Marco wanted to make absolutely sure that they were in the right place, so as not to make a fool out of himself in front of Sabrina.

"Yes, sir."

"Perfect. I imagine this will take about an hour, but I'll call you when we're done," Marco said, before turning to face Sabrina. "Are you ready, Sabrina?"

She looked over and shrugged. "I don't really know where we are or what we're doing, so I'm not sure how to answer that."

"You just need to trust me," Marco said, hopping out of the back seat of the cab. When he got to Sabrina's side, he opened the door for her and took her hand to help her out. "It's a surprise. But I do believe that you're going to love it."

A rush of energy surged through him as he admired Sabrina in her yellow summer dress. The thin material clung tightly to her, accentuating her womanly curves. His eyes were drawn to her hips and then back up to her supple breasts. He looked quickly, trying to make it seem more like a natural glance than a sexual stare. He didn't want her to think of him as some kind of sex-crazed man, but he was having a difficult time keeping his desires in check, especially after the amazingly passionate kiss that they had shared in the alley way just hours before.

The driver left, and the two of them stepped onto the sidewalk. Marco looked around and then pulled out his phone to double check the address.

"I believe it's around the corner," he said.

Marco was surprised at how quiet the little neighborhood was. They were in lower Manhattan, in an area called 'Greenwich Village.' It wasn't how he had imagined it would be, though. It was calm and peaceful, with very little foot traffic and just the occasional lonely car driving down the road next to them. It was quite a bit different than the other areas of New York that he had seen up to that point.

"So, can I get a hint as to where you're taking me?" Sabrina walked alongside him as she spoke.

Marco broke his gaze from his phone and looked at her.

"I can give you a hint, but I'm afraid if I do, you won't want to accompany me," he said.

She stopped in her tracks. "Marco, I thought you said I was going to *love* it."

"You *will*." Marco insisted. "Once we get there, you'll love it. But if I inform you as to what it is, you might overthink it and not want to go."

Sabrina looked at him suspiciously. "How about a hint then?"

"It's a tour," he said, taking a few steps forward in an effort to encourage her to do the same. "Please trust me, okay?"

"Okay, I'll trust you," she said, following Marco once again.

They walked around the corner and toward a small group of people who were gathered in front of one of the old apartment buildings. There were maybe five or six strangers, but they all had their cameras out and were snapping pictures of the building in front of them. Marco knew he was at the right place.

*I sure hope she enjoys this,* he thought. *If she doesn't, I suppose we could always try to find something else to do in the neighborhood.*

The two approached the group. Marco cleared his throat as they got close.

"Excuse me, are all of you here for the tour?" Marco asked. "I'm sorry to interrupt, I just need to confirm that I'm in the correct place."

"Indeed," a tall man in a black t-shirt responded, stepping out of the group and extending a hand toward Marco. "I'm James. I'll be leading you on the ghost tour. And you're just in time. We were about to head inside."

"Ghost tour?" Sabrina looked at Marco, her eyes widening.

Marco shrugged. "Now do you understand why I couldn't tell you?"

"Ghost tour, *really?*" Sabrina repeated.

"You're right, it's a silly idea," Marco said. "We should go find something else to do."

"What? No, Marco. This is an incredible idea!" she said, her lips curling up into an excited smile. "Honestly, I've *always* wanted to do one of these kinds of tours. This just wasn't what I was expecting. Seriously, though, I love it."

"Are you certain?" he asked. "You don't have to agree to it just because it's something I want to do. There are plenty of other things we can do today that would be fun as well."

"Yes, I'm completely sure," she said, her face beaming with joy. "This is going to be amazing."

It delighted Marco to see her happy and he was so glad that he had made the decision to buy tickets for the tour.

*This is going to be good,* he thought.

James, the tour guide, was still standing in front of them. "If you guys are ready to go, let's get started."

"Yes, we're ready," Sabrina said.

Marco and Sabrina walked to the back of the group, while James made his way up onto the concrete steps that led to the door of the apartment building. The structure was made of red bricks and the wood around the windows had been painted white. Marco didn't think it appeared all that much different than any of the other places on the block. At least until he heard what James had to say about it.

"Welcome, everyone, to the *House of the Deceased*," James said. "I won't spend too much time talking out here, since most of the good stuff is actually inside. But I will tell you a few things that you might find interesting. First off, for those of you who didn't know, New York is said to be the most haunted city on the entire planet."

The crowd drew in a breath in unison and everyone looked at each other.

"Yes, it's true," he continued. "And on top of that, the building we are currently standing in front of is said to be the most haunted building in New York. What does this mean? It means we are about to step inside of the most ghost-inhabited structure in the United States. This apartment was built in 1890 and at the time, was often used for prostitution, underground slavery and all-around bad things. That's not the interesting part, though. What makes this place special is the countless sightings of ghosts from all who have ever stayed here. Of course, nobody lives here now. My company owns the building. But I'll tell you right now, there is no way in hell I'd ever spend a night in this place."

"Why not?" Sabrina asked, her voice sounding loud over the quiet crowd.

James looked toward her. "According to history, there have been at least twenty murders here, including several murder-suicides. Mark Twain, the author, actually stayed here in the year 1901 and claimed to have experienced supernatural incidents, even before he knew that the place was haunted. Also, in the mid 1950's, there were three different tenants who were all sent to psych wards after just one month of living here. It's said that they all told similar stories to their psychiatrists; something about a man on the stairs outside of their door whispering to them while they tried to sleep."

The tour guide looked very serious as he spoke, but it only made Marco smirk. He assumed that it was all part of the show. Sabrina, on the other hand, was obviously becoming a little nervous. She had wrapped her hand into the crook of Marco's elbow and was squeezing him tight.

"Now, if you will all follow me, we'll go inside," James said, spinning around to open the door.

The rusty hinges let out a loud groan as he pushed it open. It almost sounded like the building was crying out, hurting from all of the torment that had gone on there over the years. Marco looked over to Sabrina as they walked up the concrete steps.

"Are you alright?" he asked.

"Yeah, I'm fine," she said, still holding onto him with a death grip. "This place just suddenly feels a whole lot scarier now that we heard a little bit of its history."

Marco tried to act tough and stoic, but he couldn't deny that a few goosebumps had popped up on his arms after hearing the story about the ghost on the stairs. A few more popped up when they stepped into the entryway of the apartment. The wood floor beneath their feet creaked louder than the door had and the smell of old mothballs entered his nose. The place looked infinitely more drab and creepy on the inside than it did on the outside. The only light came from a small window at the top of the first flight of stairs.

"If everyone will follow me up to the second floor, that's where we'll start our tour," James announced.

The group followed him up. Marco and Sabrina were at the back of the crowd. She was squeezing him firmly as they ascended the stairs and it put a smile on his face. He liked that he was making her feel safe. He would protect her from any ghosts they happened to come across.

They all got to the top of the stairs and the group followed James into the first apartment on the right. Marco and Sabrina were still out in the hallway when they both suddenly stopped in their tracks and looked at each other.

"Did you feel that?" Marco asked.

A light breeze had blown across the back of his neck. It was ice cold and sent a chill through his entire body.

"I definitely felt something," Sabrina said, rubbing the top of her shoulder. "It felt like a burst of wind."

They glanced up and down the stairwell. There was only the one window and it appeared to be painted shut.

*It's an old building,* Marco thought. *A breeze could have come from anywhere. But it is strange that it was so cold. It's a hundred degrees outside.*

Marco wrapped an arm around Sabrina's shoulders to comfort her. He could tell that she was getting nervous about being in the haunted building.

"I'm confident it was just a draft," he said, leading her into the apartment to meet up with the rest of the tour group. "Or possibly the air conditioning."

James overheard Marco and brought his attention to him. "Air conditioning? This old building doesn't have A/C. Did you feel something out there?"

Marco didn't want to make a big deal out of a light

breeze, even though it couldn't be explained. "No, nothing. We were talking about something else."

Marco held Sabrina close as they positioned themselves in the back of the group. The apartment where they stood looked like it had been neglected for decades. The paint was peeling off the walls and the floorboards were warped, twisting around like ribbons underneath their feet. It was the most dilapidated place Marco had ever seen in his entire life, even worse than the houses he helped fix in Haiti after a hurricane.

"I know that you're all wondering why I took you into this particular apartment," James said. "This is where a very famous axe murderer lived for a short time during her young life. Her name was Lizzy St. James."

Every jaw in the place dropped as they heard James' words. Marco felt as Sabrina wrapped her arms around him, pulling herself as close as possible.

"But don't worry, Lizzy only lived here for about two months," he said. "So not a very long time, but still long enough to commit three murders in this very room."

"What?" Sabrina's eyes widened. "Are you serious?"

"Yes, completely," James said. "In fact, where you're standing is where one of them took place."

Marco and Sabrina gasped as they looked down at the floor. Maybe it was his imagination, but Marco was sure he saw the remnants of an old blood stain in the wood. Before he could react, the door of the apartment opened up a few inches, letting out a loud creak. The entire group, including James, looked over at it.

"What was that?" Marco asked, looking toward the sound and then back to James. "Who pushed that open?"

James let out a chuckle, though didn't smile. His expression remained stern. "That's Lizzy. Every single time I do a tour of this apartment, she lets herself in. The door opens a little further. Every time."

"How do you know it's her?" one of the woman participating in the tour asked.

"It's just a guess," James said. "But it only happens in this particular apartment and only in the middle of a tour, specifically after I mention her name. I have a hard time believing that it's just some sort of coincidence."

There was a silent pause as everyone stared at the door. Marco wasn't sure what he was expecting to happen on the tour, but definitely didn't think he was going to feel this uneasy. Between the breeze on the back of his neck and the unexplained opening of the apartment door, he was now thinking that this tour was the real deal. This apartment building was absolutely haunted.

*If someone didn't believe in ghosts, they should give this place a visit,* he thought. *I have a feeling it would change their mind about the paranormal.*

"Well, I think we've had enough time in here," James said. "I get the feeling that we're invading Lizzy's space and I don't really want to make her mad. Let's head up to the fourth floor."

Marco looked over to Sabrina, who was still latched onto him. She was frozen, just staring at the doorway.

"We can most certainly leave if you're not enjoying this," Marco said, as he affectionately rubbed Sabrina's back. "This is a bit more frightening than I thought it would be."

"No way," Sabrina said. "I mean you're right, it's terrifying. But that's a good thing, right? Who would want to go on a ghost tour where nothing happens?"

"Are you certain you want to stay?" he asked. "I want you to have a good time."

Sabrina took a long breath, as if readying herself to

follow the group out of the apartment to see what was next on the tour. "I'm fine. I just having the weirdest sensation in here, you know? This apartment feels like there's actually someone else in it, even though it's just the two of us."

Marco let the idea sink in. It caused a shiver to crawl up his spine. Now that the tour had gone upstairs, it was just him and Sabrina in Lizzy's apartment. And Sabrina was right. There was an undeniable feeling that they weren't alone there. It was like someone was watching them, quietly observing.

"I feel like we should catch up with the group," Sabrina said, as she walked toward the door, dragging Marco along with her.

"Yes, that's a great idea," he said, following her to the stairs.

Despite the fact that Marco was a little agitated the haunted apartment, he still felt a giddy happiness inside. The way Sabrina clung to him made him feel like she was his girlfriend and he liked that feeling very much.

The two walked up the second flight of stairs and into the mouth of an empty hallway. They looked down toward the end, noticing closed doors on both sides. Silenced filled the air and the only sound that could be heard was their breathing.

"Did we lose the group?" Sabrina asked, her words piercing through the quiet.

"We must have," Marco said, stepping into the hallway and straining his ears. "Were they going to the third or the fourth floor? I can't recall what James said. Maybe they're in one of these rooms down here."

He started to walk, but Sabrina grabbed his arm and pulled him back. "Marco, we can't go down there without the guide. I don't want to stumble into some haunted room without knowing it. What if we get possessed or something? We have no idea what we'll be walking into."

Marco spun around and pulled Sabrina toward him. She brought her gaze to his and he smiled at her. Her blue eyes were big and beautiful. They mesmerized him and demanded his attention. He couldn't help but to stare.

She licked her lips nervously, and all he wanted in that moment was another kiss. He wanted to taste her again. He knew it might not be the best place or the best time, but he didn't care. His heart wanted her close once more, despite the fact that they were in a building filled with ghosts. Without a thought, he leaned in and kissed her.

Sabrina didn't pull away. In fact, she leaned and let out a soft moan. It was as though she'd been waiting all afternoon for Marco to kiss her again. Marco felt a surge of energy as he caressed Sabrina's soft lips with his own. Their tongues darted out, colliding with passion. It turned Marco on so much. He couldn't believe how badly he wanted this innocent girl from Memphis. Every part of his being craved her, with a desperation that was foreign to him.

It felt incredible. Marco's hands drifted down her body, gently touching the top of her hips, before making their way back up. He wished they were in his hotel room instead of on the tour, because he so badly wanted to take off her clothes and kiss so much more than just her lips.

Suddenly, Sabrina jerked away from Marco, breaking the kiss. She quickly took a step back and looked around. Her eyes were wide and filled with terror. Her chest rose and fell as she took in heavy breaths. "What in the hell was that, Marco?"

Confused, Marco shrugged. "Huh? What was what? I don't know what you're talking about."

Sabrina rubbed the back of her neck. Then she brought

her hand into the stream of light that was coming in through the small window at the end of the hall. Her fingers were soaking wet.

"Is that water?" Marco asked.

"I don't know," she said, wiping it on the front of her pants. "But this place is creepy as hell. I want to get out of here."

A few drops of cool liquid fell over Marco's shoulder, causing his heart to leap out of his chest. He didn't want to scream like a school girl, but it was difficult to remain stoic after their experience in Lizzy's room.

"I just felt something land on me as well," he said, as he wiped the back of his neck with his sleeve.

It was too dark to tell what exactly the liquid was, but it didn't matter. One way or the other, they had both just experienced something completely out of the norm. He wanted to leave, but oddly enough it wasn't for his own safety. It was for Sabrina's. He felt the need to protect her and keep her safe. What had dripped onto their necks was likely just water from a leaky pipe, but there was always the chance that it was something much more evil. For all Marco knew, this was how ghosts possessed the living.

*Maybe it starts out with a few drops of water. Next thing you know, our heads are spinning around and they're calling in an exorcist from the church to try to save what's left of our souls,* he thought.

"Maybe we should call it a day," he said, ushering Sabrina toward the stairway. "Let's head back to the hotel. I think we've had enough excitement."

They turned to head down the stairs. Sabrina appeared scared out of her mind and ready to run out of the building at full speed. But before they could descend, Marco heard the sound of a man's work boot. He turned around, expecting to see a ghost hurtling toward him only to find a man in a black t-shirt. It was the same shirt that James, the tour leader, had been wearing. The stranger was standing in the shadows near where Marco and Sabrina had just kissed. The man was carrying a small bottle of water and had a devilish grin on his face.

"Sabrina, hold on a moment," Marco said, rolling his eyes. "That wasn't a ghost. This guy splashed some water on us."

The man stepped out from the shadows. "Dammit, I didn't think you guys were going to see me back here. I had you pretty good with the water thing, though, didn't I?"

"I must assume that you're employed by the ghost tour company?" Marco asked, though he knew it was the case, based on the man's shirt.

"Yes, that's correct," he admitted. "Sorry to scare you like that. But it's my job."

Sabrina came back up the stairs. She had a relieved smile on her face. "You scared the crap out of me."

"Then I did a good job," he said, with a smirk. "The rest of the tour is on the fourth floor right now. You should go catch up with them. But don't tell them that you caught me down here. I want to scare them when they come back down."

"So wait, if you did the water thing, did you also do the cold breeze outside of the apartment?" Sabrina asked.

The man shook his head, his smile fading. "Absolutely not. Anything else you've noticed has been real. Seriously."

"Come on," Marco said, taking Sabrina's hand. "Let's go catch up with the group."

They made their way up to the third floor. They were laughing now, shocked by their overreaction to a few drops of water on their necks. They found the tour group inside another apartment. James was going on about some murder that had taken place there in the mid-1800's, but Marco didn't pay much attention. Neither did Sabrina. They just stood at the back of the group, holding each other, with their necks still wet from the over-ambitious special effects guy.

"This has been an interesting tour, don't you think?" Marco whispered. "Are you enjoying yourself?"

"I'm having a lot of fun," she replied. "I can't believe how bad that guy scared me with the water. I do kind of wonder if he had something to do with the cold breeze and Lizzy's door opening, though. I mean it would definitely make sense if that was all set up."

Marco listened and watched her lips as she spoke. He wanted to lean in and kiss her again, but he held back. It wasn't the right place or time. But he knew right then that Sabrina was the girl for him.

He didn't know exactly why, because it didn't make sense. She wasn't what he had expected. She was sweet and optimistic. Her smile never wavered and she was determined to succeed. He'd never met anyone like her before. She stirred up emotions inside of him that he hadn't ever experienced. Emotions that no other girl had ever come close to creating.

He wasn't going to let her slip through his fingers. He had a very short amount of time with this beautiful Southern belle and he refused to waste any of it. Marco was a prince of the realm, and he always got what he wanted, and right now, he wanted Sabrina.

# CHAPTER 10

*abrina*

SABRINA SMILED the entire ride back to the hotel. The ghost tour had been amazing and she couldn't stop thinking about it. But her joy was caused by more than just the tour. Her happiness was mostly due to the man sitting next to her in the backseat of the car. Marco, the wealthy foreigner who could have been an underwear model in a different life, had just taken Sabrina on something that very closely resembled a date.

She knew that probably wasn't really his intention, and in all actuality, Marco had likely just wanted to check out a ghost tour for his own entertainment. But the thought of it being something more than that made her happy. The idea that a simple, penniless girl like herself could be taken out on an actual date with a man like Marco had her smiling from ear to ear, and kept her heart thumping loudly behind her rib cage.

"That was *so* much fun," Sabrina said, as the two of them stepped off of the elevator and walked down the hallway toward their hotel rooms. "I still can't believe how badly that guy scared me with the water."

She brushed her hair back over her ear, suddenly feeling a bit embarrassed by how much of a wuss she had been.

"I'm glad you enjoyed yourself," Marco said, smiling. His dark eyes sparkled with laughter at their adventure. "It turned out to be even more entertaining than I thought it would be. I'm fairly convinced the employee was behind the effects."

Sabrina nodded, as she pulled out the key card from her purse and slid it in her door. "Yeah, it's possible. I guess we'll never know, though."

There was a pause as Sabrina stood there in front of her door. She didn't want the night to end yet. It was still early and she had absolutely nothing to do in her hotel room, besides watching the boring infomercials that would inevitably be on TV.

"I guess I'll see you tomorrow," she said, with a sigh. "Valetta set up some sightseeing opportunities for you tomorrow, so I'll make sure everything is ready."

"You're going to bed already?" Marco asked. "Why don't you come enjoy a drink with me in my room? There are some decent vodkas stocked in the refrigerator."

"That sounds great," Sabrina said, not hesitating to accept the invite. In fact, it was exactly what she had been hoping for. She quickly put her key card back into her purse. "Just promise me that there won't be any orange flavoring in it this time."

Marco chuckled as he opened the door to his room and held it for Sabrina. "I think we both had more than enough orange flavoring last night. I was thinking of making something simple, like a vodka tonic."

Sabrina stepped inside and glanced around. Marco's oversized suite was was still neat and orderly from the work she had put in earlier that day. His clothes were folded and the bed made in the bedroom and the front sitting room was organized and clean. She knew the bathroom was spotless and she'd vacuumed as well as any housekeeping staff. She definitely didn't mind the work at all, but she looked forward to the day when her future college degree would pave the way to a job that didn't include manual labor.

Marco stepped past her and went straight to the bar to fix some drinks. Sabrina took a seat at one of the bar stools and watched him. Her mind was swimming with thoughts as she admired the way he moved around the kitchen. Everything about Marco was elegant, from the way he dressed to the way he spoke. She was drawn to it, with the fascination of a child. His refinement in everything was such a far cry from all she had ever known.

But there was another side to him that she had seen as well. She saw it when they had run from the paparazzi and she noticed it in the haunted apartment building. During those moments of stress, Marco had made a distinct effort to protect Sabrina. It seemed as though he would have happily stood in harm's way to keep her safe.

"Here you go," Marco said, spinning around with two bubbly drinks in hand. "Vodka tonics, with a squeeze of lime. It should be a little more refreshing than the drinks we had last night."

Sabrina took the glass from him and then held it in the air. "Here's to a very interesting day."

"Salut," he replied, clinking his glass against hers. "The

most interesting day I've had in quite some time. I'm glad you were there with me to witness it."

Sabrina took a sip and Marco did the same. She watched his mouth as he tasted the liquid and smiled. She wondered if she kissed him, would he taste like the vodka? Or would he taste sweet like before?

Something about the privacy of his room and the fact that her lips still tingled from their kiss at the haunted apartment made her keenly aware of her own intentions. She wanted to kiss her boss again and it made her nervous. He was leaving for his home in a few short weeks, but until then, he was still her employer.

*Maybe he treats every woman like a princess. What would make me so special?* she thought, taking another sip of her drink. *I'm nothing like the women he's probably used to. I wear clothes from a second-hand store and live in a trailer park. There has to be a catch. Why does he like me?*

"How would you like to hear some music?" Marco asked, shaking Sabrina from her thoughts. "I'll play you something from my home."

"That sounds nice," she said. "What kind of music is it?"

Marco walked swiftly to the bedroom and returned with his computer. "It's kind of like salsa music. It's for dancing."

Sabrina swallowed, feeling a burst of nervousness fill her. She hoped that he wasn't going to ask her to try to dance. She was horrible at dancing. She didn't have rhythm and was cursed with two left feet.

Marco started up the music. It began with a simple drum beat, but soon flutes and horns chimed in. The music was extremely complicated and sounded like a combination of jazz and blues, mixed with salsa. Underlying the melody, though, was a rhythmic beat that actually caused Sabrina to tap her toes.

"Do you like it?" Marco asked, as he stepped close to Sabrina and placed his hand onto her lower back. "I imagine it sounds quite a bit different from the music that is made here."

Sabrina nodded. Her bangs fell into her eyes and Marco reached up, pushing her hair across her forehead and behind her ear. It was such a simple act, but meant so much to her.

"My hair is a mess," she said, desperately filling the silence with anything she could think of.

"I think you look beautiful," Marco said, sliding his fingertips down her cheek. "The most beautiful girl in New York City."

Sabrina bit her bottom lip and looked at the ground, unable to fully accept such a compliment. How Marco saw her and how she saw herself were two entirely different things.

"That's really sweet," she said, bringing her gaze back up to his eyes. "Thank you."

Marco leaned in and kissed her. Her eyes widened at first, surprised by the sudden affection. They resumed what they had started at the haunted apartment, though this time with even more passion and far fewer ghosts. Sabrina stood up from her stool without breaking the kiss. She brought her hands to the top of Marco's shoulders, pulling herself close to him. Her body tingled all over as their tongues danced.

Somewhere, in the very back of her mind, Sabrina knew that she was falling for this guy. And she realized that it put her at risk of getting hurt. She'd had her heart broken before, and she understood that it could likely happen again. But Marco was different. She wanted to believe that he would never hurt her.

She felt his hands slide down her sides, gliding easily along the smooth fabric of her shirt to the band of her pants. His touch turned her on, and a surge of excitement pumped through her. She breathed in, letting the soft scent of Marco's cologne fill her nose. She placed her hands onto his face. His beard stubble scratched at her fingertips as she drew her hands downward, all the way to his neck and then to his chest.

Marco slowly broke their kiss and looked into her eyes. Sabrina saw that his pupils had dilated and he was breathing harder now. Her hands were still on his chest and she noticed the rise and fall of each breath.

He wrapped one arm around her waist and lifted her from the floor, cradling the backside of her knees with his other arm. She was surprised by his strength as he carried her effortlessly away from the bar and to the darkened bedroom. It was as though she was in a trance, unable to take her gaze away from him. His masculine features, the beard stubble and his chiseled jaw, which were half-covered by his shoulder-length black hair. This was every woman's dream come true, and she was living it. Sabrina put a note in the back of her mind to pinch herself when this was over, just to make sure that it was all actually real. Until then, she didn't want to wake up.

Marco carefully laid Sabrina down on the bed. Her eyes stayed locked on him as he crawled over the top of her and resumed their kiss. She moaned softly as a surge of passion filled her. With Marco's body on top of hers, the craving inside of her intensified and she became wet with desire. There was no hesitation any longer and all she wanted was to have him, all of him. Her hands wandered, moving up and down Marco's back while their tongues dances inside each others' mouths. After a few seconds, Marco slowly pulled away. Sabrina noticed that her own breathing had quickened. She was practically panting, as desperation filled her core.

"Take off your shirt," she told him, surprised by her own assertiveness.

"Why don't you help me?" he asked with a flirtatious grin. "I want you to do it."

Sabrina sat up and brought her hands to Marco's pecs. Slowly, she undid the top button of his shirt, revealing a little skin and a bit of his chest. Then she dropped her hands to the next button down, undressing him a little bit at a time until his entire front was exposed.

*Whoa. He's even more gorgeous than I imagined,* she thought, as Marco let the shirt fall off of his shoulders.

She knew he was athletic since it had been clear from the first day they had met. But she never knew he looked quite like this.

*Is he an Olympic swimmer or something?* she wondered, as her gaze moved up and down his body. *His island is in the Mediterranean, maybe he's actually a Greek god in disguise.*

Marco reached forward and touched the waistband of her pants. Slowly, he undid the top button, exposing her stomach and the sliver of silk fabric underneath. She bit her bottom lip and did her best not to feel self-conscious. She wriggled her hips, leaving her with just the her underthings and her t-shirt.

"Your turn," she said, looking up at him. "Can you help me take this off?"

It was as though Marco had been waiting patiently for years to hear those words come out of Sabrina's mouth. He slowly pulled the shirt upward until it was bunched up over the top of her breasts.

"Lift your hands up," he whispered, his breath landing across Sabrina's bare cleavage.

Sabrina did as he asked and brought her hands above her head. Marco pulled the shirt off and let it fall to the floor beside the bed. She was now in front of him wearing only her underwear. It was just a simple white bra and underwear since she didn't have the money to afford anything fancier.

Marco didn't seem to mind one bit. His eyes told Sabrina everything that she wanted to know. There was an animalistic lust behind them, an instinctual desire that was apparent in the way he looked at her. It stirred a deep emotion inside of her and caused all logical thought to escape her mind. Without even realizing it, she had reached forward and brought her hands to Marco's belt. She unclasped the buckle quickly, with a newfound urgency. She wanted what was underneath there, and she wanted it badly.

After loosening his belt, she slipped her fingers into the waist band of his slacks and pulled them down. It revealed his black boxer-briefs, which concealed the firm bulge of his cock beneath. Another wave of excitement filled her at the sight. This was really happening, and she was ready for it. Marco's pants were bunched up at his knees and the current position he was in kept them from coming off. He crawled off the bed and finished what Sabrina had started, letting his pants fall to his ankles. He then reached for his underwear. Sabrina watched intently, as her body filled with fire.

*He's absolutely beautiful,* she thought. *Am I dreaming? I must be dreaming. Yep, that's what's happening right now. I'm in my bed in my parent's trailer and this is all a figment of my imagination. But I don't have an imagination, or at least one that's creative enough to come up with something as incredible as Marco.*

Sabrina licked her bottom lip as Marco hooked his thumbs behind the elastic waist strap of his underwear. Her eyes went from his face, past his muscular chest and all the way down his abs. She followed the lines of his hips, as he pulled his underwear down. Inch by inch, he slipped them off until they got past his knees and fell to the floor at his feet. He now stood next to the bed, gloriously naked and fully erect.

Marco kicked his pants and underwear to the side and then got back on the bed. This time, though, he sat behind her. He pulled her hair to the side and kissed the back of her neck, sending a pleasurable chill down Sabrina's spine. She let out a slow breath, as his soft lips grazed her sensitive skin. His hands were on her sides and she leaned backward a bit, pressing her body against him.

She closed her eyes and focused on the sensation of Marco's hands. He had wrapped his arms around her and his fingertips danced along the outside of her hips, teasing the top of her panties. His hands were warm and his contact was sensual and safe. The way he touched her and kissed her neck made her feel like she was the most beautiful woman in the entire world. And for the moment, she was at least the *center* of Marco's world, and that was enough for her.

His hands wandered around to her back and then up to the clasp of her bra.

"May I?" he asked, with a little chuckle.

Sabrina nodded. "Yes, of course."

Marco undid the clasp and then carefully slid the shoulder straps off until the bra fell down her arms, exposing her chest to the air. She leaned back toward him, encouraging him to touch her. Marco's hands went to her belly and then upward, cradling her breasts in his hands. An electric shock of pleasure pulsed into her. His touch was gentle yet firm, as he fondled her. She moaned softly, unable to find any words as his touch stole any ability to think.

Marco growled softly, his lips grazing the outside of her neck until he brought his lips to hers. His hands were all over her as he sat behind her on the bed. She wanted his touch, and too much of it would never have been enough. After a moment, though, she broke the kiss. The desperate ache inside of her had become too strong, and there was only one thing that could quench the fire. She scooted over a bit on the bed and then laid back, resting her head on the pillows.

Marco laid beside her. He touched her breasts, gliding his fingers carefully over her hard nipples. It sent a shiver of sensation into her and she groaned softly, pressing her chest out. Marco then crawled over the top of her. He placed his hands onto the bed, just above her shoulders and held himself up like that. His breathing was deep and intense now, and the look of lust in his eyes were more prominent then before. He licked his lips and then brought his face down to her breasts, flicking his tongue against one of her nipples.

He licked the sensitive nub a few times and then brought his mouth over it. Sabrina gasped, as bliss continued to fill her. She moved her body, gently grinding her hips upward against Marco's. The movement caused him to slide between her legs. She still had her panties on, but she could feel everything. His length pressed against the thin cotton, creating friction against her.

Sabrina drew in a breath through her teeth. Marco slowly pulled his mouth away from her breast, creating a wet kissing noise as he withdrew. He licked his lips again and then brought his face over her other nipple, giving it the same attention. Meanwhile, Sabrina continued to buck her hips upward, grinding against his cock. The double pleasure had her squirming beneath him.

After a moment, he pulled his face away and then brought his lips to the center of her cleavage. He kissed there and then made his way downward, dragging his lips and tongue in a straight line. When he got to her belly button, he didn't stop. He pressed on all the way to her panties. Sabrina opened her eyes and watched him. He looked up at her and smirked, as he gently tugged on her underwear.

As if to say, *"Yes, take them off"*, she lifted her butt from the bed to aid him in getting her undressed. Marco pulled her panties down and slipped them all the way off. Then he immediately brought his mouth back to where he had left off, which was just a few inches below her belly button. Sabrina opened her legs, as Marco dragged his tongue downward. Anticipation filled her as he neared her most sensitive area. He let his lips dance just above it, delicately teasing her.

Sabrina reached down and gently gripped a handful of Marco's hair. She was aching now, needing his touch. The teasing was only making it worse.

"Marco, please," she begged, her words stumbling out in a breath.

He kissed just above her pussy once more and then moved his face downward. As his tongue collided with her clit, a powerful wave of ecstasy filled her. She squeezed the handful of his hair and pulled his face against her. He let out a growl. The vibration from his throat transmitted toward her, making the pleasure even more intense. Then worked the same magic on her flower as he had on her nipples. He lapped at her sensitive clit, with just the right amount of pressure.

Sabrina leaned her head back into the pillows. She let go of Marco's hair and then brought her hands to her sides, firmly grabbing the comforter below her. It was sensory overload. Every part of her body lit on fire. Each lap of Marco's tongue brought another pulse of sensation. Her legs trembled as she relaxed them over his shoulders. He pleasured her like this for just a minute or so and then he finally pulled away. She looked forward, watching as Marco crawled off of the bed and went to the dresser to get a condom. As he walked back, he slipped it on and then positioned himself in front of her once again.

She was tingling now, every cell in her body rippling from the after effects of the sensations that she was experiencing. Her eyes were locked onto Marco, as he opened her legs and positioned himself between them. He was erect between her thighs and his tip brushed her opening.

Marco clenched his jaw as he held his body over Sabrina's. Their eyes were locked as he moved his hips into the right spot. Then he pressed forward, slowly entering her. Her eyes rolled into the back of her head and her jaw dropped as a deep wave of sensation filled her from head to toe. Marco slid his entire length in. Sabrina wrapped her hands around his back, digging her fingers into his muscles, as they made love. He started slow, but it wasn't long before he had quickened his pace. Their bodies were entangled, moving steadily in a rhythmic dance that had Sabrina's head spinning.

She watched him as he moved. His muscles flexed and relaxed to his cadence. His fair fell down across his face, messy and tangled from when she had grabbed at it. It made him look sexy, though. It gave him an edgy appearance, like something a rock star would have.

Marco leaned forward and kissed her. Sabrina wrapped her legs around his waist. The small change of position caused the pleasure to intensify. Marco's thickness was now creating a powerful friction against her clit with each thrust. She squealed out in pleasure, gripping his shoulders at the same time.

"Yes, like that," she panted. "Just like that."

He kept pace, entering her with the movement of a piston. He was rhythmic and steady, going in as deep as possible each time. Sabrina became lost in ecstasy, too overwhelmed with bliss to even remember to breath. The pleasure intensified with each pump of Marco's cock. The sensation built up inside of her, pushing her further and further toward orgasm.

Once again, she clutched the blanket on either side of her. A soft moan escaped her lips as the pleasure combined into one glorious moment of orgasm. She drew in a breath, letting the final wave of ecstasy soak through every part of her being. A burst of wetness flowed out of her and onto Marco's cock. She kept her eyes closed for a moment, frozen by the onslaught of sensation. When she finally opened them, she let go of the blanket and noticed that her hands were trembling.

Marco slowed his pace down but continued making love to her. A light layer of sweat now covered his skin, accentuating his muscular definition even further. Sabrina touched his forearms, dancing her fingertips all the way to his shoulders.

"You are so gorgeous," he said, locking his eyes with hers. "I want you on top of me."

Sabrina nodded and her lips curled up into a playful grin. "Okay."

Marco pulled out and then laid on his back. Sabrina straddled over his lap, letting his crown hover just below her entrance. His hands went to her breasts. His eyes moved up and down her body. The way he looked at her was special. She could sense it. It made her feel like he truly meant it when he called her gorgeous.

With her hands on Marco's chest, she dropped her weight, allowing his length to slide inside once again. He let out a groan and closed his eyes, fondling her breasts at the same time. Sabrina began to ride him, moving her body up and down slowly. It felt amazing, but what she enjoyed the most was watching the look of pleasure that was written all over Marco's face. Each of her movements caused his eyes to roll back a little further and his hands to squeeze her breasts a little harder. She enjoyed the feeling of being able to give him the kind of pleasure that he had given her.

It didn't take long. Within a couple of minutes, the expression on Marco's face changed. His cheeks flushed and the outside of his lips curled into a grimace. He dropped his hands to her thighs and squeezed them. Then he took control of the movement by bucking his hips upward.

"I'm coming," he groaned, his hands slipping around to her behind.

Sabrina bit her bottom lip as she watched Marco climax. Every inch of her was burning for him, wanting this moment. He drew in a breath and held it. His eyes were closed and his muscles tensed. There were a few seconds of quiet, followed by an animal-sounding grunt escaping from Marco's throat. Slowly, Marco opened his eyes. He looked dazed yet content.

Sabrina leaned close and Marco placed his hand on the

back of her head, pulling her in for a kiss. She touched his cheek, letting her fingers get tickled by his beard stubble. Her legs still trembled as she straddled him, the after-effects of her intense orgasm still seeping through her. She slowly pulled her lips away from his and then laid next to him on the bed. She was exhausted, but in the best of ways.

"You're amazing," Marco said, turning to face her.

She cuddled up to him, wrapping her arm over his torso. "You're pretty amazing yourself."

It was, with no exaggeration, the best sex she had ever had in her life. It was filled with passion, lust, desire, attraction and... love?

*Is it possible that I could actually fall for this guy this quickly?* she asked herself, as she drew imaginary circles over his abdominal muscles. *It hasn't even been a week.*

Sabrina couldn't deny the emotion inside of her. Marco was everything she could have ever wanted. But that wasn't enough to allow her to open her heart to him just yet. Sure, the sex was incredible, but there were still so many unanswered questions.

*I don't even know where he's from, or how he got all this money, and I can't find out,* she thought. *The only thing I know is that being with him feels amazing. But is that enough?*

She closed her eyes, resting into Marco's warm body. Her thoughts faded in and out as a much-needed sleep approached. Questions bounced around her brain. She wondered if this was just a casual event for Marco or if he really liked her and would be interested in something more serious. In an effort to avoid disappointment, though, she decided she'd be okay with no matter how things turned out.

*Worst case scenario, Marco and I will get to enjoy each others' company for a couple of weeks until he goes home,* she thought. *And I guess I can live with that.*

Safe in Marco's arms, Sabrina let her thoughts pass. With her mind relaxed and her body exhausted, she drifted off into the deepest sleep she had had in years.

# CHAPTER 11

arco

MARCO FOUND HIMSELF IN A DREAM. In it, he was standing on a beach, his bare feet digging into the hot sand. He looked out across the ocean as the warm breeze blew the smell of saltwater toward him. He knew where he was, and didn't even have to look around to find out. Orsino Island, his home. It was obvious, because even though he was dreaming, he could feel the nostalgia of that point on the beach. He'd spent countless summers there as a child and many days there as an adult. It was a place that only he knew about. A place where he could go to get away from all of the stresses of life.

But in this dream, something felt noticeably different. There was a hand gripping his own. It pulled his attention away from the ocean view and when he looked over to his side, he saw a beautiful and fair-skinned girl standing next to him. She was wearing an elegant white dress, which fell almost all the way to the sand. She glanced toward him and smiled, taking Marco's breath away.

*Sabrina,* he thought. *What's she doing here?*

She gazed into his eyes, her lips curling up into a warm smile. His knees became wobbly, but his heart burst with joy. Somewhere in his mind, he knew that this experience was only a dream, but it felt so real. The sunshine warmed his skin and he could taste the air. He was even pretty sure that he could smell Sabrina's perfume. The moment was perfect and he didn't want to wake up. He could have stayed there forever.

There was so much he wanted to tell her. He wanted to make sure she knew exactly how he felt, how much she made his heart pound with joy.

Marco parted his lips to speak, but before he could utter a sound, a flash of lightning hit nearby. It shook the ground and when he glanced back toward the ocean he noticed that the sky had turned black. A violet storm had come rushing in within seconds, taking them by surprise.

"Marco, we should go," Sabrina said, pulling on his hand. Fear filled her voice.

But Marco couldn't budge. He couldn't stop looking toward the ocean. Just above the horizon, there was a face in the clouds. It was unrecognizable at first. But as the sky shifted, it became more and more clear. It was the image of his stepmother, Magdalena. Her face filled an area the size of the sun. Her lips were curled into an evil grin and she was laughing hysterically.

"What in the hell is going on?" Marco asked. "What are you doing, Magdalena?"

Magdalena stopped laughing. Dark clouds swirled around her face in the sky, as if they were trying to avoid her. She brought her gaze past Marco and straight to Sabrina, her eyes sharpening. "You don't belong here, *commoner*." Her wretched voice boomed and shook the ground harder than the thunder.

Marco became defensive, wishing to protect Sabrina, who was still tugging on his arm to leave. Strikes of lightning shot from the sky and collided with ground, just a few feet away from them. The sound was deafening and the energy from it nearly knocked Marco over. But he didn't care. He wasn't going to budge. He was going to stand there and get hit by the lightning if that's what it took.

*Sabrina is not a commoner,* he thought. *And I'm done getting pushed around by stepmother.*

He was about shout at Magdalena and give her a piece of his mind, but then everything became quiet. The lightning stopped and the image of his stepmother in the sky faded away as the dark clouds cleared. A moment later, the only sound that could be heard was that of a honking horn.

*What the...* he thought.

Marco's eyes shot open and he squinted immediately as the morning light from the hotel window entered them. The sound of the horn that had pulled him from his dream was still there, followed by someone shouting in traffic outside the hotel. Marco sat up, letting the blanket fall to his waist. Beads of sweat dotted his forehead and his heart beat rapidly in his chest.

*What was that all about?* he asked himself, as he tried to get his heart rate back to normal. *I haven't had a dream that intense in a very long time.*

When he looked over to the other side of the bed, he saw Sabrina laying there, still sound asleep. The sunlight blanketed her face, illuminating her features. A strand of her light brown hair fell across her forehead, contrasting against her fair skin. Marco couldn't help but to smile as he gazed at her. And the warm feeling he had experienced in the dream, the one before Magdalena had shown up, returned to him. It was the feeling of love, or maybe just a serious crush. He couldn't be sure. All he knew is that he felt *something* toward Sabrina and it was powerful.

*Could I love this girl?* He asked himself. *Is it possible that she's the real reason I came on this trip? Was I destined to meet her?*

Marco was most certainly one to pay attention to his dreams. He never wrote them off as meaningless and would constantly try to make a point to find their reason.

With that in mind, he realized that there were two main themes that he had noticed during his dream. One, was that he was falling in love with Sabrina and he couldn't deny it to himself. The other, was that Magdalena would most certainly disapprove of it. Of course, Marco didn't need to have a dream in order to realize that Magdalena wouldn't approve of his choices, but it did bring to light the fact that she would be the biggest hurdle he'd have.

It wouldn't have been the first time, either. Every time Marco had ever wanted to get serious with a girl, his step-mother would step in to prevent it somehow. She'd sabotage the relationship one way or the other, usually with the excuse that the particular girl was "no good for the royal family." Marco knew that Sabrina would be no different in Magdalena's eyes. But his heart ached longingly for this so-called commoner who laid next to him in the bed. This girl was different and special.

*I want to be able to love whomever I want,* he thought. *This is my life, isn't it? Shouldn't a man be able to live it how he sees fit and love whatever woman steals his heart?*

He quietly crawled off the bed, so as not to disturb Sabrina. After slipping on his black silk robe, he walked out to the living room and sat on the couch. He'd tried to fight it at first, but it was becoming clear to him that he was legitimately falling for this woman. She had taken him off guard from the moment they met for her interview. Something about the way she carried herself, so innocent yet strong. And genuine. Sabrina was the most genuine girl he'd ever met and was beautiful in ways that he couldn't put into words.

*There is no way that I can let a girl like this slip through my fingers,* he thought. *I don't care what Magdalena or my father will say about it. If she'll have me, I will be her man, regardless of the opinions of my family. Tradition will not stand in my way.*

Marco was resolute in his thinking. The decision to attempt an actual relationship with Sabrina excited him. Traditions and royal blood lines were a thing of the past. Sabrina was his future. He had a couple more weeks before he had to go back home and he hoped that he'd be able to convince her to go with him once that time came. Granted, he had no clue whether or not she'd actually *want* to but he figured by the time the vacation was over, he'd at least have a pretty good idea.

He got up from the couch and walked to the kitchen to make a cup of coffee. He also ordered room service for the two of them from the TV menu. This included eggs, bacon and bagels. After he was done with that, he walked across the hotel suite and outside to the back patio. The morning sun warmed his skin and he closed his eyes as he faced it.

*I've got just a couple of weeks to convince Sabrina to be my girl,* he thought. *A few more days in New York and then we'll be heading to Hawaii for the remainder of the vacation. Is that enough time to convince a girl that I'm the one for her? I guess it'll have to be.*

Marco's mind whirled with ideas. He wanted to squeeze

every drop he could from the short amount of time that he had left with Sabrina. There was not a minute to waste.

*I'm not sure what I'll end up doing about Magdalena, but I do know that if I really love this girl then I need to show it in as many ways as I can. She and I need to have a solid and firm relationship if we are to have a chance at facing Magdalena's wrath. Of course, all of this hinges on whether or not Sabrina feels the same about me as I do her. That's something I need to find out.*

Sabrina became Marco's focus. Sure, he was excited about doing a little bit more traveling, but he was quickly becoming much more interested in the girl he was with. New York City seemed drab and boring compared to the beauty she carried in a single smile. He was looking forward to the next couple of weeks to see what it would bring.

The image of the dream he had experienced earlier that morning flashed into his mind. He thought about the beginning of it when he had been standing on the beach, holding hands with Sabrina. His heart swelled as he relived it, hoping that there was a chance that at least that part of the dream could become a reality. Meanwhile, he prayed that the second half of the dream when, the part when Magdalena reared her ugly head and ruined everything, was only a figment of his imagination.

*I guess I'll find out soon enough how things will play out,* he thought, as he turned around and walked back inside as he heard Sabrina rise from the bed. *Meanwhile, I've got to make the most of the time Sabrina and I have together.*

# CHAPTER 12

S*abrina*

SABRINA FELT the warmth of the morning sun on her face, but didn't want to open her eyes quite yet. She was so cozy and comfortable underneath the blanket. Even the honking horns and revving engines from the traffic outside didn't disturb her.

In the living room, she could hear Marco walking around and humming quietly to himself. Her lips curled up into a smile as she listened.

*I guess it wasn't just a dream,* she thought.

His footsteps got closer and she felt his hand touch her shoulder.

"Wake up, sleepy," he whispered. "We have a lot do to today."

She rolled over to face him and opened her eyes. Marco stood next to the bed, wearing nothing but a black robe.

"Good morning, beautiful," Marco said, smiling. "I

ordered room service and it should be here in a few minutes."

"What time is it?" Sabrina asked, as she sat up in bed and stretched her arms above her head.

When she did, the blanket fell off of her front and exposed her naked chest. She squealed in embarrassment and did her best to cover herself with her hands.

"Sorry, I forgot I was naked under here," she said, scrambling to pull the blanket back up.

Marco sat on the edge of the bed and gently touched the top of her arm. "Please don't ever apologize for that."

Sabrina laughed. "How long have you been awake?"

"Just a few minutes," Marco said, still tenderly touching her shoulder. "Just long enough to order room service. It's only nine in the morning but I wanted to wake you so that we can get going. I've made a change of plans."

"A change of plans?" she asked, her eyebrows rising. "What do you mean?"

"I know that we had originally planned on being in New York for another week, but I got to thinking this morning," he said, taking a dramatic pause. "I want to take you some place special, some place romantic."

Her heart swelled as he listened to him speak. Nobody had ever wanted to take her any place special before.

"I like the sound of that," she said, reaching forward to squeeze his hand. "Where are you thinking?"

Marco's smile widened from ear to ear. He looked like a kid who was about to open up the biggest Christmas present under the tree. "How would you feel about spending the rest of this vacation in Hawaii?"

Sabrina's eyes widened and her jaw dropped. There was no way that she had heard him correctly.

"Hawaii?" she asked, as a burst of excitement filled her.

"I thought you wanted to check out California and maybe New Orleans."

"I *did*," he said, leaning in a little bit closer. "But let me ask you something, Sabrina. Have you ever been to Hawaii?"

"No, of course not," she said, shaking her head. "I've hardly been outside of Tennessee."

"That's why I want to take you there," he replied. "A city will be full of people that want to take our pictures and force us to blend in. Let's take a flight to Hawaii today and make this the best trip of our lives."

Her heart was beating wildly now. She felt like jumping up and down, and she probably would have if she wasn't still naked underneath the covers.

"That sounds incredible," she said, as she brought her face closer to his.

Their lips collided and that exact moment was when she felt it. It was as though the entire world shrunk down and the only two people that existed in it were she and Marco. This man, the one who was the last person she should have ended up with, was also the same one who had her heart. She couldn't put the feeling into words or even an organized thought, but in that moment she realized that this was a man she could truly love. Of course, only if she allowed herself to do so.

Marco broke the kiss, but kept his eyes locked with hers. "So that's a yes?"

"Of course that's a yes," she said. "I'll call Valetta and get the trip scheduled. You said you wanted to leave today, right? I'll run down to the front desk in a bit to tell them that we'll be checking out early."

Her words stumbled out of her mouth quickly. She was so excited that she could hardly breathe. She had known that this job would entail some traveling and sight-seeing, but never could she have imagined that it would take her to a place as magnificent as Hawaii. But in addition to being excited about the hot sun and the warm water of Hawaii, she was also looking forward to spending the time there with Marco.

*This is going to be so romantic. Hawaii, really? Could this job get any better?* she thought. *I can't wait to tell my parents about this. They probably won't even believe me when I tell them where I'm headed.*

"WELL, WHAT DO YOU THINK?" Sabrina asked Marco, as the cab driver dropped them off at the end of a paved driveway.

They gazed up the hill to where a beautiful little cabin stood, its backdrop the lush jungle. Huge windows overlooked the both the greenery and the ocean on the other side.

"I think this is absolutely perfect," he said, throwing his duffel bag over his shoulder and then grabbing Sabrina's hand.

"Valetta suggested a hotel, but I thought this would be better," Sabrina explained. "Here, we don't have to worry about anyone else."

"I think that this will be so much better than a boring hotel," he said, squeezing her hand. "Besides, this place is only a few minutes from the beach. What more could we ask for?"

Marco's private plane had landed them on the big island of Hawaii a half an hour prior and they had taken a private car to their place. Sabrina was tired from the long journey, but had a renewed energy now that the reality of the situation had finally settled in.

*I can't believe I'm actually in Hawaii right now,* she thought.

The closest she had ever come had been while looking at travel magazines during a dentist's visit. She'd always get lost in the articles, imagining what it would actually feel like to be there. She had always thought of it as a place reserved for rich people, but those ideas faded quickly as she walked up the driveway toward the cabin.

The house was stunning. Huge floor to ceiling windows seemed to line every wall, giving amazing views of both the jungle and and the ocean. Several of them were open, allowing in the scent and sound of the water. Sabrina set her bags down and walked around back. She could hear the ocean and wanted to see just how close they were.

"Whoa," she whispered, stepping out onto a wooden deck through an open door.

The large opening in the trees behind the cabin revealed a panoramic view of the ocean. The water was deep blue in color, contrasting against the white sand. It was breathtaking and Sabrina found herself staring at it. She wasn't sure exactly why, but a tear came to her eye and slid down her cheek. Standing there, looking at the ocean that she thought she'd never see, was a very emotional experience for her. It represented a lot. She'd come so far in life and seeing the ocean was proof to her that dreams sometimes actually do come true.

The moment was bittersweet, though. She thought of her parents, who were back home working hard to just pay the bills. She felt a bit of guilt, wondering why she got to be so lucky and they never had the chance.

*Maybe someday when I'm making steady money and have a good career, I can take them out here to see this,* she thought. *I can already imagine my mother's smile. Even Dad might smile if I told him I was flying them to Hawaii.*

A clattering sound came from the cabin and Sabrina spun around. She ran inside, where she saw Marco standing in the kitchen looking down at a broken plate.

"I'm terribly sorry," he said. "I was going to make us a quick dinner so that we could take a walk before it gets dark. Clearly, though, I've no business attempting to cook."

Sabrina put her hand over her mouth to keep from laughing. Marco looked so disappointed, but she found it to be cute. "It's just a plate, Marco. It happens. I'll clean it up."

She found a broom in the closet by the front door and went to sweep up the remnants of the porcelain plate. Marco stood outside of the kitchen, as though he were afraid he'd break something else if he got too close. Once the floor was swept, Sabrina looked across the room to Marco. "What were you going to cook, if you don't mind me asking?"

Marco shrugged. "While you were outside, I looked through the cabinets. I saw a pack of dry noodles and I was going to add some eggs and vegetables to them."

The cabin came fully stocked, which was another reason Sabrina had chosen to go with it over the hotel. A full fridge and pantry meant that they wouldn't have to run to the grocery store, which in turn meant that it would be less likely someone would find out that Marco was in Hawaii.

"That's sweet of you," she said, her heartwarming from the kind gesture. "But I'm happy to cook some food. There are lots of things to eat here."

"I'm sure you're exhausted from the flight, though," Marco said, hesitantly stepping back into the kitchen and next to Sabrina. "We can go get food somewhere. I'm certain there are restaurants nearby."

"It's completely up to you," she said. "But I'm happy to finish the meal you had started. Then we can take that walk you were talking about."

Marco nodded in agreement. "As long as you don't mind."

Sabrina put her hands on her hips and cocked her head to the side. "Marco, you're paying me to help you out. I certainly don't mind making us food."

He smiled warmly. "Fair enough. Let's cook a meal tonight and we'll go out for a nice dinner tomorrow night. How does that sound?"

"Sounds like a marvelous plan," she said, spinning around to start the food.

It didn't take long to cook. She quickly boiled some noodles and then added fresh veggies to it, topped with some tomato sauce. It wasn't too fancy, but she didn't want to waste too much time. It was already dusk and if they wanted to take a walk then they needed to hurry.

While she had been hard at work in the kitchen, Marco had slipped away around the corner, where the only bedroom was located. He showed up a few minutes before the food was finished and he had a giant smile.

"Look what I found in the back of the closet," he said, holding up a wicker picnic basket. "How would you feel about an evening picnic on the beach?"

"Now tell me, Marco, how could I possibly say 'no' to something like that?" she said, with a giggle. "I'll pack up the food and a bottle of wine. We can head out in less than five minutes."

She pulled the noodles off of the stove and decided to change into something more comfortable while the food cooled. She made her way to the bedroom and heaved her suitcase up onto the bed. After digging through her clothes, she finally found something that she considered suitable for a dinner on the beach. It was a silky black dress with red flower petals on it. Her mother had found it at a second-hand store, but even though it hadn't cost very much, it still looked expensive. It was probably the nicest dress Sabrina owned and she decided that their first night in Hawaii would be the perfect opportunity to wear it.

So she stripped off her clothes and then stepped into the dress. She brought her hands down her sides, feeling the smooth material. Then she walked over to the mirror that hung above the wooden dresser. As she brushed her hair, she thought about her deepening feelings toward Marco.

*Where is this really headed?* She asked herself. *And when do I just come clean to him about my feelings?*

Her mind and heart felt separated. A battle waged between them. Her heart knew exactly what it wanted. It wished to open up and fall in love with Marco, carelessly throwing all she had at him. But her mind quarreled, unable to fully accept a relationship with him as a real possibility. Doubt crept just below the surface and she continued to question just how it could work out.

The door to the bedroom slowly creaked open and Sabrina glanced over to see Marco in the doorway. He was holding the picnic basket in one hand and an unopened bottle of red wine in the other. He leaned against the door jam and tilted his head, causing his hair to fall across his face.

"You've been in here a while," he said. "I just wanted to make sure everything was okay."

"Everything is fine," she said, with a nod. "I guess I was caught up in my own mind for a minute. Are you ready to go? I still need to pack up the food."

"One step ahead of you," he said, holding the basket up in the air. "I'm ready when you are."

Sabrina glanced out of the bedroom window, noticing that the sky had begun to turn a shade of orange.

"If we hurry, we can catch the sunset," she said, as she slipped on a pair of sandals and followed Marco out the door.

The two of them walked quickly down the hill behind the cabin, making their way through the lush foliage that separated them from the beach. Sabrina hurried ahead, running straight to the edge of the water and pausing at the wet sand before dipping her toes. She held the hem of her dress up as a single wave washed over her feet.

The sun was sinking quickly, but the air was still so warm. Sabrina brought her gaze to the horizon and gasped when she saw the view. The sky had become an explosion of color, a combination of blue, purple and orange. Rays of light shot through the few clouds that hovered above the ocean, making the scene look more like a painting than reality.

"It's amazing," she whispered. "Oh my gosh, so beautiful."

Marco stepped side her and placed his hand onto her lower back. She looked over at him, admiring the way the colors of the sunset reflected on his dark eyes and gave his face an orange glow. By the time she looked at the horizon again, the sun had sunk a little further and the colors in the sky changed to a deeper purple.

"I have to say that I'm very glad I decided to bring us here," Marco said as they walked back to dry land. He pulled a blanket out of the picnic basket and spread it out on the sand. "New York was great, but I prefer a view like this any day."

Sabrina nodded in agreement. Marco had been right when he said that a city was just a city. There were buildings, cars and people. But the paradise they stood in now was so much more intriguing. She took a seat on the blanket and Marco sat across from her. A light breeze blew off of the ocean and caused Marco's hair to fall across his face. He looked up and smiled at her. Her heart swelled when she realized that the view of him trumped the view of the sunset.

He reached into the picnic basket and pulled out the bottle of red wine. Sabrina watched as he opened it and poured two glasses. As soon as the wine was poured, Marco crawled across the blanket and sat next to her. Together, they sipped their wine while watching the last few minutes of the sunset.

A realization occurred to Sabrina. She found herself happier in this moment than she could ever remember being in her entire life. There was a deep peace inside of her. Maybe it was the warmth of the air, or the fresh breeze. Or maybe it was that she was there with Marco.

*I'm living a life right now that I only ever dreamed of,* she thought.

Marco scooted a bit closer to her and wrapped his arm around her back. Sabrina closed her eyes and leaned toward him, placing her head against his shoulder.

*There is literally no other place on Earth where I'd rather be right now,* she thought. *This is perfect. This is what life should feel like.*

"This is perfect," Sabrina whispered.

"And we have a whole two weeks more," Marco whispered before kissing the top of her head.

Sabrina grinned and relaxed against him. She couldn't imagine a better two weeks.

# CHAPTER 13

 *abrina*

"Picnic again?" Marco offered, holding up the basket.

Sabrina laughed. "We've had a picnic every night for the past eight days," she informed him. "And I still say yes every time. So, yes. I'd love a picnic on the beach."

Marco grinned at her and his dark eyes sparkled as he helped her gather a simple meal with a bottle of wine to enjoy on the beach. It had become something of a tradition for the two of them now, and the fact that there were only a few days left before Marco needed to return home to be with his father broke Sabrina's heart.

She never wanted this to end. She wanted their happy days to continue on forever, even though she knew they couldn't. There were signs of change coming. The pantry was running low on supplies and they only had two more bottles of wine left. Restocking was as simple as making a phone call, but it still meant that time was passing.

Hand in hand, the two of them walked along the sandy path to the beach to watch the sunset over the ocean. These days were paradise. They made love on the beach, played in the water, and then would go back up to the house to make love again.

Which reminded Sabrina that food wasn't the only thing that needed to be restocked if they were going to stay in their perfect paradise.

Marco stood and stared at the horizon as Sabrina finished unpacking the last few things for their meal.

"What are you looking at, Marco?" she asked, following his gaze out across the ocean. The sky was just starting to change from blue to pinks, but he wasn't looking at the color.

"Just thinking of home," he replied. He shook himself and sat down on the blanket next to her. "I want to show it to you someday."

Everything she wanted to tell Marco came bubbling to the surface. Her heart had been aching for the opportunity to tell him how she felt and this quiet moment on the beach seemed like as good of a time as any.

"Marco, can I ask you something?" Sabrina said, as she opened her eyes to see that the sky had grown a darker shade of purple in just a few seconds.

He was silent for a moment, as he took a sip from his wine. Then he set the glass down next to him and kissed the top of her head. When he pulled away he said, "You can ask me anything."

Sabrina's chest tingled with anxiety. She was about to put herself on the line and risk embarrassment.

"I'm not really the best at this sort of thing," she said, nervously fidgeting with her hands.

Her confidence waned and she suddenly wished she

hadn't brought it up. It had sounded like a good idea until she actually started telling him.

"Actually, never mind," she said, shaking her head.

She leaned forward and let out a discouraged sigh. Marco brought his hand up her back, gently massaging her shoulders.

"Sabrina, please," he said. "Tell me what's on your mind. I promise that I would never judge you. You can tell me anything. Really."

She turned to face him and his expression was one of legitimate concern. He stared straight at her and smiled warmly.

"Really?" she asked.

"Yes," he said, still massaging her shoulders. "Really."

Sabrina drew in a breath and exhaled slowly. "Marco, I've had more fun on this trip than any other time in my entire life. At first, I thought it was simply because I was getting to see new places and eat at nice restaurants. But I've realized that those things weren't the real reason I've been enjoying myself so much. It's because of you that I've had so much fun. Even when things were crazy, like running from the paparazzi, I was still having a good time because it was with you."

Her face felt hot and she knew she was blushing, but she had come too far with spilling her guts to turn back now. Marco sat silently and appeared to be listening intently as she spoke.

"I know that you're not from here and that you have a home to go back to," she continued. "But even so, I can't stop thinking about the fact that we're perfect for each other. We have so much fun and there's so much passion between us. I really like you, Marco. A lot. I'm sorry to dump this on you all at once. But if I didn't at least tell you how I felt, I'd kick myself for the rest of my life."

Marco lips parted and he leaned in close to Sabrina. She was stunned when he kissed her. He pressed his lips to hers with a passion unlike anything she'd ever felt. She hardly had time to realize what had happened before Marco broke the kiss and looked her in the eyes.

"Sabrina, I'm overjoyed to hear you say this," he said. "I've been thinking the exact same thing and have been merely waiting for a proper opportunity to tell you. You're all I've been able to think about since we arrived in New York. I've never felt like this about someone. You excite me in ways that no other woman has and you make me feel at ease when I should be stressed. You've brought peace to my life that I didn't expect when I hired you. I thought I was hiring someone to help me cook and clean, but it turned out that I hired the girl of my dreams."

His words were so sincere and hearing it made tears well up in Sabrina's eyes. She was so relieved that he felt the same way and her concern of losing him washed away.

"Like you said, though, I do live far away and will inevitably end up going home at the end of this trip. I have to, for my father. He needs me there," Marco said. "But, if you're willing, I'd love nothing more than for you to come with me."

A tear fell down Sabrina's cheek and Marco pushed it away with his thumb. She was shocked by the invitation. It was what she had hoped, but didn't expect for him to ask so soon.

"Where is 'home'?" she asked. "I still don't know where you're from, Marco."

"Orsino Island," he said and for the first time Sabrina

found out something about his life. "It's a small island in the Mediterranean."

"An island?" she asked, unable to hide her girlish smile. "Like the one we're on?"

"It's similar in many ways," he said. "But also very different. It's a paradise, just like here."

Sabrina's mind whirled with thoughts and emotion. She imagined living on the beach, soaking up the sun every day and coming home to Marco each night. She thought about what it would feel like to be treated so well for the rest of her life. It sounded incredible and there was no way that she could turn this kind of opportunity down.

"Let's do it," she said, affirmatively. "I want to come with you."

Marco's face lit up brighter than she had ever seen and he kissed her again. They embraced on the blanket while the sun finished it decline behind the horizon. Even as the sky went dark, they continued to kiss. They kissed for what seemed like a blissful eternity to Sabrina and once again, she didn't want the moment to end.

But in the very back of her mind, there was a nagging voice. It was the whisper of doubt, the same voice that had caused her to hesitate her entire life. This time, though, what it said actually made some sense to her.

*I'm in love with a mystery man and I just agreed to move to the other side of the planet with him,* she thought. *That's not going to work. I need to find out who he is.*

Sabrina decided that she would start asking very pointed questions about Marco's life, like who he really was and what he did for a living. She wondered what the legal ramifications would be now if she looked up his island and figured out who he was.

*I want to know everything about him, but I'm not going to ruin tonight with a bunch of questions,* she thought. *He will tell me everything tomorrow.*

arco

THE SOUND of Marco's cell phone ringing pulled him out of his slumber. He opened his eyes to find that his arm was still wrapped around Sabrina, in the exact position that they had fallen asleep. They were both fully clothed, though. They hadn't had sex that night, only snuggles and kisses. He didn't want the entire relationship to be built around sex anyway, so he was content to have an evening where they just held each other and talked.

The phone continued to ring on the nightstand and he rolled over to see that the call was coming from the palace. He quickly sat up and answered it. He hadn't heard from his father in several days and was growing concerned. The only contact he had was now through Magdalena.

"Hello?" he said, standing up from the bed and scurrying out to the kitchen. "Father is that you?"

"Marco." The voice that replied was as cold as a witch's heart and sent a chill down his spine.

Marco sighed. "Good morning, Magdalena," he said. "And to what do I owe the honor of hearing your voice today?"

"Don't get a big head, Marco," she shot back. "I was merely called to double-check that you'll be home for the ball and for your father's surgery. I didn't want you to forget."

"Yes, I will absolutely be there," he said, as he paced the kitchen. His blood pressure rose easily five points just to the sound of her voice, but he did his best to stay calm. "May I speak to my father?"

"He's resting," she stated.

"He's been resting every time I've called him," Marco growled. "Yet, you always have his phone so he cannot call me."

"He needs his rest and I'm making sure he gets it," Magdalena informed him. "He's only got a few days before the ball and he needs to be in tip top shape."

"So you've called just to check in on me?" Marco asked. "No other reason?"

"I think that's reason enough," she said, with a chuckle. "A boy like you needs to be checked in upon, as I'm not certain you can take care of yourself."

Marco cleared his throat, and took a seat in a wooden chair at the corner of the living room. The memory of the dream he had had the day before flashed into his mind, where Magdalena's snarling face had shown up in the clouds. He could see it now, imagining her in the same form as she spoke.

"You've accomplished what you needed to then," Marco

said. "You've checked in on me and I've told you that I will most certainly be at the ball. If that's all you wanted, then I must let you go. I've things to do and places to see and don't have a moment to spare."

"I certainly wouldn't want to interrupt your vacation more than I already have," she said, sarcastically. "I'll go and tell your sick father that you're having fun while he's in bed. I'm sure that's exactly what he wants to hear."

"Tell him whatever you want, stepmother," Marco said. "I'm sure by now he knows that most of what you say is a lie anyhow."

"You sound more like a commoner every day you're away," she replied.

"Good day, Magdalena," he said.

Without giving her a chance to respond, he hung up the phone and tossed it onto the couch nearby. He let out an agitated sigh as he kicked his feet up onto the coffee table in the center of the living room. His hands were clenched in anger.

*Sometimes I wonder what happened in that woman's life that turned her into such a horrible human being,* he thought.

His attention moved toward the bedroom, when he saw Sabrina standing in the doorway. Her hair was a mess and she let out a yawn, at the same time rubbing the sleep from her eyes with the back of her hands.

*Oh no, I must have woken her,* he thought. *I was speaking so loudly.*

"Good morning," he said. "Did I wake you?"

Sabrina nodded as she took a seat on the couch across from Marco.

"I've been awake for a little bit. Your phone woke me a few minutes ago," she said. "Sorry to be nosey, but I heard your phone conversation."

Marco swallowed, realizing that most of his conversation with Magdalena would be sure to raise questions for Sabrina.

"My stepmother is a witch," Marco said with a smile, in an attempt to lift his mood.

"It sounded like you don't get along very well with her," Sabrina said. "Did I hear you say something about a ball?"

"You did," Marco said.

"A ball is being held at your home?" she asked, covering her mouth as she yawned. "That sounds rather fancy."

Marco sighed and nodded his head. "Sabrina, I need to tell you some things that you don't know about me. I've hidden a lot from you and I think it's time to lay everything out on the table."

Sabrina sat up on the edge of the couch and leaned forward, bringing her elbows to her knees. Her eyebrows rose and she seemed extremely eager to hear what Marco had to say.

"I couldn't agree more," she said. "I know that I already agreed to move with you to your home, but I need to know more about you before I can say for sure that it's what I want to do."

"I understand," he said. "But before I tell you, please realize that the only reason I haven't given you this information until now is because I had no clue that I'd fall for you so hard. If you had stayed as just my employee, this all would have remained a secret."

"I know," she said, with a comforting smile. "The only reason I haven't looked it up is because I was your employee, but I think I should know what I'm getting myself into."

Marco's heart beat rapidly in his chest. This girl who sat across from him deserved to know who he was, but he feared that it would be shocking to her. He hoped that news of his royal blood would not be something that would sway her from wanting to be with him.

"Do you remember yesterday, when I told you where I came from?" he asked.

Sabrina nodded. "Of course. You said Orsino Island."

"Yes," he said. "But that's not the whole story. Orsino Island is not only where I reside, but is also the country that my family rules."

She stayed silent, her eyes sharpening as Marco spoke.

"You know me simply as Marco," he said, sitting up in the wooden chair. "But the rest of the world knows me as 'Prince Marco of Orsino Island'."

He held his breath after speaking the last sentence. He waited for the repercussion of the news, figuring that Sabrina would either jump for joy or pass out from shock. She did neither. Instead, a hesitant smile crossed her face. "You're joking, right?"

"I would never joke with you about something like this," he said, standing up from his chair so that he could sit next to Sabrina. "I realize this is probably not what you expected, but it is the truth. I'm from a royal family."

"*Prince* Marco?" she said, her expression still a bit suspicious.

"My father is the King of Orsino," Marco stated. "My stepmother, the one whom I was just speaking with on the phone, is his wife, Queen Magdalena. She's the one who scheduled his surgery and she's the one who decided to have a ball in his honor the night before."

"Is this for real or am I on some kind of hidden camera show?" she asked, as she scooted away from Marco. She glanced around the room, looking for hidden cameras.

Marco gently took her hand in his and gazed into her

eyes. "Sabrina, I would never lie to you. I didn't tell you before because I wanted my identity to remain a secret for this trip. There's no better way to keep a secret than by not telling it. But, I'm telling you now, though. I promise not to hide anything from you ever again."

"I'm just in shock right now," she said, her eyes welling with tears. She took three deep breaths that got shorter and more panicked with every inhale. "Marco, you're a *prince* for crying out loud. Do you know who I am? I'm a poor girl from the wrong side of the tracks in Memphis, Tennessee. What business would I have being you? I just... I don't know. I don't know about any of this anymore."

He squeezed her hand reassuringly. His heart ached as he heard her speak, because her doubts resembled the same rationalizations that had come from Magdalena's mouth. She'd said similar things about commoners and royalty not being suited for each other, but to hear it from Sabrina's lips pained him much more.

"Look at me," Marco said, putting his fingertips on her chin.

Sabrina turned to face him and he noticed that the tears had begun to fall down her cheeks. He loved this girl more than anything and seeing her cry made him hurt.

"You have to understand that I care about you," Marco said. "I realize we haven't known each other for very long, but that doesn't change the facts. I want to be with you and I don't care that we come from different walks of life. That doesn't matter to me."

She sighed and wiped her cheek with the back of her hand. "That's sweet of you to say, but I'm not stupid, Marco. This is real life. Look at me. I'm barely fit to clean your throne, let alone be with you on it. How would I possibly fit into the world that you come from?"

"You'd fit in, because you're beautiful in every way," he said. "I know where you're from, Sabrina. And it hasn't stopped me from getting close to you. Do you think I care where your clothes come from or how much they cost? It means nothing to me. I care about *you* and your heart and your dreams."

His words were able to get Sabrina to finally smile through her tears. "I just can't believe you're a prince. I've been hanging out with a freaking *prince* for the past few weeks. I guess it explains quite a bit, though. I suppose that's why the paparazzi chased us that day, because there was royalty sitting there eating beignets."

Marco smirked and lifted his shoulders into a shrug. "Your guess would be as good as mine as to why they'd want to film something like that."

Sabrina laughed and playfully pushed Marco's shoulders. "This is a lot to absorb. I'm sorry to act so overwhelmed, but this was the last thing in the world I thought you would have told me this morning."

She paused and the two of them sat silently for a moment. Then she looked over to Marco once again. "I hope I'm not stepping out of line by asking this, but if something happened to your father then you'd become…"

"King." Marco finished the sentence for her. "And in fact, nothing has to happen to my father for that situation to take place. He's stepping down from the throne after his surgery, though the public doesn't know this yet. But when he does, I will take the crown."

"You're not just a prince, you're going to be the king in the near future?" Sabrina brought her hand over her mouth and her eyes widened with shock. "I'm sorry, but this a lot to take in this early in the morning."

"Don't be sorry," Marco said, touching her hand reassuringly. "It *is* a lot and I'm sorry to deliver it all at once. But you need to know who I am if you are to come back home with me. I'd be a terrible person to not tell you."

"I'm glad you're telling me, honestly," Sabrina said. "In fact, I planned on asking you more questions to find out about you. But really, I'm sitting next to a king right now?"

"Just a prince, at the moment," he said, with a boyish smirk. "But yes, I will be king soon. It's been my destiny for as long as I can remember."

"Are you nervous?" Sabrina asked. "I mean, I'd be nervous."

"I've been groomed to be king my whole life," he replied with a shrug. "I've already taken over many of the responsibilities, but the formal passing of the title will happen soon."

"King Marco, huh?" Sabrina bit her lip, and shook her head, still processing his words.

"Yes, King Marco." He smiled at her. "That's part of the reason that my father's sickness has weighed so heavily on me. And also why I decided to take this vacation in the first place. With the news of Father's cancer, it became clear that time may not be on his side, and that I will likely become King sooner than later. I wanted to see some more of the world before my royal duties took over."

"And that woman, the one you were on the phone with… you said that was your stepmother," Sabrina said. "So that means you were arguing with the Queen of Orsino?"

Marco chuckled. "Yes, even though we are a royal family doesn't mean that we don't quarrel. She's a very difficult person to deal with."

The sun had completely risen now and tropical birds began making their calls outside of the cabin. Its sound reminded Marco of home.

"Sabrina, if you don't want to come with me when I go back home, I'll understand," he said. "I'll be heartbroken, but I won't blame you in that decision."

"I just have a lot to think about," she said. She held up her hand. "I'm not saying no, but let me have some time to allow this all to sink in."

"Of course," Marco said, happy to hear that Sabrina was still willing to consider it.

He'd told her a lot about his life, but one thing he had avoided mentioning was his stepmother's hatred for common folk. It was on his mind, but he'd thrown enough at Sabrina for one morning and didn't want to scare her. Magdalena had most of the politicians in court on her side. She was a powerful woman in Orsino politics, and not someone to be taken lightly.

*I refuse to let Magdalena have an influence on my decisions,* he thought. *I love Sabrina and I want to marry her. That's the bottom line.*

"I just want you to know that I'm serious when I tell you that being with you makes me the happiest man in the world," Marco said. "I've been spoiled with the finest clothes and food and home for all of my days, but I never realized what true happiness felt like until I met you."

Sabrina sighed and snuggled up next to him. Her touch put Marco at ease.

"You make me feel beautiful," she said. "And that's something that no amount of money or hard work could have ever afforded me."

He kissed the side of her neck, breathing her in as he held her close. They embraced for a while, letting the morning sun warm them as it poured in through the back patio doors.

*I can make this relationship work and I need to show Sabrina that,* he thought. *Never in my life have I felt this way about someone and I won't let anything ruin this. Not Magdalena, not my father and not my position of royalty. From now on, I'll be completely open with her. I'll tell her everything. No more secrets, no more hiding.*

# CHAPTER 15

SABRINA STOOD ON THE DOCK, the sea air whipping her hair around as she watched as Marco speak with the boat captain. Marco had scheduled a boat tour around the island, which included a stop at one of the largest active volcanoes in the world. She was super excited about it and planned on taking lots of pictures so that she could send them to her parents.

"Marco, how long until we leave?" she asked. "I need to make a phone call."

Marco looked up and then exchanged some words with the captain, an older gentleman who wore a tan fishing vest. After conversing for a minute, Marco said, "Take as much time as you need. We're just getting the boat ready, but there's no rush."

"Okay, thanks." Sabrina said as she stepped off of the dock and back onto the beach. She dug into the front pocket of her shorts and pulled out her cell. There was only a couple of days until Marco would be leaving for Orsino Island. Sabrina still hadn't made up her mind as to whether or not she'd be joining him. She needed the counsel of someone she trusted, someone who would give it to her straight, someone whose advice she cherished more than anything. So she called Aunt Faye.

The phone rang two times before Faye picked up. She sounded very excited to receive the call.

"Bean!" she cried out, her accent coming through strongly. "What in the world has taken you so long to call me?"

"Sorry, Aunt Faye," Sabrina said. "This job has been taking up most of my free time."

"No need for apologies," Faye said. "It's so good to hear your voice. How are things going? Are you enjoying your travels?"

"Very much so. We went to New York first and that was amazing. But you'll never guess where I am now." Sabrina walked down the shore, her bare feet sinking into the hot sand with each step.

"You know I'm horrible at guessing games," Faye said. "Where are you, love?"

"Hawaii," Sabrina said, proudly. "I'm walking on the beach as we speak."

"That's incredible," Faye said, her excitement mirroring Sabrina's. "Have you told your parents where you are? They'd never believe you."

"They didn't believe me until I sent them pictures," she said, stopping her trek through the sand to take a seat under a palm tree.

"Make sure to send me pictures as well," Faye demanded. "If your parents got some, I want some too."

"How are they doing?" Sabrina asked. "Did Dad find work yet?"

"No, not yet," she said, with a sigh. "But he's hanging in there. I know he'll find something soon, as long as he doesn't get discouraged. Unfortunately, there's not a lot of work to go around at the moment, especially for factory workers. Your dad is creative, though. He'll make something happen."

Sabrina closed her eyes, squeezing them firmly to keep a tear from leaking out. "I really miss everyone back home. But I'm glad to hear that things are going okay overall. You're right, Dad will figure something out."

"Bean, what's on your mind?" Faye asked. "I can tell by your voice that there's something you want to tell me."

*How does she do that every time?* Sabrina thought. *Is she psychic or something?*

"You know me too well, Aunty," she said. "I called hoping for some advice on a situation."

"A situation?" she asked. "That doesn't sound good."

"It's actually a very positive situation," Sabrina said. "But I'm still a bit unclear as to what I should do."

"I'll help you if I'm able to," Faye said. "Tell me everything."

Sabrina spilled everything to Faye. She told her about Marco and how she'd fallen for him quickly, even though he was technically her boss. She explained the mutual attraction between then and how she could see herself really loving him. Sabrina even told her about the paparazzi chase and the kiss that they had shared in the haunted apartment building.

"He sounds like a really great man, Sabrina," Faye said. "It's a shame that he's going home early. But you know, sometimes things aren't meant to be. God shows us that through situations that we can't control."

"I haven't finished telling you everything, though, Faye," Sabrina said. "Marco invited me to move home with him once the vacation is over."

"You mean, permanently?" Faye asked, clearly shocked. "Bean, I don't know."

"Faye, I love this man, or at least I know that I *could* love him with a little more time," she said. "I'm falling more in love with him every day."

"But do you really *know* him?" Faye asked. "You've only been working with him for a couple of weeks."

"You're right," she told her aunty. This was the moment of truth. She checked with Marco, and she could now tell family about his identity. "But I'm learning more about him every day. In fact, there's something I want to tell you about him, but you have to promise to keep it a secret."

"Who would I even tell a secret to, bean?" Faye replied with a laugh. "I promise I won't tell a soul."

"Marco is a prince of an island."

She'd expected Faye to yelp out in excitement or to at least hear a gasp on the other end of the phone line. But there was nothing but silence. Sabrina waited a few seconds, wondering if she had lost the cell phone connection with her aunt.

"Hello? Aunt Faye, are you there?"

Faye cleared her throat. "Yes, honey, I'm here. Sorry, I just wasn't sure if I had heard you correctly. You said Marco is a prince? He's royalty?"

"Yes, he's the Prince of Orsino Island," she repeated.

"This is not what I was expecting to hear," Faye said, after a few seconds of pause. "I'm happy for you, Sabrina, and I can hear the excitement in your voice. I want you to be careful, though."

"What do you mean?" Sabrina asked, standing up from the ground to brush the sand off. "Why do I have to be careful? Marco is a good guy, he wouldn't do anything to hurt me."

"That's not what I mean," Faye said, her inflection sounding more motherly than before. "I just know that members of the aristocracy don't tend to mix very well with ordinary people."

"I understand what you're saying and to be honest, I felt the same way at first," Sabrina said, as she began walking back toward the boat where Marco was. "But I expressed those concerns to Marco and he assured me that it wouldn't matter. He said he didn't care where I was from or how much money I had, he just wanted to be with me."

Faye sighed and Sabrina could tell that this news was weighing heavily on her.

"Love, I just don't want you to get hurt emotionally," Faye said. "Marco sounds lovely. I'm sure he's got good looks, money and charm. On top of that, he's also a prince. On the surface, it would be crazy for me to try to talk you out of it. Who wouldn't want to be with him? But even so, you've only known him for a couple of weeks and you don't really *know* him."

"But I do, Aunt Faye," Sabrina said quietly. "I do know him."

"He's a noble," Faye said the word like it tasted bitter. "He comes from an entirely different world. He may say that he doesn't care where you come from, but I don't know that he fully understands how different those two world are."

Sabrina listened to her words and allowed them to soak in. She trusted Faye with everything and didn't take her opinion on the matter for granted. However, her Aunt wasn't giving her the kind of encouragement that she had been seeking.

"I thought you would be supportive of this," Sabrina said, kicking the sand.

"I'm supportive of *you*," Faye said. "Because of that, I don't know if I can fully get behind this decision to move across the world for him. The decision seems a bit rash. Call me old-fashioned, but I think it would be better to wait for a while."

"Aunty, I wish you could see how he treats me," she said. "He makes me feel beautiful and special. I've never been this happy in my entire life. I don't want to be with him because he's a prince and he's rich. I want to be with him because he makes me excited about my life and nobody has ever done that before."

Faye was quiet for a minute and Sabrina thought she heard her sniffle. "I suppose I can't argue with that logic. And, I have to admit, that it makes me proud to hear you stand up for something like this. You must really believe strongly in your relationship with Marco."

"I believe in it so much," Sabrina said. "If I didn't, then I wouldn't risk moving across the planet for him."

"Hearing you speak with such passion reminds me of when I was younger," Faye said. "I guess sometimes, I forget what it feels like to be young and in love. It's a special time and even though I'm hesitant about you moving away, I want you to know that I have your back. Always."

"You're the best, Aunty," Sabrina said. "I love you."

"I love you, too," Faye said. "Call me again whenever you get the chance. I hope that I get to see you sooner than later."

"We'll see each other soon, Faye," Sabrina promised. "I'll

be in touch and let you know the details about where I am and when I'll be back in town."

"Okay, love. Have a fun time in Hawaii and go take a dip in the ocean for me."

"I will. Bye, Aunt Faye.

"Bye bye, Bean."

They hung up and Sabrina drew in a breath of air as she put the phone back in her front pocket. Marco was already on the boat, walking around and examining the rigging. Sabrina chuckled. Of course he'd be a sailor on top of everything else. He did live on an island.

Sabrina made her way back down the shore, with mixed emotion. She was surprised by Faye's reaction to the situation. Normally, Faye supported absolutely everything Sabrina did, but that's not what happened during their conversation.

*Faye seemed so adamant about dating a person of royalty could never work*, she thought. *It makes me wonder if something happened to her once, maybe something to do with aristocrats. She is from Britain after all, so it's not out of the realm of possibility. And there are certainly a lot of things that I don't know about Faye's former life.*

"Come on, gorgeous, let's start our tour," Marco said, as Sabrina neared the dock. He walked toward her and took her hand, leading her onto the small sail boat. "Is everything okay? You look a bit shook up."

Sabrina smiled genuinely. Hearing his voice put many of her doubts to rest. "Actually, yes. Everything is fantastic."

"Good, I'm happy to hear," he said. Then he turned to the captain of the boat. "Sir, all parties are accounted for. We're ready to go when you are."

*I* CAN'T BELIEVE *that Marco scheduled a private boat tour around the island. He's such a sweetheart,* Sabrina thought, as she watched the captain open up the sail on the catamaran. It was a small ship, built to hold only a handful of people, but Sabrina rather liked it that way better. It felt more intimate.

There were only three on board, though; the captain, Marco and Sabrina. Within minutes, they had left the dock and were sailing quickly away from shore. The wind was strong and Sabrina was glad she had something to tie her hair back.

She could hear the captain and Marco speaking. Marco sounded slightly annoyed. She watched as he looked at the sky and then shrugged. He didn't seem too concerned, so she wasn't worried.

"This is really nice," Sabrina said, as she sat with her feet hanging over the edge of one of the hulls. Beneath her, blue water flew past as they raced across the ocean. She looked up to see Marco frowning slightly at the sky.

"I'm glad you like it," he said, reaching over to touch the top of her knee. "I'm excited to see the volcano. While you were on the phone, the captain told me that the island grows larger every single year because of the molten lava hardening in the ocean."

"Believe it or not, I actually knew that," she said. "I've spent a lot of time looking at travel brochures for Hawaii and researching it on the Internet."

"It makes me happy that I've able to take you here then," Marco said.

She smiled at him and then turned back to the water. Deep water was dark and mysterious beyond them. The boat rocked and she gripped at the rail.

"Everything okay?" Marco asked, turning to face her. "You seem lost in thought."

Sabrina nodded. "Yeah, I'm great. Just enjoying the moment, that's all."

They sailed in silence for a while, feet hanging off the side. She thought of laying down in the netting between the hulls and taking a nap, but instead just sat where she was.

Sabrina closed her eyes, soaking up the sun while taking a little cat nap. It was so calm and peaceful. But the peace didn't last long. The next thing Sabrina knew, the light breeze that she had been enjoying had turned into powerful gusts of wind. It flapped against the sails and the sound caused her eyes to shoot open. She lifted her gaze toward the front of the boat. Dark clouds had begun to roll in over the horizon. It was clear that a storm was moving toward them and it was moving quickly.

"We weren't supposed to hit that," he murmured, rising to a standing position.

Sabrina turned to Marco. "Those clouds look pretty ominous. Are you sure we should be doing this?"

Marco looked to the front of the boat and a concerned look crossed his face again. It made Sabrina worry even more, because if he looked worried then there was most definitely something wrong.

"Captain, did you notice this storm up ahead?" Marco called out, his words drowned out by the increasing wind. "I thought you said we were sailing away from it."

The old man turned around from his post and shrugged. "Just a little storm. Shouldn't be a big deal. They happen sometimes and usually pass before the water gets too rough."

As the Captain explained himself, Sabrina spun around to see how far they had gotten from shore. Her heart sank when she noticed that the land which they had left behind was now barely visible.

"Can we at least get a little closer to shore?" Sabrina shouted to the captain. "That way if something does happen, we won't have far to go to get back to land?"

The captain placed his hand on top of his head to keep the wind from blowing off his hat. "We can't do that. The coral reef makes the water too shallow that close to the beach. We have to stay out this far if we want to travel to the other side of the island."

The wind picked up again, so powerful that the main sail became as taut as could be, and Sabrina felt the boat shift against its pull. A burst of adrenaline pumped into her veins and her heart rate increased. She suddenly wondered if this tour to see the volcano was worth the risk. But the captain seemed steadfast and Sabrina put her faith in his experience. Marco, on the other hand, didn't seem to have such blind faith.

"Are you sure this is safe?" Marco asked. "We were supposed to avoid this."

"It's just a little storm," the captain repeated, gripping the wheel a little tighter. "My computer is telling me that it's safe to sail, so we're sailing."

"The computer? But what about experience?" Marco said.

"I've got both," the captain said abruptly, clearly not wanting to hear it from Marco any longer.

A swelling wave rocked the vessel, and Marco stumbled to keep his balance. The clouds, which just a few seconds before had been in the distance, were now nearly straight above them.

It all happened so quickly. Sabrina didn't know what to do. The boat rocked aggressively as large waves pounded its side. Each hit came harder than the last and she gripped the railing so hard that her knuckles turned white.

*This is not what I had in store for today,* she thought, attempting to swallow down her fear. This certainly didn't feel like a little storm.

That was when the biggest of the waves hit the side of the boat. Everything that wasn't tied down was forced to the starboard side, including the captain. While Sabrina and Marco were able to grab the rail, the force was too great for the old man. He lost grip of the steering wheel and Sabrina watched as he flew straight off of the boat and into the water.

"Marco! The captain!" Sabrina shouted, as the wave passed and the boat settled again. "He fell off!"

Marco stood up and glanced overboard. The captain was in the ocean, and was flailing against the waves. He was obviously panicked and barely able to keep his head above the water. It would only be a matter of time before he got hit by another wave.

"We have to save him." Marco leaned in toward Sabrina, enunciating the words over the wind. "I can't do it on my own, though. I'll need your help, Sabrina."

"What? I don't know what to do, Marco. I'm not that good of a swimmer," she said, her voice sounding panicked. "What can we do? Let's call for help. I'm sure the coast guard or someone can get out here."

"There's no time for that." Marco walked over to a bench near the front of the vessel and lifted up the seat of it. He then pulled out some life vests, one of which he tossed to Sabrina. She held the orange device, her hands trembling as she put it on as quickly as possible. When she looked back up, Marco already had his on and he was now holding a circular white lifesaver with a rope attached.

"Now what?" she asked, already guessing the answer and hating it.

"I'm going in to get him," Marco said.

The boat rocked again and Sabrina nearly lost her balance, but managed once again to not fall over.

"I need you to crank this handle to reel us back in once I have him," Marco shouted over the wind. "It'll pull in the rope that's attached to this life preserver. Can you do that, Sabrina?"

"I don't know if I can," she said, shaking her head. "I'm not strong enough."

Marco approached her and placed a hand onto her shoulder. "You *are* strong enough, Sabrina. Trust me. Just give it everything you have and don't stop no matter what."

Sabrina doubted she'd have the strength to pull off such a maneuver, but she quickly realized she didn't have a choice. If they didn't save the captain, he'd likely drown. And with no captain to steer the boat, then all three of them had a fair chance of sharing a similar fate.

"Okay," she said, with a hesitant nod.

With the lifesaver in hand, Marco hopped the rail and disappeared into the dark blue water. He resurfaced almost immediately, though, and swam toward the captain. He appeared fearless, as he powered his body against the waves, which seemed to pull him back a little each time. It didn't matter, though. He pressed on, unrelenting and steadfast. It took a few minutes, but he finally reached the old man. Once Sabrina saw that they were both holding onto the lifesaver, she began to reel them in using the giant crank that held the rope.

The first few turns were easy, until the rope became taught. Then it took all her strength to get it to turn. She let out a grunt as she pushed it down and pulled it up.

*There's no way I can do this,* she thought. *I'm not strong enough.*

But she thought about Marco and the captain. The two of them were relying solely on her. She had to make it happen. She didn't have a choice. So she turned the crank again, using her body weight to press it down and all of the strength in her legs to pull it back up. When she turned around, she saw that the she had pulled the two men noticeably closer to the boat.

*It's working,* she thought. *Oh, my God. It's working. I can do this. I can do this.*

With a clenched jaw, she gave it all she had. She poured every ounce of energy into turning that crank, feeling the muscles in her shoulders and arms burn. She cranked and cranked until suddenly, the reel stopped turning completely. She couldn't budge it any more. By the time she spun around to see what was going on, Marco and the Captain were clamoring over the railing and back onto the boat.

"It worked," Sabrina shouted into the wind. "It worked!"

Marco helped the old man hold onto the rail. The captain seemed weary and shaken up.

"Is he okay?" Sabrina called out.

The storm was directly over them now and the waves continued to pound the side of the boat. But Marco seemed unfazed. He walked across the floorboard toward Sabrina and pulled her in for a hug.

"He's fine, just exhausted from treading water," Marco said, shouting in her ear. "I couldn't have gotten him back into the boat without your help."

"Marco, we need to get out of here," Sabrina said. "Can the captain still steer this boat?"

Marco shook his head. "I don't know. He might be able to, but to be honest, I don't trust his judgment any more. I'm not going to let him put you in any more danger."

"What are we going to do then?" she asked, still panic-stricken beyond belief.

"I'll get us back," he said, stepping past Sabrina.

She watched as Marco untied a few ropes and turned the main sail of the boat, until the vessel shifted back toward shore. Then he grabbed the steering wheel and pointed them away from the horizon. Sabrina sat next to the captain in the netting, wrapping an arm over his shoulder. He was shivering even though the water wasn't that cold.

"Are you okay?" she asked.

He just nodded. "I'm sorry. I didn't know it would get so bad, so quickly."

Sabrina didn't respond. She just held him close, trying to stabilize his body as the boat continued to teeter on top of the waves. There was nothing she could do, so she closed her eyes and held on tight. Terrified, she focused on her breathing. She counted each one, concentrating as much as possible in an attempt to shut out the danger that surrounded her.

She was able to count to twenty-three before Marco's voice broke her out of the trance.

"We're almost there," he said.

Those words were the most welcoming thing Sabrina had ever heard in her life. She opened her eyes to see the safety of land just a few hundred feet away. Marco spent the next few minutes expertly steering the vessel next to the dock that they departed just an hour prior. The only sign of the storm here was a light rain that was almost pleasant. After securing the boat, he walked over to Sabrina and helped her to her feet.

"Are you okay?" he asked, his dark eyes examining her for any sign of injury.

Sabrina nodded and took a huge breath of relief. "I'm fine. Just wet."

Marco kissed her cheek and then turned to face the captain. He helped the old man to his feet and then off of the boat. Sabrina followed them and when they got to the sand, she almost felt like dropping to her knees and kissing the ground. She didn't do it, but that was the kind of relief that filled her.

"Next time someone warns you of a storm, please take notice," Marco said to the captain. "You put both me and my girlfriend in extreme danger."

"I'm sorry, sir," the captain said. "The computer-"

Marco cut him short, "What's done is done. "

The old man nodded in agreement. "Again, I'm sorry."

The three of them walked across the sand and toward the parking lot that was a few hundred yards from the water. Sabrina's heart rate finally went back to normal, but her hands still trembled from the adrenaline. She walked beside Marco in a daze. What had started as a romantic boat tour had quickly turned into a life-threatening situation. But she was alive. She was alive and the captain was alive, all in thanks to Marco.

"I'm so sorry you had to go through that," Marco said, as he embraced Sabrina.

She held him close, more tightly than ever before. She didn't want to let go.

"I was so scared," she sobbed into his already soaking shirt.

"Me too," he said, as he rubbed her back. "Me too."

But she didn't believe him. He hadn't seemed scared at all the entire time.

"How did you know what to do?" she asked, pulling away just long enough to look him in the eyes.

Marco chuckled. "I grew up on an island. The water is my second home. Sometimes these summer storms come in quickly. It's happened to me before, but the captain should have known better."

"You've *done this before*?" she asked.

"Not exactly *this*, but I have been in similar situations," Marco said. "Let's just say that wasn't the first time I've had to go help someone who went overboard."

And once again, Marco proved to Sabrina that he was an even more amazing man that she had thought. A soft smile crossed her face as she pressed her cheek into his chest. She felt like she was hugging Superman.

arco

MARCO WOKE up early and crept quietly out of bed, so as not to wake Sabrina. He slipped on some khaki shorts and a polo shirt before making his way out of the cabin. There was a small gift shop down the road about a mile and he intended to go there to buy her something special as a surprise. He felt she deserved something nice after the boat tour had turned into a complete nightmare. Not only that, though, it was their last day in the island. It was his last chance to woo the girl of his dreams and hopefully convince her to go back home with him.

He made the walk down the winding paved road and eventually approached the gift shop. It stood just a few feet off the pavement, surrounded by palm trees. Luckily, it was open. And it seemed pretty popular, based on the handful of cars that were already parked in front of it.

Marco stepped inside, making his way through the maze

of coat racks and glass cases that held inexpensive jewelry. He wasn't sure exactly what he was looking for, but he figured he'd know it if he found it.

"Aloha," a plump man called out from behind the counter.

"Hi there," Marco replied with a smile.

"How can I help you this morning?" the man asked.

"I'm looking for a gift for my girlfriend," Marco said. "Any ideas?"

The man stood up from his stool and approached Marco, shaking his hand. "I suggest you take a look in the women's clothing corner. You might find something there."

"I'll do that," Marco said. "Thanks for your help."

Marco turned and went to the back corner of the shop. Most of what he saw there was pretty typical. There were a bunch of swimsuits, hats and sunglasses. He glanced around, but didn't see anything at first. He was about to turn and leave, when something caught his eye. There was a rack of summer dresses that were tucked in the very back. They had been hidden behind the rest of the products. There was one in front, though, that had particularly gained his attention.

"That's beautiful," he whispered, as he approached the dress and pulled it off of its hangar.

Marco held it in front of him. The dress was light blue, with a vibrant floral pattern on the front made of red and purple colors. It was short-sleeved with a narrow waist, and made of smooth silk.

*This would be perfect,* he thought. *She would look so good in this.*

He imagined Sabrina in the dress. He thought about her long legs exposed and how the material would conform to her womanly curves. It made him practically pant right there in the store. He knew right then that he had found the right dress.

Marco spun around and walked straight to the counter. The rotund man had taken his seat back at the stool and greeted him with a smile.

"Ah, that's a great item right there, sir," the man said. "Your lady is going to love that."

"I agree," Marco replied.

He set the dress on the counter and reached into his pocket for his cash. After paying for the dress, he turned to leave but hardly made it to the door before the employee stopped him.

"Sir, can I ask you a question?" he said.

Marco spun around. "Sure, what is it?"

"You look really familiar. I know I've seen your face somewhere," the man said, stroking his chin. "I can't quite place it, but man, I swear I recognize you."

Marco shook his head and pulled his hat down a little further on his forehead. "I get that all the time. I think I just have one of those faces. I assure you, you're thinking of someone else."

Then he turned and left the gift shop before the man could reply. He walked quickly back to the cabin, chuckling to himself.

*That was close,* he thought. This was exactly why Sabrina was supposed to do all his shopping.

Marco quietly opened the door to the cabin and was greeted by the inviting smell of fresh coffee. He smiled as he heard Sabrina humming to herself in the kitchen. He did his best to conceal the dress behind him as he poked his head around the corner. Sabrina was standing at the stove making eggs, wearing only a t-shirt and panties. She turned around and smiled when she saw him.

"Hey," she said, playfully putting her hand on her hips. "How long have you been standing there staring at me?"

"Not long enough," Marco said, with a smirk. "I just got back from a little walk."

"Yeah, I figured you had gone out to the beach or something," Sabrina said.

"Actually, no," he said. "I took a walk to the gift shop down the road and picked you up something."

Sabrina's smile widened and she walked across the kitchen toward Marco. He continued to hold the dress around the corner, though, to keep it hidden.

"You're not supposed to do that," she chided, but smiled widely at him and did an excited little dance. "But, I love surprises!"

Marco shrugged. "I wanted to get you something special to make up for the terrible boat tour yesterday."

"What is it?" she asked, nearly jumping up and down. "Show me."

Marco found her child-like impatience to be cute and endearing. Sabrina was so much fun and he loved that she got excited over the simplest of things.

"I'm not sure if you'll like it, but when I saw it I just had to buy it for you." Marco stepped around the corner and held the dress out in front of him.

Sabrina gasped and then jumped up and down, snatching the dress from him. "This is beautiful! Marco, *oh my gosh*, it's perfect."

She spun in a circle, her eyes fixated on her new dress. Then she carefully set it over the back of the couch and ran to Marco, embracing him in a hug. His smile was just as wide as hers. He realized that making her happy also made him happy.

"I'm glad you like it," he said, before kissing the top of

her head. "I wasn't sure. I know it's kind of bright, but I figured it would look really good on you."

"It's so perfect," she said, still squeezing him tight.

She pulled away and then stood on her tip toes, giving Marco a quick kiss. Her soft lips pressed into his and his hands drifted down her sides. He wanted more, but she spun around and walked back to the dress to admire it again.

"Should I put it on?" Sabrina asked. "What are our plans for the day? Maybe I can wear it out to lunch or something."

"Save it for tonight," Marco said, as he walked into the kitchen to pour himself a cup of coffee. "It's our last day in Hawaii and I want to take you to a beautiful dinner. I did some research and there's a really nice sushi place on the beach, just a few minutes from here. I think that dress would be perfect for the occasion."

Sabrina nodded in agreement. "Yes, that sounds great. I'll hang it up in the bedroom so it doesn't get wrinkly."

She carried the dress around the corner, leaving Marco in the kitchen. He loved to see her happy, but his own emotion was still brought down by the fact he would be leaving for Orsino Island the following morning. Sabrina still hadn't made up her mind about going with him. He deeply hoped that she'd agree to accompany him back, but the thought of her not doing so created a sinking feeling in his gut.

*I'm not sure what I'll do if she won't go to Orsino with me,* he thought. *She's the only girl in the entire world that I want to be with. Now that I've spent time with her, I can't imagine my life without her. She's the one for me.*

Sabrina reappeared from the bedroom. She walked with a spring in her step, clearly excited about the surprise gift from Marco.

"I seriously can't wait for tonight," she said, making her way back into the kitchen to turn the eggs in the frying pan. "I'm so looking forward to wearing that dress."

"It'll be a great night," Marco said. "You're going to look amazing."

*I just hope that tonight isn't the last night that I get to spend with you,* he thought.

MARCO AND SABRINA were seated at a small table on the patio of the restaurant. He'd reserved the seats earlier that day, asking the hostess to put them as close to the ocean as possible. He wanted the evening to be perfect.

"Look at this view," Sabrina said, turning to face the ocean.

Marco much preferred to look at the view of the woman he loved, who sat across the table from him. Sabrina's new dress looked amazing on her. The silk held to her curves and he hadn't been able to take his eyes off of her since she'd put it on.

"I think it's a full moon," she said, reaching over to touch Marco's hand.

He looked over to the horizon and nodded in agreement. "I'm certain that it is."

The sky was clear and the moon shone brightly down over the ocean, giving the tops of the waves a silvery glow. The fact that the moon was full brought more meaning to Marco than just its beauty, though.

"Where I come from, a full moon is considered auspicious," he said, bringing his attention back to Sabrina. "We think of it as good luck and therefore, a time when people should celebrate and make important decisions."

"Really?" she asked. "Where I come from, the full moon is when people turn to werewolves."

Marco chuckled. "I suppose that could happen too. But not on Orsino. You should see it, Sabrina. The people all gather into giant groups on the beach during the full moon. Right now, I'm sure hundreds of citizens are dancing on the sand on Orsino, praying and celebrating. It's a giant event every single month."

Sabrina brought her fists to her chin as she listened to Marco tell the story. "That sounds like fun."

The waitress approached, delivering a bamboo platter completely covered in different types of sushi. From fresh unagi, to spicy tuna rolls, to sashimi, it was all there.

"Anything else I can get you two?" the waitress asked.

"Can we get some hot Saki, please?" Marco requested.

"Of course," she said. "I'll be right back with that."

Sabrina was staring at the plate of food as though she had just seen an alien. "I don't know what any of this is."

"You've never had sushi before?" Marco asked, tilting his head to the side.

"I haven't," Sabrina admitted. "But I'll try anything."

The waitress brought them the Saki Marco had ordered and filled up the two porcelain cups, before walking away to help the other restaurant patrons. Marco held the cup in the air and Sabrina did the same.

"Here's to adventures," Marco said. "Sometimes they're exciting and sometimes they're terrifying, but we're always better for having sought them out."

Sabrina smiled and clinked her glass to his. "Yes. Here's to that."

They sipped the rice wine and then dug into the food. Marco was surprised by Sabrina's willingness to try every type of sushi, even the ones that were completely raw. In fact, the only one she cringed at was the octopus. She still managed to chew it up and eat at least one piece, though. After the meal, the waitress took away their plates and left them to themselves to enjoy their Saki and the view.

Marco reached across the table and held Sabrina's hands. He gazed into those beautiful blue eyes of hers, wishing he could just get lost in them forever.

"It's hard to believe that this trip will be over tomorrow morning," Marco said, trying hard to savor every ounce of the moment that he possibly could.

"It's gone by so fast." Sabrina squeezed his hands. "It feels like yesterday that I was doing the interview for the job."

Marco sighed, his eyes still locked onto hers. This was the moment of truth. He needed to find out whether or not she was going to come home with him to Orsino. It scared the hell out of him to ask, for fear that the answer would be "no". But he couldn't ignore the topic any longer.

"Sabrina, I know that you had some hesitations about coming with me to Orsino," Marco said, leaning closer. "But I'm wondering what your current thoughts are about it."

Sabrina nodded. "I've been thinking a lot about that."

Marco stayed silent. His heart pounded in his chest, eager to hear her decision.

"You're right. I did have some hesitations about going with you," she said. "I was so scared about a girl like me being with a guy like you. I thought that you and I could never mix. We come from such different backgrounds. I told myself this, over and over, until I started to believe it. Even my Aunt Faye, who I've confided in about the situation, said the same things."

Marco looked down at the table as his heart sank. "You aren't coming with me, are you?"

Sabrina dropped his hands and gently touched his cheek. "Marco, look at me. I'm not finished saying what I need to say."

He looked back up, to see her eyes shining in the moonlight.

"The part of me that didn't think something could work between us was the same part that had kept me stuck in the trailer park in Memphis for all those years," Sabrina said. "I've been full of doubt for most of my life. I thought that nothing would ever get better, that I would be forced to work random jobs forever and just squeak by, like my parents always have. But look where I am now."

She motioned her hands to the beautiful scenery around her and then upward toward the moon.

"I'm sitting here with the most incredible man on a beach in Hawaii," she said, now tearing up. "I've been to New York and seen buildings and places I had only ever dreamed of."

Marco's heart swelled as he listened. He was so deeply touched by her words.

"What I'm trying to say, Marco, is that I'm no longer listening to the voice inside of me that tells me beautiful things can't happen to common people," she said, as she reached forward and squeezed Marco's forearms. "I'm not listening to that voice of doubt ever again."

Marco smiled hesitantly. "Are you telling me what I think you're telling me?"

Sabrina bit her bottom lip and nodded. "I'm going with you, Marco. I'm going back to Orsino Island with you."

The words hit Marco's eardrums and it took a second for it to register in his brain. He couldn't believe what he had just heard.

"You're serious?" he asked. "Please tell me you're serious.

I need to hear it."

Sabrina shook her head, as she grinned. "I'm not messing with you. I want to be with you, and if that takes moving across the world, then I'll do that. I'm coming with you."

Marco jumped up from his chair and stepped over to Sabrina. He wrapped his arms around her and kissed her passionately in front of everyone at the restaurant. He knew the other patrons were watching, but he didn't care. The girl of his dreams was going to be coming home with him. Nothing in the entire world could bring him down. His heart was filled with the kind of joy and excitement he hadn't ever experienced.

That was when he said the words. It was as though his heart said them, not his brain. They just came out without a second thought.

"I love you, my beautiful Sabrina," he said.

Sabrina gracefully touched his cheek and looked deep into his eyes.

"I love you, too." Her words caused goose bumps to pop up in Marco's skin.

They were silent for a moment, their eyes locked with the moon above them. The *full* moon, the auspicious one. It was part of the reason that things were working out so well, at least that was what Marco believed.

"Let's get out of here and go back to the cabin," Sabrina said, with seductive eyes. "We have some celebrating to do."

MARCO HAD ONLY one thing on his mind as he opened the cabin door and held it for Sabrina. He wanted to get that dress off of her and kiss every square inch of her skin. He wanted to celebrate her decision to go with him, giving her as much pleasure as he possibly could.

As soon as they were both inside, he closed the door. The only light that was on was in the kitchen, but it lit up the living room with a romantic glow. Sabrina turned around. She was biting her bottom lip and Marco could tell that she was just as turned on as he was. No words needed to be spoken. The passion between them was obvious and talking would have dampened the mood. It would have watered down the lust in the air.

He stepped up to her, bringing his hands to her hips. Their bodies collided, but he didn't stop there. He took another step forward, until Sabrina was pressed against the wall that separated the kitchen and the living room. She exhaled with a soft moan and looked up into Marco's eyes. Her expression was one of desire and seeing it caused Marco's cock to get hard.

They kissed and Marco felt her hands wander up and down his sides. Her typically delicate touch was not so delicate this time. She tugged on his clothing, un-tucking his shirt and removing his belt in a matter of seconds. Meanwhile, he brought his hands to the bottom of her dress and slid it up to her belly. He could feel the heat from her core, radiating toward him. He dropped his hands down and touched the bare skin of her upper thighs, letting his fingers dance over her panties.

By the time he broke the kiss, Sabrina had managed to unbutton his dress shirt completely. She reached forward and tugged it away from his shoulders. Marco shimmied it off, letting it fall to the floor behind him. They were both breathing harder now, panting with need. Nothing mattered in that moment besides their attraction toward each other. It made no difference that he was a prince and that she was a broke girl from Memphis. Right there, in that cabin on Hawaii, the only thing that mattered was how they'd satisfy the craving they both felt.

"I want you so bad right now," Sabrina whispered. "Take me."

Marco's eyes drifted down her body. Her nipples were hard and pressing against the silk dress, begging to be released. The bottom part of the dress was still bunched up around her belly. When his eyes got to her panties, his cock throbbed underneath his slacks. She was so turned on that the front part of her underwear had become wet with desire.

He stepped forward once again, this time slipping his fingers into her underwear and tugging them down. She leaned her head back against the wall and closed her eyes as he shimmied the panties off of her, all the way to her ankles. Then he dropped to his knees in front of her. He wanted to taste her and pleasure her at the same time. He wanted to spoil her like the future queen that he hoped she would be.

Marco lifted one of her legs and draped it over his shoulder. Sabrina kept her back pressed against the wall and slowly bucked her hips toward his face. He looked her up and down quickly, then leaned in. As soon as his tongue touched her clit, she moaned out and gripped a handful of his hair.

"Yes," she whispered, pulling his tongue into her.

His hands went to her thighs as he flicked his tongue sensually against her, changing pace and pressure in accordance with her squeals of pleasure. He sent her flying into beautiful oblivion, not just once, but twice. By the time he was done, Sabrina's leg was trembling over his shoulder.

She reached down and placed her hands on his cheeks, forcing him to look up at her. Her eyes were dilated and her chest rising and falling rapidly.

"Let's go to the bedroom," she said.

Her words sounded more like an order than a suggestion, but Marco didn't mind one bit. He got up from the floor and followed Sabrina to the bedroom, his eyes glued to that magnificent butt of hers as she walked ahead of him.

As soon as they got there, she pulled the dress off over her head and set it on top of the dresser. She was now wearing only a bra. Marco stepped behind her and undid the clasp that held it on, letting it fall off of her shoulders. Then he turned her around to face him so he could kiss her again. This time, Marco's hands were able to roam all over her naked skin. He pulled her close, feeling her wetness as she collided with the front of his slacks.

Their tongues continued to dance, while Marco took off his slacks and underwear. He stepped out of the clothing and bucked his hips forward, sliding between her thighs. The top of his dick dragged against her entrance, causing both of them to moan together softly. He gritted his teeth, wishing to just lay her down on the bed and enter her right there. But he slowly pulled away and held his index finger in the air.

"One moment," he said, with a smirk.

He went straight to his suitcase and pulled out a condom. They were going to need more of these soon. He slipped it on as he approached her once again.

"Now where were we?" Sabrina asked, taking the words right out of his mouth.

Marco let out a growl as his hands went to Sabrina's rear. He lifted her from the floor and carried her a few steps over to the bed, setting her down. Her hands were wrapped over his shoulders, her breath hot against his naked chest. She leaned in and kissed him, gently biting his lower lip as she pulled away. When she laid back, she wrapped her legs around Marco's waist, putting his cock in the perfect position to enter her. He was still standing on the floor next to the bed, looking over the love of his life who laid before him.

*How in the world did I get so lucky?* he thought to himself.

Everything about Sabrina's body turned him on. Her beautiful hair, blue eyes and innocent smile. Her firm breasts, the lines of her hips and the way her legs flexed when she walked. She was, in no exaggeration, absolutely perfect in Marco's eyes.

He paused for a moment, just admiring her. She brought her hands to her breasts and gently fondled them, teasing him with the action. It only made him want her more.

"Take me," she said for the second time that evening. "I need you."

Marco slowly pressed into her. Sabrina gasped and leaned her head back, closing her eyes. He entered her, feeling her wetness wrap his cock until he was all the way in. Pleasure pumped through him as he bucked his hips back and forth. While he continued the movement, he leaned forward and kissed the top of her breasts. The sweet smell of her perfume was on her chest. He breathed it in as he danced his lips around her nipple.

This moment was incredible for him, but for so many more reasons than just the sex. He was on cloud nine because he knew that he was going to marry the girl he was making love to. This wasn't just a fling or a one-night stand. This was the real deal. This was what his heart had been seeking for years and he finally had it.

Marco circled her nipple with his tongue, gently flicking against it. It grew firm to his touch and he moved his face over to give the other one equal attention. He was so turned on by her that he had to slow down the pace of his thrusts to keep from climaxing too soon. He wasn't usually one to orgasm so quickly, but Sabrina did something to him that no other woman ever had.

"That feels so good," Sabrina whispered. "God, I love you."

Marco slowly pulled his face away from her breasts and looked into her eyes. She looked dazed, with a half smile of pure bliss. He loved that expression of hers. It made him want to go harder and deeper. He grabbed her legs and pressed them toward her chest, then increased his pace. Ecstasy filled his body as he pounded her.

Sabrina's breasts swayed up and down to the cadence of his thrusts. A thin layer of sweat had begun to cover her skin and there was just enough light in the room to make her shine. He could have admired that view all day and all night for the rest of his life. But when she begged him to flip her around, he couldn't say no.

"I want you to take me from behind," she whispered, before biting her lip.

Her words took Marco's breath away and he found himself more turned on than ever before. He took a step back and then gently turned her over on the bed. She bent over in front of him and looked over her shoulder. His eyes moved downward, noticing those two little dimples on her lower back that he loved so much.

*God, she's perfect,* he thought.

Grabbing her hips with both hands, he stepped forward and slid his length back in. The pleasure filled him again, only this time it was more intense. His jaw dropped and his eyes closed, as he rocked his body against her. The feel of her flesh in his hands, the way their sweat-covered skin collided, the wetness of her flower around his length. It all added up to be the perfect experience for Marco. There was no other place on the entire planet that he would have rather been than in that cabin with Sabrina. That was his heaven.

When he opened his eyes, he saw that Sabrina was facing away from him. She had buried her face into a pillow, muting her yelps of pleasure which had grown significantly in volume. She was climaxing and Marco knew it. So he increased his pace, pounding his body into hers with more vigor than before. Within a few seconds, she lifted her head and drew in a quick breath. He watched her grip the blankets on the bed with both hands as she let out a guttural moan. At the same time, Marco felt her clamp around him.

While keeping the same pace, he reached forward and fondled her breasts. He let her nipples slide between his fingertips, gently pinching the firm nubs to give Sabrina the extra sensation.

She went silent for just a moment and then exhaled, relaxing her head into the pillow in front of her. When she released her grip from the blanket, Marco noticed that her hands were trembling. A contented smirk crossed his face, knowing that he had made her climax.

But Sabrina wasn't the only one who couldn't hold back any longer. Marco's loins ached for release. He brought his hands back to her hips and continued rocking his body against hers until all of the pleasure and sensation culminated into one perfect moment of orgasm.

He closed his eyes and held himself inside of her as his body exploded with ecstasy. His cock swelled and his balls clenched, releasing all of his sexual tension and passion in just a few short seconds. After the intensity had passed, he opened his eyes and took a breath, feeling dizzy with bliss.

"You're amazing," he said, shaking his head in awe.

Sabrina laid on her side and Marco crawled up next to

her. They cuddled up, entangling their naked bodies. A cool evening breeze blew in from the open window, falling lightly upon their skin. It felt refreshing to Marco and the smell of the nearby ocean was nostalgic. It reminded him of home.

He kissed her forehead and wrapped an arm around her back, pulling her close. They were silent for a while, just enjoying the sound of the waves outside in the distance. Marco was still in shock that his life was coming together in such a positive way. Things were really falling into place for him.

"I'm glad you're mine," he whispered, as he affectionately touched Sabrina's bare shoulder.

"Me too." She lifted her gaze and smiled. "I'm really excited to see Orsino Island and to meet all of your family."

Marco nodded. "It's going to be wonderful. Orsino is a paradise. I'm looking forward to sharing it with you."

Sabrina snuggled her face toward Marco's chest and giggled. She seemed just as excited as he was about it.

*The fact that she's willing to accept my unusual circumstances says so much about her. She's uprooting her entire life to come with me and that's not something an average woman would do,* he thought. *This girl is worthy of everything I have to offer. She deserves to be a princess and spoiled with the greatest of all things. I hope that I'm able to offer her all that she desires in life.*

Marco grabbed the edge of the blanket and wrapped it over the two of them. Then he relaxed into the bed. His mind was filled with the best of thoughts. He especially looked forward to the following day, when he'd get to introduce the woman he loved to both his father and his country.

*And what better way to show her off than at the ball Magdalena has arranged?* He thought, as he drifted off into a deep sleep.

# CHAPTER 17

Sabrina's face was practically part of the window of the car as she and Marco were driven up the long and winding paved driveway toward the Palace. After a nine-hour flight, the two of them were finally on Orsino Island and she was about to see the castle that Marco called home. She was beyond excited about it, but also desperately nervous. This wasn't just about seeing where her lover lived, this was also about meeting his family. That by itself would have been enough to make a girl nervous, even in a normal situation. But this situation was anything but normal.

"Are you okay?" Marco asked, reaching across the back-seat to touch Sabrina's shoulders.

She nodded, but inside she felt nothing but turmoil. Her heart was pounding out of her chest and her hands were clammy. When she turned to face Marco, she was greeted by his warm and reassuring smile.

"I can tell you're nervous," he said, bringing his hand affectionately down her back. "But I assure you, there's nothing to be nervous about. You're going to love it here. I promise."

Sabrina smiled and scooted close to him. "I already love the island. It's beautiful here. Reminds me a lot of Hawaii, actually. I'm not nervous about that, but I *am* a little bit anxious about meeting your family."

"My father is going to adore you," he said. "Trust me. It will all work out."

*Except for the fact that I'm the last person they'd expect to be your girlfriend,* Sabrina thought.

"I hope you're right." She fidgeted with her hands as she spoke. Then she turned to face the window once again. Her jaw dropped as the palace at the top of the hill came into view.

The massive structure stood tall against the blue sky and appeared to be at least as wide as a few city blocks. It was made of white marble, which was beautifully complimented by the red-colored roof and an ornate gold design surrounded the building, just below the roof line.

*It's like the White House, only far more intricate and dazzling,* she thought, taking in the view.

She glanced over to Marco and then back toward Orsino Palace. She couldn't believe her surroundings. Her reality was quickly becoming more grandiose than anything she could have ever dreamed.

The driver pulled the car up to the front of the Palace and an armed guard in a black suit opened the rear door. Sabrina smiled nervously as she stepped out. Marco was close behind her. He placed his hand on her lower back and led her toward the stairs.

"Welcome to Orsino Palace," Marco said, leaning toward

Sabrina. "I'm glad you're here with me."

Sabrina's heart beat wildly as they walked up the grand staircase that led toward the front entrance. Armed guards lined the edge of the stairs. They stood at attention, their facial expressions completely stoic as they kept their black rifles in hand. They appeared to be ready for anything.

The two got to the top of the stairs and approached the massive front door. One of the guards gave Marco an affirmative nod.

"Prince Marco, it's wonderful to see you again, sir," he said, reaching for his radio.

The guard said a few things into the radio and a moment later, the front doors opened up. Sabrina gripped the crook of Marco's elbow as they stepped inside the palace. Her eyes were immediately drawn to the massive stairway in the center, which was covered in elegant red carpet. She glanced around, admiring the white marble which most everything seemed to be made of. It felt like she had just walked into the picture of a magazine or onto one of those documentaries where they showcase the world's richest people.

*It's so beautiful,* she thought, clearly overwhelmed by her surroundings.

A man in a black suit with yellow accents hurried over to Marco and whispered something in his ear. Marco sighed and turned to face her.

"I have a few things to attend to, now that I'm home. I need to check in with my father and Queen Magdalena, and touch base with some of the other nobles. I'm sorry to leave you, but it must be done."

"I understand," she told him with a gentle smile. "You're important here."

It was true. He stood taller here. In just the few moments of being inside the palace, she could already tell that this was where Marco belonged. He fit. She wasn't sure that she did yet, but he belonged in the castle as much as the marble in the walls did.

"Your room is on the third floor. Just take the stairway up and then turn right when you reach the top. Go all the way down to the end of the hall and it's the last door on the left," Marco said, bringing his hands to Sabrina's shoulders. "I wanted to show it to you myself."

"You can show it to me later," she replied with a suggestive wink. It made him smile before he glanced at the waiting man in black and schooled his face. He checked his watch.

"Winston will find you shortly," he told her. "He's the man I told you about, the one who will help you prep for tonight's ball."

Sabrina nodded, and the ball of nerves started building in her stomach again. The ball. She wasn't sure she was ready to be presented to a room full of royalty.

"Winston will teach you everything you need to know for tonight," Marco promised her. "He's amazing at what he does."

The man in black cleared his throat and Marco frowned.

"You should get going," Sabrina told him. "I'll be fine. I'll head up to the room and freshen up before I meet with Winston. The next time you see me, you'll barely recognize me."

"I'd recognize you anywhere," he told her.

Marco kissed her cheek and followed the man in black around a corner, leaving Sabrina by herself in the grand entryway of the palace. She took a deep breath, trying not to feel completely overwhelmed. She'd just make her way up to the bedroom, and then go from there. One step at a time.

She walked slowly, taking in all the details of the palace.

She noticed a few people, but none of them appeared to be from the royal family. One of them was obviously a janitor, based on the cleaning cart he pushed. And she also saw a woman in a gray maid's outfit. But no royalty.

When she got to the top of the stairs, she stopped and looked around. Marco had said that her bedroom was to the right, but something toward her left caught her eye. There was movement and when she looked over, she saw an attractive blonde-haired woman in a long purple dress walking quickly down the hallway. She was probably only twenty years or so Sabrina's senior, but she moved with grace that Sabrina knew she would never have. Following this lady, like an obedient little puppy dog, was a muscular man who was only wearing swim trunks. Sabrina watched them until they made it halfway down the hall.

The woman giggled and kissed the younger man before pulling him into an open door. The door slammed shut, and the giggling was cut off.

*What was that all about?* She thought to herself. *I might be wrong here, but it definitely felt like that lady and that guy were about to have sex. They seemed pretty eager.*

She didn't know who they were, but the woman was dressed very nicely and Sabrina thought for sure that she could have been royalty. Maybe it was the way she carried herself or possibly the dress, but something told Sabrina that the woman was most definitely not a maid.

"Huh, oh well," she whispered.

Then she faced to the right, pointing herself the other direction. She walked down the hallway and got to the end, where she saw that the door on the left was open. Inside, a young woman with blonde hair was standing at the foot of the bed. She was carefully straightening the bedspread, but turned around when she saw Sabrina in the doorway.

"Oh goodness, where are my manners," the young woman said, dropping to a knee and bowing her head. "I didn't know you were standing there, Ms. Wise. I'm so sorry."

"How do you know my name?" Sabrina asked.

"Everyone knows your name, Ms. Wise," she said, with a thick accent that was similar to Marco's. "Marco informed us of your arrival. And actually, you're the reason I'm in his room right now. He told me to pick out something for you to wear."

Sabrina stepped forward. "Please, stand up. I appreciate the gesture, but you certainly don't need to bow for me."

The girl hesitantly stood up from the floor. She appeared to be about the same age as Sabrina.

"What's your name?" Sabrina asked.

"Marla, Ms. Wise," the girl said. She motioned to the bed behind her. "I hope you like what I've picked out so far."

Sabrina looked past Marla to the three dresses that were hung along the wall. Her eyes widened as she took notice of the beautifully colored silk that each of them was made of. They weren't just dresses. They were gowns. One of them was royal blue, another was a pale honey color, and the last was bright white. Each was floor length and looked like something fit to wear on the red carpet.

The blue had a slightly poofed skirt, where the honey was slim and would hug every curve. The white dress was her favorite, with clean lines and just a hint of sparkle.

"They're lovely," Sabrina said, with a warm smile.

A knock near the bedroom door caused Sabrina to turn around. An older gentleman in a formal dark gray suit stood in the doorway.

"My apologies for interrupting, Ma'am," he said, his

voice low and scratchy, but somehow soothing to Sabrina. "I trust you must be our young prince's Sabrina?"

Sabrina smiled wide and nodded. "Unless there's another Sabrina I don't know about."

The man chuckled. "Not that I'm aware of, Ma'am. I'm Winston, the head butler here at Orsino Palace. Welcome to the Island."

"Thank you, Winston," Sabrina said. "This place is amazing."

As soon as she said it, she realized how stupid it sounded.

*Of course it's amazing,* she thought. *It's a palace on an island. Dammit, Sabrina. Don't sound like a tourist.*

Winston just kept the warm smile on his face, though. "If you're ready, my dear, I can show you a few things on the main floor."

Sabrina turned toward Marla. "Do you mind?"

Marla looked over and said, "Of course not, m'lady. I'm sure I'll see you soon, though. I'm always around the Palace, doing this or that."

"Sounds good, thank you," Sabrina said, as she turned and followed Winston back down the stairs toward the entryway.

Winston led her down one of the hallways and stopped at a row of pictures that were hung along the wall. He turned to face her before speaking. "Ms. Sabrina, pardon me for asking, but I'm curious as to where you are from. I can hear your accent, but I can't quite place it. American, I know, but there's something a little different about it."

"I'm from Memphis, Tennessee," Sabrina said, suddenly realizing how heavy her accent probably sounded to everyone there. "It's in the South. We have a different accent than people from other parts of the United States."

"Indeed," Winston said. "I've never been to the States myself, but we do get visitors sometimes. But you're the first from Memphis, at least as far as I know."

"It's a nice place, but nothing like Orsino Island," Sabrina said. "I'd almost say it's the complete opposite, actually."

Winston nodded as he listened. The lines around his eyes showed his age, but gave him a distinguished and wise appearance. Sabrina felt safe with him, as he didn't seem to judge her.

"Maybe one day I'll get to visit," he said, with a chuckle. "If I ever retire, that is."

Her heart reached out to him. She and Winston probably weren't so different. They both knew what it was to work hard for a living. The way he smiled reminded her of her father.

"At any rate," he continued. "The reason I took you down here was to show you these pictures. This way, you will be able to recognize them later tonight. This first one here is of King Carlo, father of Prince Marco."

Sabrina looked at the picture of the man and instantly saw the resemblance to her lover. He had the same nose and sharp eyes. In the picture, the King was seated on a golden throne with a red velvet seat. He was wearing a dark blue robe, with intricate yellow designs sewn into it. The King's hair was white, but just as thick as his young son's. It took her a moment, but she recognized one of the photos from her interview as him.

"He looks a lot like Marco," Sabrina whispered, just loud enough for Winston to hear.

"And he's just as charming," Winston said, with a wink. "But, like they say, the apple never falls far from the tree."

"Very true," she said, as she followed Winston a few steps further down the hall.

They approached the next picture and when Sabrina saw it, she did a double-take. She recognized the woman immediately.

"This photo is of the graceful Queen Magdalena," Winston said. "I'll presume you don't know the history, but the Queen is not Prince Marco's mother. She was wed to King Carlo many years ago and has reigned as Queen over our wonderful country ever since. She is a powerful woman."

*That's the woman I saw upstairs,* Sabrina thought. *That's the lady that was running down the hall and into the bedroom with the shirtless man.*

Shock filled her body and she couldn't stop staring blatantly at the photo. Winston took notice immediately.

"Everything okay, my dear?" he asked. "You look like you've seen a ghost."

"Oh no, I'm fine," she said. "It's just that I think I saw that same woman a few minutes ago upstairs leading a half-naked man into a bedroom. But I must be mistaken, because the man that I saw with her wasn't the king."

"You'd have to be more specific for me to understand," he replied.

"It's probably nothing, but I saw an older woman with gray hair down the hallway across from Marco's room," Sabrina explained. "She was leading a younger man to a bedroom and they seemed quite... *eager.*"

Sabrina's cheeks burned as she spoke and she wondered if she should have even brought it up. She worried she may have overstepped her bounds.

Winston looked over his shoulder before leaning in close to Sabrina. "Now I know what you saw. And you were correct, when you thought you saw the Queen." He drew in a slow, measured breath before continuing. "The man she was with is her lover and no, it's not the king."

"What?" Sabrina said, her voice echoing down the hall.

"Speak quietly," Winston said, bringing a finger up to his lips. "You see, Sabrina, there are some things that happen here that must remain a secret to the outside. What you saw this morning is one of those things."

"The queen and that guy, they're... lovers?" she whispered, now self-conscious about the volume of her voice. "I don't understand. How does the king not know about an affair that's happening in his own palace?"

"I never said anything about the king not knowing," Winston said. "It's the general public and the staff that can't find out. If they did, it would create an uproar that nobody in the noble family would be prepared to deal with. It's about keeping the peace. Some things are better left unspoken."

Sabrina was absolutely floored by the news, although it did help explain some of Marco's distaste for his stepmother. But she couldn't understand why the king would allow such a thing. Clearly, though, there was a whole lot about royalty that she'd yet to learn.

"I'm a little confused," she said. "Why doesn't anyone say anything?"

"She is usually more discrete, so not many know." Winston smiled again and placed a hand onto her shoulder. "But all you need to know is that loose lips sink ships, and it would be wise of you not to repeat to anyone what you saw going on upstairs. Especially to anybody in the public. She is a powerful woman, and I'm afraid you would be an easy target for her to destroy to save her reputation."

"I wouldn't say a word," Sabrina said. "I promise. My lips

are sealed."

"Good," Winston said. "Now, moving on…"

He led her down the hall and continued showing her pictures. She saw one of Marco and a few of other nobles who were somehow related to the family. She noticed that each person in the pictures either had a purple or a green pendant attached to their collar.

"What do those pendants mean?" she asked.

"Glad you asked," he said. "It's information that will help you at the ball tonight. The ones wearing a green pendant are members of the noble family, but not related by blood. They're typically knights and priests who have been sworn in. They're as loyal to Orsino Island as the royal family. The ones wearing a purple pendant, as you may have guessed, are members of the royal lineage."

"That really is good information," Sabrina said, with a nod. "Anything else I should know before the ball tonight?"

"Do you know how to curtsy?" Winston asked.

Sabrina laughed and then quickly realized that Winston wasn't joking.

"Like this?" Sabrina carefully tucked one leg behind the other and and dipped.

"That, my dear, was atrocious. It's high time you learned," he said, shaking his head. "Trust me, you won't get very far going around and high-fiving people, or whatever it is that you Americans do."

Winston sighed and pretended to act annoyed, but Sabrina could tell that he was excited to show this naive westerner some culture.

"Thank you, Winston," Sabrina said. "I'm all ears and ready to learn. I'll happily accept any information that can possibly make the celebration tonight go a little bit smoother for me."

# CHAPTER 18

 *abrina*

THANKS TO WINSTON, Sabrina became fully versed in the art of the curtsy. He'd made her practice it in the Palace library until she had it down perfectly. Now she stood in her new bedroom in front of the over-sized mirror on the wall. She was only wearing a towel around her body as she curtsied a few more times, just to make sure she had it down.

"A pleasure to meet you, your majesty," Sabrina whispered, reciting the lines that Winston had told her to memorize. It was "your majesty" not "your highness". Winston had seemed scandalized that she could even confuse the two. "It is a true honor to be here on Orsino Island."

Her nerves were causing her hands to tremble. She drew in a long breath and stared at herself in the mirror.

"You can do this, Sabrina," she said, locking eyes with her own reflection. "Just try to stay calm and have fun. This will be a great night."

*As long as I don't screw anything up,* she thought.

The ball was only twenty minutes away. Sabrina had already taken a luxurious bath in the over-sized tub. She now smelled of lavender and rose pedals, which Marla had put in the water before drawing the bath for her. The royal hairdresser and makeup artist had already turned her into a masterpiece fit for a magazine cover. All that was left was to get into her dress.

A light knock came from the bedroom door and Sabrina spun around. "Come in."

Marco popped his head in and grinned. Sabrina's eyes moved up and down his body. In the time he had been away, Marco had changed into a formal outfit. He was dressed in a dark blue suit, with gold designs on the shoulders and gold buttons on the front. His hair was combed neatly to the side and he'd cleaned up his beard stubble. For the first time since they'd met, he appeared like the prince that he was. Sabrina yelped in excitement and ran toward him, embracing him in a hug.

"Hey, lovely," he said, kissing her cheek. "I trust Winston gave you a proper tour?"

"He showed me around a little bit, but there really wasn't enough time for an in-depth tour," Sabrina said. "But he *did* teach me a few things that he said would help me to fit in around here."

Marco raised his eyebrows. "Like what?"

Sabrina gracefully bent her knees and bowed, at the same time bringing her hands up to her side as if she were holding the bottom of a dress. The perfect curtsy.

"Look at that," Marco said, with a chuckle. "I must say that I've not often seen a more refined bow. Clearly, Winston knows what he's doing. Should we promote him to curtsy teacher?"

Sabrina laughed and playfully pushed against Marco's chest. "To be fair, I think Winston saved me a lot of embarrassment by teaching me the proper way to greet your parents."

"He's a good man," he said. "I've known him since I was a child."

Marco closed the bedroom door and then looked past Sabrina toward the array of dresses that were laid out on the bed. He grabbed Sabrina's hand and walked her toward them. "What do you think?"

"I think I love every single one of them," Sabrina said, with a childlike smile. "They're all so beautiful."

"They are indeed," Marco said, carefully running his fingers over each one. "Have you chosen one for tonight, though? The ball starts soon and we must be on time."

"There's one that I really like," she said, stepping toward the white dress that was draped over the foot of the bed. "But I wanted to get your opinion on it first."

She picked up the dress and held it in the air. The look on Marco's face told her everything she needed to know. His eyes widened, along with his smile. He nodded as he looked between Sabrina and the dress.

"You'd look amazing in that," he said. "Please, try it on."

Sabrina nodded and then grabbed a pair of panties and a bra from her suitcase. Then she pulled off the towel that was wrapped around her, letting it fall to the floor. She stood naked in front of the Prince, and watched as his eyes dilated.

"If only we had more than a few minutes," he said, his eyes moving up and down her nude body.

"You be good, Prince Marco," she said, flirtatiously. "We have a ball to attend."

She turned and walked to the bathroom. As quickly as possible, she got into the dress. She was amazed at how perfectly it conformed to her curves. It was as though the dress had been stitched just for her. She stared in the mirror for a moment. The woman in front of her was a princess, transformed by a fairy godmother.

When she walked back into the bedroom, Marco stood up from the bed. His expression was one of complete awe as he eyed her up and down.

"I've never seen someone so lovely," he said. "Sabrina, you look incredible."

Sabrina pushed a loose strand of her hair behind her ear and smiled. "Thank you. You're so sweet."

"Here, let me button up the back for you," Marco said, stepping behind her.

He pulled the back of the dress together and buttoned it up. Sabrina closed her eyes and relaxed her shoulders. Marco leaned close and kissed the back of her neck as he clasped the top button. When he pulled away, he said, "Okay, you're all set."

Sabrina spun around and kissed him. She let her hands wander over his shoulders and down the front of his shirt, letting her fingers bounce over the gold buttons. The smell of his cologne entered her nose and for a fleeting moment, she wondered if they could possibly fit in a bit of intimate time before the ball.

But when she broke the kiss and looked at the clock, her eyes widened.

"It's almost time to go," she said. "We've only got a few minutes."

"Indeed," Marco said, with a half smirk. "Are you ready?"

"As ready as I'll ever be," she said, with a nervous sigh.

～

DRESSED TO PERFECTION, Marco and Sabrina made their way downstairs and to the back of the building, where the grand hall was located. Winston had walked her by it earlier that day, but they weren't able to go inside due to preparations for the celebration that evening. But now the place was filled. Elegant people, with elegant attire, were lined up out the door. They turned to look when Marco and Sabrina walked toward them and the ones who weren't wearing a green or purple pendant on their collar stepped to the side and dropped to a knee out of respect.

"Good evening, everyone," Marco said, as he and Sabrina walked by.

The two made their way into the main room and Sabrina's gaze moved toward the very back, where the King of Orsino sat on his throne. He looked regal and proud as he gazed out at the audience. Seated next to him was Queen Magdalena. She sat with a smug expression on her face, as though she was too good for even her own party.

Surrounding the royalty were guards, but also guests. Many of them appeared to be nobles, based on their expensive dress and the elegant way that they carried themselves. Sabrina's nerves were through the roof as she walked alongside Marco toward the throne.

*I wonder how many other girls out there can say that this is how they "met the parents,"* she thought, swallowing down the lump in her throat.

She squeezed Marco's arm firmly and he looked over.

"You're doing fine," he said. "Just relax."

Sabrina didn't respond as she tried to keep her cool. She became utterly self-conscious, suddenly worrying about each step she took. The last thing she wanted to do was to trip and fall in front of the royalty, making herself look like a total fool.

Her heart was racing and she felt like she could have thrown up from nervousness. Each inch they got closer to the throne caused another butterfly to release into her gut. Her hands were trembling and her knees were weak by the time they got to the back of the room.

"Father," Marco said. "I'd like to introduce you to the beautiful Sabrina."

The man in the throne sat up and smiled. He appeared to be much older than the man in the picture that she had seen. He looked pale and sickly, with dark bags under his eyes. His hair, though thick in the photo, was weak-looking and sparse.

"Marco, my son," the king spoke, his deep and authoritative. "Bring her closer. My eyes aren't what they used to be."

"Of course, Father," Marco said, leading Sabrina up the stairs toward the throne.

Sabrina felt the room shrink as the king and queen both brought their attention toward her. Luckily, the training that Winston had given her earlier kicked in. She let go of Marco's arm and did the perfect curtsy in front of everyone.

"It's a pleasure to meet you, your majesty," she said, dipping down toward the ground. "It's a true honor to be on Orsino Island."

"And it's an honor to have you here," the king said.

Sabrina finished her curtsy and stood up straight. King Carlo was looking at her with curiosity, while Queen Magdalena sat in silence, her face unreadable.

"I appreciate the formalities, but come closer still," King Carlo said. "Let me get a look at you."

Sabrina stepped toe to toe with Carlo and he took her hand. Their eyes were locked as he spoke. "Where are you from, Ms. Sabrina?"

"Memphis, Tennessee," she said, her accent suddenly

feeling more thick than usual. She usually tried to keep her accent as minimal as possible, but it often came out stronger when she was stressed.

"I can hear it," he replied. "It's soft, but there."

"Yes, I was born and raised there," she said.

"Welcome to Orsino." King Carlo squeezed her hand. "I'm confident that you'll love it here once you get settled. It's a beautiful place with a lot to offer."

"Marco has told me a lot about it, but I'm excited to explore." Sabrina smiled, relieved by the small talk. She glanced at the queen, still unsure because the woman had yet to say a word.

"It really is a pleasure to meet you, King Carlo," Sabrina continued. "It's nice to finally be able to put a face to a name."

"I can say the same about you," he said, before turning toward the woman next to him. "Since we're making introductions, I'd like to officially introduce you to my wife, Queen Magdalena."

Sabrina curtsied again. This time a warm smile filled her face. Something about it felt off, but Sabrina couldn't place it. Perhaps it was that it didn't seem to touch her lavender colored eyes as most smiles usually did.

"How lovely to meet you," the queen cooed. "I'm so excited to hear of your travels with our young prince. Thank you for keeping him so entertained in his travels."

Sabrina did a double take. Both Marco and Winston had mentioned to her that the queen hated commoners and to expect her to be cold and cruel to her. Yet, the queen was smiling and being pleasant. *Perhaps, I misunderstood them,* Sabrina thought, looking at the queen's warm smile. *She seems nice enough. Maybe she just speaks her mind and is considered cruel for it.*

"Father, there's something that I want to announce," Marco said, clearing his throat.

"By all means, Marco," Carlo said. "Take the floor. I'm certain most everyone who will be attending tonight is present now."

Sabrina turned around to see that the room had filled. Most of the attention from the guests was directed toward the front, where Sabrina stood with the royal family. Marco nodded to a man in black holding a large staff. The man banged it on the floor twice. The idle chatter went quiet.

"I have an announcement to make," Marco said, his voice booming over the silent guests.

A pin drop could have been heard. It was clear just how much respect everyone held for Marco. Sabrina stood next to him, not knowing what this announcement was about. He certainly hadn't mentioned anything to her.

"First off, I want to thank everyone for coming," he said. "This ball, as you may already know, is in honor of our great King. King Carlo."

Marco stepped to the side to give the audience a better view of the king and the crowd went crazy. They clapped and shouted, giving praise to their leader. Once they settled down, Marco continued. "For those of you who were wondering where I've been the last few weeks, I was on holiday in the United States. It's a beautiful place, but I have to say that I've never been so happy to be back. I learned something while I was there and it's that Orsino Island will always be my home."

The crowd got loud again, but this time Marco held his finger in the air.

"Please, let me finish," he said. "Even though I love Orsino Island, I will never regret my time spent away. It's because of that time, that I was able to meet the most beautiful woman on the entire planet. In just a few short weeks, she's become my everything."

Sabrina's jaw dropped and her heart swelled as she faced Marco. This speech was taking her completely off guard, but in the best of ways.

"When I met her, I knew that there was something special about her," he said, as both Sabrina and the audience hung onto every word. "It was in the way her eyes lit up when she smiled. It was her genuine curiosity about the world. It was how she made me feel happy. But most of all, it was Sabrina's deep love of life that had me hooked from the very beginning. With all of that being said, I'd like to ask Sabrina something in front of all of you."

Marco faced Sabrina and took both of her hands in his. She practically melted in front of him. In that moment, she felt more loved and cared for than ever before in her life. He gazed at her for just a second and then dropped to one knee. The audience gasped and so did Sabrina.

"Sabrina, will you marry me and become the princess of Orsino Island?" he asked, his words echoing out over the silence of the crowd.

Sabrina's lips curled up into the widest and most uncontrollable smile she'd ever had. His question took her breath away and tears instantly burst down her cheek. She brought her hand over her mouth and nodded, unable to speak at first. The audience stayed silent, as they waited to hear her answer.

"Will you marry me and make me the happiest man in the world?" Marco asked again, this time a bit quieter. He spoke the words so that only Sabrina could hear them.

"Yes," she managed to say, in between sobs of joy. "Yes, of course. Yes!"

The crowd went insane and the room filled with

applause. Marco pulled a beautiful single-set diamond ring out of his pocket and slipped it on over her finger, before standing up. He gave her a peck on the lips and pulled away, gazing into her eyes.

"I love you," he said, then paused for a moment. "Princess Sabrina."

Sabrina's chest was filled with excitement. Somehow, a handkerchief was pressed into her hand to wipe the tears from her eyes. She looked over the crowd of strangers, who were standing up from their chairs, still clapping in celebration.

"I love you, too," she said, turning back to Marco. "You never cease to surprise me, you know that?"

"If that's true, then I've succeeded in my goal," he said, placing his hand on Sabrina's lower back.

They both faced the crowd and Marco waited patiently until the noise had died down and the guests had taken their seats once again.

"Thank you for the love. And thank you for welcoming Sabrina in such a beautiful way," Marco said to the audience. "Now please, enjoy yourselves this evening. This is a celebration of my father's reign and of Orsino Island's economic success in the previous year. We all have a lot to be thankful for and to celebrate. My only request from each and every one of you, is that you fill your bellies with drink and food, and dance like it's the last day on Earth."

The crowd clapped again at the traditional request and Sabrina sighed. She was overwhelmed with emotion. She glanced down at the ring that Marco had slipped on her finger and shook her head in amazement. Never in a million years could she have imagined that she'd step into the shoes of a real princess.

Marco took Sabrina's hand and led her down the steps

toward the center of the room. Music began to play from a small band in the corner. There were flute players, trumpets, trombones and violins. Sabrina recognized the sound immediately. It was the same band that Marco had played for her at the hotel in New York.

"Will you do me the honor of a dance?" he asked Sabrina.

The crowd made way, giving the two of them space in the room. Sabrina, not one for dancing but only because she didn't know how, decided that if there was ever a time for her to expand her horizons it was right then.

"Yes, of course," she said. "But you have to lead."

"My beautiful fiancée, I'd be honored," he said.

The band continued to play and Marco carefully held Sabrina's hands. He swayed back and forth with her, starting slowly. The crowd surrounded them and the music intensified. Marco began spinning her and dipping her with the rhythm. He led so well that Sabrina hardly had to think. She just went along with his movements, giggling and laughing as he expertly maneuvered both of them around the dance floor.

The audience watched the two, but only for the first few minutes. Then they all began to dance. The entire room became alive as everybody grabbed a partner and joined Marco and Sabrina. There were so many things that could have caught her attention, like Queen Magdalena still on her throne and giving her a dirty look, or Winston in the corner dancing with Marla, or King Carlo tapping his foot to the music. But she didn't really give much mind to any of these things. The only thing she was focused on was Marco. She just couldn't take her eyes off of him.

~

After dancing for three full songs, Sabrina needed a break. She pulled Marco to the side of the room, walking with a new-found confidence. Not only did it turn out that she was a decent dancer, but she was also going to be getting married soon. There was an obvious spring in her step.

"Marco, this is so much fun," she said into his ear, having to speak loudly because of the music. "I still can't believe you asked me to marry you in front of everyone. That was the most romantic experience of my life."

"I was so nervous," he admitted. "I'm unbelievably relieved that you said yes."

"I can't wait to tell everybody," Sabrina said, bringing her hands to Marco's chest. "My parents are going to be so excited."

She took a moment and thought about her parents and how they would benefit from her new position as princess.

*I can save them from their misery,* she thought. *I can give them the kind of life they deserve.*

"You've made me the happiest man on earth, you know that?" Marco said, leaning closer to Sabrina.

"You've done the same for me and more," she replied.

King Carlo approached Sabrina from across the room. His thick and elegant robe made him look healthier than he was. It gave the illusion that he wasn't sickly and thin, but Sabrina could see the truth in his face and neck and his slow and careful movements.

"Congratulations, love. You and Marco will make a beautiful team. I couldn't be happier that you're part of our family now," he said, placing a hand onto Sabrina's shoulder.

"Thank you, your majesty," Sabrina replied.

"Sabrina, please," he replied. "You're practically my daughter now. Call me Carlo."

"Okay," she said, with a smile. It felt wrong after Winston's drilling earlier, but to disobey the king would be a true disgrace.

"Now, if I can steal away your husband-to-be, just for a moment, I would be ever so grateful. I've something important to discuss with him." Carlo placed his other hand onto Marco's shoulder, giving it a firm squeeze.

"Of course," Sabrina said. "I'll go get a drink and mingle while you guys talk. I'm sure you have a lot of catching up to do."

"I promise to have him back to you in just a few minutes," Carlo promised.

The King and Marco turned and walked away, disappearing through a door at the back of the room. Sabrina watched them until they were gone and then made her way to a nearby table that was piled with food and drinks. She intended on getting a glass of something to quench her thirst. But she hardly made it two feet before she felt someone tap her shoulder strap of her dress, stopping her in her tracks.

"What the..." Sabrina said, spinning around.

Standing there, with the kindest smile she'd ever seen on a person, was Queen Magdalena. "I do hope you realize what's going on.."

Sabrina took a step back. "What are you talking about, your majesty?"

"He's afraid his father is going to die," the queen informed her. Her accent wasn't from Orsino. It was British, just like Aunt Fayes.

"I don't understand," Sabrina said, shaking her head. "Why would that have anything to do with what Marco just did."

"Oh, you sweet, innocent young thing." The queen

clicked her tongue and shook her head. "He is afraid is father is going to die, and so he proposed so his father would see it. He's trying to give his father something to live for."

"I beg your pardon," Sabrina said, taking a step back. "Marco asked me to marry him because he loves me."

"You really believe that, don't you?" The queen's delicate features filled with pity. "Marco always did have a way with the ladies."

Sabrina had no idea what to say. Her mouth hung open and she knew that later tonight, she'd have a million smart remarks to say back, but unfortunately the only thing she managed to get out was a childish, "You're lying!"

"I wish that I were, child," Queen Magdalena replied. "But he can't marry you. He legally cannot marry you. I'm surprised he hasn't mentioned it, to be honest."

"Marco wouldn't lie to me," she hissed. One of the guests turned and gave Sabrina a dirty look, but the queen just waved him on.

"He lied to you about being a prince, didn't he?" Magdalena shrugged. "Is it so hard to believe that he would lie about this as well? Or, is it possible that he simply found a gullible American to come play the part of loving daughter-in-law-to-be in order to give his father something to fight for? All the man wants is to see his boy happily married."

"No," Sabrina replied, shaking her head. "He wouldn't do that."

"If you say so my dear," Magdalena replied with a sad shake of her head. "But perhaps you should ask him about the Law of Princely Marriage. It's a law that's been a part of our country for countless generations. He would have learned of it as a boy."

"You must be mistaken," Sabrina told her. She glanced

around, wishing that Marco or Carlo would return so she could get away from Magdalena's insinuations that Marco didn't love her.

"The law states that a prince or princess or Orsino must marry someone of noble blood," the queen informed her. "As you come from, well..." Queen Magdalena seemed to be searching for the right words, something that would offend without being vulgar. "Well, not anything noble anyway, you are ineligible to marry him. He knows this. He has to know the laws as a prince."

"He wouldn't lie to me," Sabrina repeated. But the doubt didn't disappear from her mind as easily as she said the words. Marco *had* lied to her about being a prince. A lie of omission, anyway.

Magdalena put a hand on Sabrina's shoulder. Her fingers were cold against Sabrina's bare skin. "Either, Prince Marco doesn't know the laws of the land- the laws that he had to recite daily as a child, or..." Queen Magdalena shrugged and let the rest of her sentence hang in the air.

"No," Sabrina repeated, taking a step back. "He wouldn't do that to me."

The queen laughed. It was cold and cruel. "Why? Because he loves you? Love is just a word people use to get what they want. My mother claimed to love my father, but she abandoned him with an infant child. He gave her every-thing, but just like Marco, she left him with nothing."

Sabrina's cheeks stung as if she had been slapped. "That's not true," she whispered.

"If you say so, my dear." The queen shrugged. "But perhaps you should consult the law before you throw your life away for him. The library is just over there and the book's open to the page."

With that, the queen turned on a heel and spun smiling

to mingle with the crowd. Sabrina stared after her, shocked and shaken to her core.

Marco and Winston had been right. The woman was evil. She would stop at nothing to destroy any happiness that she saw around her. This was supposed to be one of the happiest nights of Sabrina's life, and now she was ready to cry.

"It can't be true," she whispered, more to herself than to anyone else. Yet, Queen Magdalena's words seeped into her soul like poison.

Sabrina looked around again for her husband-to-be. She found him animatedly discussing something with a very attractive woman in a low cut dress. The woman touched his arm, gazing up at him in adoration.

Sabrina could see the door to the library from where she stood. If the law book was open like Magdalena had said, then she could read the law for herself. It probably was something from the days of knights and armor that no longer applied. She had her phone on her. She could check the law, and then check her phone and see if it was as Magdalena said.

She glanced over to see Marco laugh at something the other woman said. With quick steps before she could change her mind, Sabrina hurried to the library.

The room was quiet as the party went on in the adjacent rooms. Books of all shapes and sizes lined every square inch of wall space, but sitting on a reading stand in the center of the room between beautiful leather furniture was a large open book.

She approached it with hesitation. For a moment, she considered simply leaving the room without reading anything. If she didn't know, then it wouldn't be true.

Except she was already at the book.

*"The Law of Princely Marriage: The royal heir, be it male or female must wed of noble blood. No other suitors may be entertained."*

"No," she gasped, but the words stayed the same. Frantic, she pulled her phone out of her clutch and googled the law. It was a real law. There were no repeals. All Orsino marriages were of noble heritage. The latest one listed was between King Carlo and Lady Magdalena Dunhill.

She had been telling the truth.

"No," Sabrina whispered, sinking into one of the leather couches. "This can't be right."

"No," she said, stronger this time. "There has to be an explanation. He loves me."

Sabrina stood up and left the library determined to confront Marco.

"I told you, didn't I?" Magdalena asked as soon as Sabrina left the library. "You are nothing but a worthless commoner and you will never be royal."

"I will marry Marco," Sabrina informed her. She could see her beloved just across the room. He smiled at her and motioned that he would be there in just one moment.

Anger flashed across Magdalena's beautiful features. Heat flared in her lavender eyes as she realized her plan hadn't worked. She cocked her head and smiled cruelly.

"You haven't won. You will never marry him. You only want him for his title," Magdalena shouted. Everyone in the room turned and looked.

Sabrina looked around, suddenly feeling very small.

"You don't belong here," Magdalena growled, so loud that everyone could hear it.

Sabrina's cheeks burned as she blushed from embarrassment.

"I'm sorry you feel that way," Sabrina whispered.

Out of the corner of her eye, Sabrina saw Marco approaching. He marched up to them quickly.

"What's going on over here?" he asked, staring straight at Magdalena.

"None of your business, Marco," Magdalena snapped. "Why don't you go back to your father and leave me alone with your little princess?"

"I don't want to have this argument," Sabrina said. "I just want to have a good night."

Magdalena let out an exaggerated scoff. Then she reached forward and grabbed the shoulder strap of Sabrina's dress.

"Nothing in this palace belongs to you," Magdalena said, her voice more raspy and evil than before. "*Nothing.* Not even this dress."

As soon as she finished speaking the words, she tugged down firmly on the shoulder-strap, causing it to rip off of Sabrina's shoulder. Sabrina squealed in surprise and took a step back, holding the top of the dress up with her hands to keep from exposing her breasts to the entire party.

"How dare you try to swindle our prince!" Magdalena shouted.

Marco turned an absurd shade of red as the ballroom ground to a halt and everyone turned to watch the scene unfolding before them. Marco grabbed Magdalena's arm, pulling her away from Sabrina and toward his father.

While Marco and Carlo were arguing with Magdalena, Sabrina was left standing by herself. The tears that she had been desperately trying to hold back finally welled out of her eyes and down her cheeks. Never in her life had she felt so embarrassed and discriminated against.

She stood there for a moment, just holding up the top of the dress. The shoulder-strap, now torn at one end, hung loosely by her side. She waited, hoping that Marco would come and comfort her. She needed him in that moment. But he didn't come to her. He stayed with Carlo and Magdalena.

*Why isn't he coming over here?* She thought.

Sabrina watched as the royal trio walked away. She couldn't hear what they were saying, but it was pretty clear that the words were not civil. They all appeared to be shouting and their hands were flailing in the air with anger.

*I can't believe this,* she thought. *I never should have come here. This was a mistake. Everything about this was a huge mistake.*

Tears flowing, Sabrina turned and ran toward the doors. She looked at the ground to avoid eye contact from the guests, not wanting to feel any more embarrassment. She made it to the main entryway of the palace, but saw a group of people standing there. They turned to face her, but she didn't want to chat. The only thing Sabrina wanted was to get out of there.

So she ran down the hallway that Winston had shown her earlier that day. She passed the pictures of the nobles that were hung on the wall. Her stomach turned as she passed the one of Magdalena. When she got to the end, she pushed through the double doors and into the sunlight.

*I don't know where I'm going. I just want to be anywhere but here right now,* she thought.

Sabrina ran down the steps and into a large courtyard. It was surrounded by parts of the palace, with a large fountain in the center. She slowed her pace down to catch her breath, but continued to move across the courtyard. Once she had reached the opposite side, she stepped into a door.

*Another hallway,* she thought.

This one was empty, thankfully. But she still didn't know where she was or how to get out of the palace. She walked around for a bit, until she found another door that led outside. She pushed it open and focused her eyes. Toward the bottom of the hill was a main road. It was the same one that Marco and Sabrina had taken to get to the palace earlier that day.

"That's my way out of here," she whispered.

She couldn't believe she was about to leave, but staying there didn't feel like an option to her, though. Not only had the queen made it very clear that she wasn't welcome, but Marco hadn't even attempted to console her after seeing Magdalena tear her dress.

*He saw what she did to me, but he's done nothing,* she thought. *And why hasn't he come looking for me? I know I ran off, but surely he'd be able to find me right now if he wanted to. He knows this place like the back of his hand. Doesn't he care about me?*

Magdalena's accusation that he was simply using her to give his father hope for the future echoed in her ears.

Sabrina glanced back, getting one last look at the palace, the place that was supposed to be her new home. A tear trickled slowly down her cheek, but she quickly wiped it away. She made her way down toward the main road, with the decision that she'd go find a hotel somewhere and check in under a fake name. At the very least, that would give her some space and time to sort everything out in her mind. It would also give her a chance to find some proper clothes and to call her Aunt Faye for advice.

"At least Faye will be there for me. I can always rely on her," she said to herself, as she continued her trek through the dirt and grass. "That's more than I can say for Marco, apparently."

# CHAPTER 19

MARCO STOOD with his arms crossed and his eyes glaring. Magdalena was in front of him. Rage pumped through his veins and all he wanted to do was to let it all out on her. After seeing what she had done to his beautiful fiancée in front of everyone, he was beginning to care less that Magdalena happened to be the queen.

"How dare you embarrass Sabrina like that," Marco said, keeping his eyes locked with hers. "And for what? What point were you trying to make, Magdalena?"

They were still standing next to the outer wall in the grand room. The music was playing once again and people were dancing. The ball continued on, even though the hosts weren't currently participating.

"Marco, please, we need to keep this civil," Carlo said, placing a hand onto Marco's forearm. "Come on, let's go somewhere quiet so we can discuss things."

"Father, how can you expect me to remain civil after seeing what Magdalena is capable of?" he asked. "You saw it, too. She attacked my fiance in front of the entire party. Is there no justice for something like that?"

Magdalena rolled her eyes. "Don't act like a spoiled little brat, Marco."

"What do you have against her anyway?" Marco asked. "I'm well aware of the fact that you hate everything and everyone, but your aggression toward Sabrina seems elevated. Even for you."

"She's a commoner," she said, matter-of-factly. "I could tolerate her being here, but marrying her? You must be insane."

"Maybe it's none of your business who she is or where she's from," Marco said.

"I suppose you'd be right," Magdalena said, with a smug smile. "That is, if you didn't drag her home with you. But now she's here. So she has *become* my business."

"Both of you, stop this at once," Carlo interjected. "We will meet in my chambers in five minutes to discuss this. No more arguing here, though. The last thing we need is for this drama to get out of hand again."

Marco sighed. "Fine. Sabrina and I will meet you there."

"Sabrina is not welcome in this meeting," Magdalena said, before Carlo could reply.

"Yes, actually, she *is*." Marco corrected her. "She's my fiancée and therefore, she has as much right to be there as I do. In fact, I'm going to go find her now and make sure that she's okay. I'll see you in you a few minutes, Father."

Marco spun around before getting a response. He scanned the audience, looking for his lover, but didn't see her.

*Maybe she went for a breath of fresh air,* he thought, as he left the room.

A group of nobles from a nearby island stood at the entrance. They were sipping champagne and chatting among themselves when Marco approached.

"I'm sorry to interrupt," Marco said. "But have any of you seen Sabrina? There was a bit of a mishap and it's important that I speak to her."

One of the men turned to face Marco and gave him a nod. "Prince Marco. Pleasure to see you again. I regret to tell you that Sabrina ran out of here a few minutes ago. She looked very upset and was crying as she left."

*Oh no,* Marco said. *This is not how I wanted her to feel on her first day here. This has gone horribly wrong.*

"Thank you for the information," Marco said, running quickly out the door and to the front of the palace. He approached the first guard that he saw. "Have you seen Sabrina? My fiancée, she's left and I don't know where she's gone. She's wearing a white dress. You can't miss her."

"I'm sorry, sir, but I haven't seen her," he said.

"*Find* her!" Marco demanded. "I'm going to check the bedrooms upstairs, but something tells me that she's gone further than that."

The guard reached for his radio as Marco ran upstairs. He poked his head into his bedroom, but it appeared to be untouched, as expected. He ran down the hall, opening every unlocked door and peering in just to make sure. But there was no sign of Sabrina. Panic filled him.

*She was already nervous about being here and then all of that happened with Magdalena,* he thought. *She's probably devastated and trying to figure out a way off of the island.*

Marco quickly descended the stairs and approached the same guard. "I need you to call me when you locate her.

Search everywhere. It's important that I find her as soon as possible."

"Of course, sir, we're on it," the guard replied.

Marco's gut clenched into a ball of anxiety. His love for Sabrina was stronger than even he had realized and the thought of her being upset pained him beyond belief. This wasn't how he had hoped things would turn out. And there was only one person to blame.

*Magdalena,* he thought, as the image of the queen put a scowl on his face.

"That rotten bitch," he whispered.

While the guards began the search for Sabrina, Marco marched straight toward his father's chambers.

*I'm going to get to the bottom of this right now,* he thought.

WITH HIS BLOOD BOILING, Marco pushed open the double doors that led into King Carlo's chambers. He found Carlo and Magdalena seated at a large table near the back of the room. Carlo looked a bit flustered, while Magdalena sat with a contented smile on her face. The expression made Marco even angrier as he walked toward them.

"My fiancée is missing, *thanks to you,*" Marco growled, as he stared blatantly at Magdalena.

"Such a shame," she said, sarcastically. "I suppose everything happens for a reason, though. Maybe it just wasn't meant to be."

Marco walked up and slammed his fist down on the center of the table. "This has gone too far!"

"Marco, I understand that you're upset," Carlo said, in his calm tone. "But don't feed the fire. Just take a seat and we'll work through this."

"I can't sit and do nothing," Marco said. "Sabrina is nowhere to be found."

"She's likely taken a walk to clear her head," Carlo said, patting his son on the shoulder. "There's nothing to worry about. Have you told the guards to look for her?"

"Yes." Marco ran his fingers through his hair and looked upward in despair. "They're searching."

"Then it's out of your hands." Carlo squeezed his shoulder. "So just relax."

Marco sighed and then faced forward, catching Magdalena's gaze. For the life of him, he couldn't understand why the queen had made it her life mission to make his life a living hell. And why she hated commoners so much was another thing that he just couldn't wrap his head around. It just didn't make sense to him that she could put so much energy into something that really didn't affect her.

"Father, I apologize for any way that I've acted out of line today or for anything I've said," Marco leaned forward and put his palms onto the table. "But all that I want is to be able to marry the woman I love. She's an amazing girl, commoner or not, and she's the one who I want to spend my life with. Why does this have to be such an issue?"

Carlo swallowed and looked down at the table. Magdalena was still smirking, as she crossed her arms and leaned back in her chair. The room was filled with silence.

"What's going on? Why isn't anyone saying anything?" Marco asked.

"Go ahead, Carlo, tell him," Magdalena said, looking amused as could be. "Why don't you tell him the law?"

"Magdalena, you agreed that you'd be civil," Carlo said, his voice catching . He coughed twice. "If you continue to be domineering, then I will not allow you to participate in this conversation."

Marco smiled on the inside, as Carlo put Magdalena in her place. It was nice to see once a while, since she was usually the one running the show since he fell ill.

"All I was saying is that you should tell Marco he should repeat his childhood laws more often," Magdalena said, faking an innocent voice. "It's very important."

"What in the hell is she talking about?" Marco asked.

"The Law of Princely Marriage," Carlo said softly. "It states that a prince or princess cannot marry someone who is not of royal blood."

Marco's stomach dropped. "What are you talking about? I can marry whomever I choose."

Magdalena leaned close and said, "No, Marco, you can't. It would be against the law."

"Is this true?" Marco asked, turning to the king. "Is this a real law or something that *she* created?"

"It is a true law." Carlo stood up from his seat as he spoke. "It's not a scenario that happens very often, so I'm a bit unclear on the details. There may be caveats."

"Oh, I guarantee you there aren't," Magdalena said. "Trust me. I've checked into it already. As soon as I got word that our young Prince was fluttering about with a commoner, I checked with the lawmen. You don't have to believe me. You can believe them."

Marco swallowed and stared at his father. His heart sank.

*What if Magdalena is right? What if the law really does say that a noble can't marry a commoner? What would I do then?* he thought.

"I need to look into this before I can say what should be done," Carlo said, taking a few steps toward the door.

"Why bother?" Magdalena said. "You'll find out what I already told you."

"I'll see it for myself then," King Carlo said shortly. "In the meantime, Marco, look for Sabrina."

Carlo stepped out of the room. The door shut, leaving the queen and the prince to themselves. They stared at each other from across the table, like dogs about to fight. The tension in the air was obvious. It was silent for a few seconds, until Marco finally just stood up. He had better things to do then waste time getting in another argument with Magdalena. He needed to go find his fiancée and comfort her.

# CHAPTER 20

SABRINA WOKE to the sound of rain outside her window. She opened her eyes and slowly sat up on the love seat. A pile of wrinkled tissues was next to her, which she had been using to dry the tears from her cheeks for the past two full days. She looked across the motel room, noticing a drip of water coming down from the ceiling and landing with a soft thud into the carpet. To have gone from spending time in a beautiful palace to this rundown motel at the edge of the island was quite a change for her, but it was the only place she could afford.

She'd managed to get away from Orsino Palace two days before. And after walking for over an hour along the highway and then hitchhiking several times, she found this motel. It was a total dump, but she knew that it would have to do. After what had happened at the ball, Sabrina wasn't ready to face any of the royalty again. In fact, she was still toying with the idea of leaving the island altogether and pretending like this part of her life had never even happened.

*Maybe I just go back to Memphis and find a regular old job,* she thought, stretching her arms above her head. *Maybe this really wasn't meant to be.*

"What do I do now?" she asked herself, as she walked to the sink to get a cup of water. "I hardly have enough money to stay here for a few more nights. There's no way I could afford the trip to get back home."

Her parents didn't have any money, so it wasn't like she could have them buy her a plane ticket. Her Aunt Faye was in a similar boat, and even if Faye could afford it, Sabrina would never ask her to do something like that. So she was stuck. Out of money and out of options.

The only thing that had kept her sane in the motel room for two days was talking to Faye on the phone occasionally. But even that only did so much. Because it was during the nighttime, when Sabrina was left with only her thoughts, that she became extremely depressed about the situation.

She plopped back down on the couch and as soon as she did, someone knocked on the door of her room. She froze and held her breath, listening to the sound of her heartbeat. The knock came again, this time a little louder.

*It must be Marco,* she thought. *Did he finally try to find me? Took him long enough.*

She got up and walked toward the door, both excited and nervous to see him again. After a long sigh, she turned the handle and opened it up. When she saw who was standing in the doorway, she nearly fell over from shock. Her head cocked to the side and her eyebrow raised.

"Faye?" she said, looking the older woman up and down.

"Oh, Bean," Faye said, stepping into the motel.

Aunt Faye was soaking wet from the rain. Her hair was a matted mess on top of her shoulders. She was dressed in just a simple t-shirt and jeans, and didn't even have a jacket on.

"Faye, I was just thinking about you. What are you doing here? How did you find me?" Sabrina asked, her eyes wide.

Faye pulled her close for a hug. "I have my ways. Besides, I've never heard you sound more upset than you did last couple of days. I knew that I had to see you, so I spent my money on a plane ticket and got here as fast as I could."

Tears fell down Sabrina's cheeks as she held her Aunt. She was completely shocked to see her, but so grateful for her presence. Her broken heart began to feel a tiny bit better just having someone familiar there with her, especially after being by herself for two days.

"Aunty, I can't tell you how happy I am that you're here right now," she said, between sobs. "You shouldn't have spent the money, though. That ticket must have cost a fortune."

Faye pulled away and looked at Sabrina directly, her light purple eyes glowing. "It's just money, Sabrina. Some things are far more important. And your happiness is priceless to me. I'd spend every dime I have on it."

"I still can't believe you're here," Sabrina replied, looking her over. "You're soaking wet. Let me get you a towel."

She turned and ran to the bathroom to get Faye a dry towel. When she returned, she found Faye sitting in the small chair near the front door.

"Here you go, Aunty." Sabrina handed her the towel and Faye used it to dry her hair.

As soon as she was done, Faye said, "Now that I'm here, we need to discuss your situation."

Sabrina replied instantaneously. "I want to go home."

"Back to Memphis?" Faye asked, looking shocked by Sabrina's sudden decision.

"Yes," she said. "I've been going back and forth for two days now, but seeing you makes me realize that there's still a place on earth where people love me. It's home. It may not be the nicest place in the world, but at least the people there understand me."

Faye slowly pushed herself up from the chair and approached Sabrina. She seemed a bit weary and Sabrina placed her hands on her shoulders to help her balance.

"You should sit, Aunty," Sabrina said. "You must be exhausted from the trip."

"Nonsense," Faye said. "I'm fine. But you must listen to me, child, because I didn't fly all the way out here just to take you home. In fact, I came here to do just the opposite."

"What do you mean?" Sabrina asked.

"I've been alive a long time, Sabrina," Faye said. "And during that time, I've been in love. Not all of the time, of course. But some of it. Enough to know that true love is a rare thing and not everyone is lucky enough to experience it."

"It's very rare indeed," Sabrina agreed. "But I don't know what you're getting at, Faye. I'm not in love, apparently. If Marco loved me, why isn't he here right now?"

"You *are* in love, Bean," Faye said, with a smile that caused the skin around her eyes to wrinkle. "You might be upset right now, but that doesn't mean you're not in love. The way you spoke of Marco over the past few weeks told the whole story. I've never heard you so happy and excited about life."

"That was before everything went to hell." Sabrina wiped the tears from her cheeks. "That was before I learned how awful people can be. You should have seen it, Faye. I've never been so embarrassed in my life as when Queen Magdalena ripped my dress and shouted at me in front of the entire party."

"I know, love, but you're not seeing my point," Faye replied. "This is one moment in time. Queen Magdalena ripping your dress and you running off and Marco not chasing after you. It all happened within a few minutes. But what's a few minutes in the scheme of things? It's nothing. Do you really want to sacrifice potential love and an amazing future for a few minutes of friction?"

"But Faye, you were the one who first warned me about dating a nobleman, remember?" Sabrina asked, putting her hands on her hips.

"Yes, but that was before I looked at the whole picture," Faye said, walking toward the kitchen. "I've thought long and hard about this and I truly believe that you need to give Marco another shot."

Sabrina followed her Aunt to the kitchen and watched as she made herself a cup of tea.

"Faye, he didn't even come and say anything to me after Magdalena attacked me," she said. "He just stood there arguing with her. And I've been here for two days and he hasn't shown up. He's the Prince, for crying out loud. You can't tell me that he hasn't been able to find me. *You* found me, why can't he?"

Faye spun around and raised an eyebrow. "I found you because you told me where you were staying."

"Fair enough." Sabrina shrugged. "But still. If Marco wanted to locate me, then he could. His family owns the island."

"Bean, I understand you're mad at him, but I'm asking you to try to forgive him," she said. "I know for a fact that he would be here right now if he could be."

"Why are you sticking up for him?" Sabrina asked. "And what do you mean he'd be here if he could be? What's stopping him?"

Faye strolled back to the living room and took a seat on the love seat. "Sabrina, there are things that you don't know about me. I'm sure you've wondered how it is that I knew so much about royal families. I never told you much about my past, because I never wanted to relive any of it."

"What do you mean?"

"I mean, that if things went the way you say they did, he has to do damage control. Magdalena shouted to a ballroom full of powerful people that you only wanted to usurp the throne." Aunt Faye shrugged. "He can't just go on national television asking for you, especially with the Law of Marriage hanging over him. Give him time to come up with a plan."

Sabrina grabbed the chair next to the front door and brought it over in front of her Aunt. She sat down and leaned forward, listening intently.

"How do you know how this works? Tell me everything, Faye," she said. "Please."

Aunt Faye took a deep breath in and let it out with a long sigh.

"You've always known me as your neighbor," Faye said. "And same with your parents. After moving into the trailer park, I told myself that I'd keep my past a secret. But now, my past seems more relevant than ever."

"What do you mean?" Sabrina asked.

"You may find this surprising, but I wasn't always just an old lady living in a trailer. When I was younger, I was married to a nobleman. A lord to be exact."

Sabrina lips parted from shock, but she stayed silent.

"Yes, I was part of a royal family when I lived in Britain," she continued. "I was married to a British Lord by the name of James Dunhill. I loved the man deeply, despite the fact that he was arrogant beyond belief. I saw through that one fatal flaw the best I could and did everything I could to continue the relationship with him."

"Faye, are you serious?" Sabrina asked. "How did I never know this about you?"

"Like I said, I never saw the need to bring it up," she said.

"I didn't mean to interrupt," Sabrina said, leaning in a little closer. "Please, continue."

"I met James in a park one afternoon," Faye said. "It was the summer after I graduated high school. I still remember the dimples on his cheeks when he smiled and the way his eyes first lit up when he saw me. We got to talking and one thing led to another. The next thing I knew, a few years had passed and we were married. I was part of the royal family."

"What happened?" Sabrina asked.

"We grew up," Faye said. "I never really learned to be a lady, though I did try. We had a daughter and after that, something changed in James. I couldn't ever figure out exactly what it was, but he just wasn't the same. He pretty much ignored me for the first year of our daughter's life and then one day, I was escorted off the palace grounds by the guards. They took me back to my old home in Britain and I was told to never contact James again, or else I'd be harassed by the law. That was when I decided to move to the United States. I wanted, and *needed*, a new beginning."

"I knew you had a daughter, but I didn't know the circumstances," Sabrina said, looking down at the floor. "I'm so sorry, Faye. That had to have been so difficult."

"Don't be sorry for me, Bean," Faye said, with a soft chuckle. "I'm glad things worked out the way that they did.

Everything happens for the best and we can't predict the future."

"I don't mean to be rude, Faye, but why do you want to me to continue trying to be with Marco when your similar experienced ended with such heartbreak?" Sabrina asked.

"Because I don't believe that James and Marco are similar at all," she said. "What you've told me of Marco has painted a picture in my mind of a man who knows how to treat a lady. He sounds like the kind of man that any girl would be proud to be with. James wasn't a villain, but he certainly was never charming or kind. In fact, he was quite the opposite. I loved him, but it wasn't the same as you and Marco. I truly believe that what you have with him is something special and I won't allow you to throw it away without giving it another shot."

Sabrina was surprised by the words. She thought Faye would have been delighted by the news of her wishing to return home. Clearly, though, her aunt saw something in Marco that even Sabrina may have overlooked.

"I guess you're right," Sabrina said. "I suppose that I can forgive Marco, since he really didn't do anything that bad. But even if I do, what about Magdalena? If I am to stay here, how can I possibly get along with her? She hates me with every ounce of her being, Faye. She'd rather see me die than get married to Marco."

Faye nodded and took a slow sip of her tea. "She'll get over it. It may take her a while, but she will. I'm confident of that."

"How are you so sure?" Sabrina asked.

"She's my daughter," Faye said, abruptly.

If Sabrina had been standing, she'd have fallen over right there. Faye's words hit her eardrums, but the reality of what she had said took a moment to soak in.

"You're going to have to say that again," Sabrina said, shaking her head. "Because I'm pretty sure that I heard you wrong."

"You heard me correctly," Faye said, drawing out a long breath. "Magdalena is my biological daughter."

"Magdalena. Like *Queen* Magdalena?" Sabrina placed her palms against her forehead. "You've got to be kidding me."

"I wish I was, but it's true," Faye said. "It's another reason why I wanted to fly out here to tell you everything. I had to tell you in person."

"But you said that James left you when your daughter was only one," Sabrina said. "How do you know Magdalena is yours?"

"My entire family still lives in Britain, Bean," Faye explained. "They've kept me up to date on the latest gossip ever since I moved to the States. Although I never really *knew* Magdalena, she's still my daughter. I tried to learn as much as I could about her. I always hoped that James would raise her right and lead her to a good life, but all I've heard is that she's as spoiled rotten as they come."

Sabrina leaned back and closed her eyes. The news hit her like a ton of bricks.

*What are the chances of this? Is the world really this small?* she thought.

"So let me get this straight," Sabrina said. "*You're* the mother of Queen Magdalena of Orsino?"

Faye chuckled. "Yes, Sabrina. I am. I know it's a bit of a shock, but I hope you can understand why I haven't been able to tell you until now. When you called me from Hawaii and told me that Marco, your new boss, was the Prince of Orsino, I nearly fell out of my chair. I've never met him, but

I've definitely heard of him. I guess he's technically my step grandson."

"And here I was, thinking that things couldn't get any more interesting," Sabrina said, finally opening her eyes.

She sat for a moment, just contemplating everything. Then she turned to face Faye.

"Can I ask you a question, Aunty?"

"Of course, anything," Faye said.

"How on Earth did Magdalena become such a rotten person when she had a mother as amazing as you?" Sabrina asked. "I know you weren't around to raise her, but certainly there has to be something genetic that could have been passed down. Something positive."

Faye laughed hard and set down her cup of tea on the coffee table. "There's always a bad apple in every bunch. That's about the best explanation I have."

Sabrina smiled for the first time in two days. Somehow, her Aunt Faye could always manage to find the humor in every single situation. Even if the situation was as bizarre as the one they currently faced.

"You really think I should fight for him, huh?" Sabrina asked, already knowing the answer. "Even with the law saying I don't have a chance?"

"I wouldn't have flown ten thousand miles if I didn't believe in it," Faye replied. "Some things are worth fighting for, Sabrina. And if you give up on those things, you'll spend the whole rest of your life regretting it. Laws can change."

Sabrina sat down next to her Aunt and wrapped her arm over her shoulder. She held her close, burying her face into her neck.

"I don't know what I'd do without you, Faye," she said. "Thank you for everything you've ever done for me."

"You're the daughter I always wanted, Bean," Faye said,

with a sniffle. "You're what gets me out of bed in the morning. So really, it's me who should be thanking you."

They held each other for a while, just listening to the rain outside. Then Sabrina got up and turned the heat up for Faye, whose clothes were still damp.

"Faye, do you have your phone with you?" Sabrina asked. "My battery has been dead since last night."

"What do you need it for?" Faye asked, with a smirk.

"I need to call my fiancé."

# CHAPTER 21

arco

MAGDALENA LOUNGED on the queen's throne. There was no one to see her, yet she still sat in the chair decked out to the nines. It made Marco sick to see her so blatantly on the throne as his father lay upstairs recuperating.

The doctors said the surgery had gone well, but King Carlo was still weak and exhausted from the ordeal. It frightened Marco to see his father like that.

"Marco," Magdalena greeted her stepson as he approached.

"Do you really believe that you have the power to stand between Sabrina and I?"

"Of course I do," she said, as though it was such an obvious fact. "I have all the power I need, because it's in the law. And royalty must obey the laws just like everyone else."

"Laws can be changed," Marco replied.

Magdalena scoffed. "*You* can't change anything, Marco. Don't deceive yourself."

"And why not?" Marco asked.

"Because if you do, I'll be sure to point out to the public that their Prince is not a law-abiding member of this country," she said, casually glancing down at the gold rings on her fingers.

"Not a law-abiding citizen? What are you talking about?" he shouted.

"You just suggested that you could change the law for your personal benefit," Magdalena said, with a smirk. "Do you understand how serious a crime that is? It's a total scandal. So please, play nice. Because if you don't, then the citizens of Orsino Island will learn that Prince Marco is trying to change the laws for his own gain."

"Are you blackmailing me?" he asked, stepping toward her.

"Call it what you like," she said. "It matters not."

She stood on the throne dias and stared down at him.

"The court is in my pocket, Marco," she told him. "While you were away playing with your little American friend, I was here. I will always be here and there is nothing you can do about it."

He was outraged, and suddenly it all boiled over for him. He was done getting pushed around.

"Magdalena, you've gone too far now," he said, slowly walking toward her. "I wasn't going to do this, but you've left me no choice."

"Do what?" she asked, crossing her arms. "There is nothing you can do. I am more politically powerful than you."

"Leave my relationship with Sabrina alone, or else the

entire population of the Island will find out about your affair with Alanso, " Marco said, with revenge in his eyes.

"You have no proof," Magdalena said, trying to call his bluff.

But he wasn't bluffing. In fact, Marco had never been so serious in his life. He'd known about her affair, just like everybody else in the Palace knew about it. It had been made very clear to him, though, that he mustn't ever let the information get released to the public. The last thing the citizens needed to hear was about a sex scandal happening within their own government. It could be the beginning of the end of the monarchy. Even Carlo had pushed the fact that it could never get found out about. But now, this little bit of information became Marco's biggest strength.

"I'm not joking with you, Magdalena," he said. "One more attempt at ruining my relationship and I'll be the one calling every journalist on this entire Island to give them the full story. I'm sure they'll love to post a story about the queen's affair. The newspapers will sell like hotcakes and your face will be plastered all over them."

She stood silently and for a fleeting moment, Marco could have sworn that he saw the expression of defeat on her face.

"I think it would behoove you to keep those secrets to yourself," she said, quietly. "I will ruin you."

"With what? The fact that I want to get an antiquated law changed to marry the woman I love?" Marco scoffed. "Who will the public prefer, the woman who cheats on their beloved king or a prince who fights for love?"

"You have no proof," Magdalena repeated, but the strength wasn't in her voice this time.

Marco pulled up his phone and began opening up a phone app. "You have been far less than discrete while I was away," he told her. He held up his screen. "Do you think I don't have my own allies to run the country? I am not as naive as you seem to think, Magdalena. I do have proof."

On his phone was a picture of her kissing someone who was clearly not the King in one of the castle hallways.

"I have more, Magdalena," he told her. "Just because I was in America doesn't mean I wasn't securing my political position here. Your ruthlessness has made you many enemies. So yes, you have power in the court, but then so do I."

"You can't do this to me," Magdaglena sputtered. "You can't!"

"I can and I will," Marco told her coldly. "Until now, I was content to ignore you for Papa's sake. I will not ignore you at the cost of Sabrina. You will leave her be."

Magdalena's mouth opened, but nothing came out.

"I think it would behoove *you* to mind your own business and stay as far removed from my life as possible. If I hear so much of a breath that Sabrina is only after my crown from anyone connected to you, I will release these photos," he replied, before turning his back to her. "Now if you'll excuse me, I have to find my fiancée."

With that, Marco spun around and walked toward the door. Magdalena began to say something, but he didn't even bother listening. He just pushed through the door and left her to herself. He was breathing hard, adrenaline still fresh in his veins. But he felt somehow refreshed. Alive. He'd just stood up to his stepmother, the queen of a country, and in a big way.

*Now, I just have to find the love of my life and tell her that I love her. I just hope she can find it in her heart to forgive me.*

# CHAPTER 22

Sabrina

SABRINA HAD TAKEN Faye's cell phone and stepped into the other room of the motel to make her call. She knew Marco's personal number by memory and she dialed quickly. She couldn't wait to finally hear his voice again and looked forward to clearing things up.

It only rang once, before Marco picked up on the other end.

"Hello?" he said, his voice instantly putting a smile on Sabrina's face. "Who's this?"

"It's me," Sabrina said.

"Oh, my God, Sabrina," Marco said, clearly relieved. "Where in the hell are you? We've been searching the island non-stop. I haven't slept in days."

"I'm so sorry," she said. "I shouldn't have done this to you, but I had to get away."

"Are you still on Orsino?" he asked. "Where are you calling from?"

"I'm using my Aunt's phone," Sabrina said.

"You went back to Memphis then?" His voice broke slightly.

"No, I'm not in Memphis," she replied. "I'm using my Aunt's phone, because she's here with me on Orsino. She came out to see me."

"Thank God," Marco said, relief flooding every word. "Where on the Island are you? The guards have been searching homes and boats, looking through every nook and cranny to find you."

Sabrina chuckled. "You missed a spot. I'm staying at the South End Motel."

"Why didn't the guards check there?" he said. "They told me they searched everywhere. Don't go anywhere. I'll be there in a few minutes."

Marco hung up the phone and Sabrina stepped back into the main room of the motel. Faye was still seated on the love seat and when Sabrina walked in, she smiled at her.

"How did it go?" Faye asked.

"He's on his way here now," Sabrina said. "He seemed very excited to see me."

"As he should be," she said. "You'll be a sight for sore eyes for him. You've been missing for two days, so I can only imagine how worried he was about you."

"I'm going to gather the few things that I have here and get ready to go back to the Palace," Sabrina said, as she picked up the living room a bit. "Are you coming with me?"

"I'd love to," Faye said, standing up from the couch. "As long as I'm invited, that is. I don't want to intrude."

"You would most certainly not be intruding, Aunt," she replied. "In fact, I really want you to be there. I need you on this. I feel like I'm about to walk into a lion's den and I don't want to go in alone."

"You know I've got your back, kid," Faye said, as she helped Sabrina clean up the motel room.

Only a few minutes passed before Sabrina heard the sound of a car pulling up to the motel. A second later and someone was knocking frantically on the door. When she opened it, Marco stepped in with open arms and pulled her in for a hug.

"Sabrina, you had me scared to death," Marco said, squeezing Sabrina so tightly that it was clear he never wanted to let her go.

She pressed her face into his chest and breathed him in. His familiar scent calmed the anxiety that had been in her heart for two days. Being in his arms again felt right, and she knew she was making the right decision by giving him another chance.

"I'm so sorry," she said. "I was just scared and embarrassed. I couldn't face anybody. I just wanted to run and hide, so that's what I did."

Marco pulled away, but kept his hands on her shoulders. He looked deep into her eyes, and Sabrina breathed a sigh of relief.

"Please come home," he said, his eyes filling with tears. "I can't live without you. I need you, Sabrina."

"I'm going back with you," she said. "But I'm still so nervous about Magdalena."

"Don't be," Marco said. "I took care of it."

Sabrina cocked her head to the side. "How so?"

"It doesn't matter," he said. "All you need to know is that she won't be bothering us anymore."

Sabrina was confused, but decided not to push the issue.

If Marco said things were fine, then she had faith that they would be.

"By the way, Marco, this is my Aunt Faye," Sabrina said, spinning around.

Faye approached and held out a hand, but Marco ignored it and instead pulled Faye in for a hug.

"Thank you for coming," Marco said. "Thank you for taking care of my girl. You're a saint."

"I'm far from a saint, I assure you," Faye said, laughing. "But you're welcome. I'm happy to be here."

"Please, come back to the Palace with us," Marco said, still squeezing Faye with a bear hug. "Stay as long as you like."

"Thank you," Faye said. "I'll certainly take you up on the offer."

With that, the three of them left the motel and walked down to the black town car that was running in the parking lot. They all clamored in the back and Marco ordered the driver to take them back to the Palace.

Sabrina and Marco couldn't take their eyes off of each other. It had only been two days, but to Sabrina, it had felt like an agonizing eternity. She had missed him so much.

"I want to apologize for what Magdalena did to you at the ball," Marco said. "You didn't deserve that and it wasn't your fault."

"It's okay," Sabrina said, scooting close to him on the leather car seat. "I just didn't know what to do, so I ran. I'll admit that I was a little upset at first that you didn't come and talk to me afterwards. It made me feel like I wasn't even there."

"I was so angry at Magdalena," Marco explained. "I saw red and she became my focus. I wanted to put an end to her nonsense so badly that I didn't consider your embarrassment by what had happened. I regret not running to you right away."

"I understand," Sabrina replied. "I didn't at first, but I do now."

Faye cleared her throat and smirked at the two of them.

"Sabrina, before we get to the Palace, do you think we should tell Marco my relation to his family?" Faye asked. "It might spare us an awkward moment in front of everyone."

"Yes, I suppose we should..." Sabrina said, turning to Marco.

THE TOWN CAR pulled up to the Palace and Marco was still shaking his head in awe from the story that Faye had shared with him about her origins.

"The universe does like to use her favorite characters," Marco commented.

A guard opened the rear door and the three of them stepped out. Sabrina walked up the stairs, with Marco on one side and Faye on the other. Her heart was beating through her chest as they neared the front entrance.

"Are you sure Magdalena isn't going to kill me?" Sabrina said, with a half-smile.

"I'm positive," Marco said. "Don't you worry about her. Besides, my father needs us now during his recovery. I don't want to waste any extra energy on Magdalena."

*Oh my God. Carlo's surgery. I completely forgot about that, since I've been so absorbed in my own feelings,* Sabrina thought.

"Marco, how did everything go with the surgery?" she asked, as the guard opened the front door for them and they stepped inside.

"It went okay, given the circumstances," he said. "He had

the surgery the morning after the ball and just got home last night. The doctors were able to remove the tumor, so hopefully it doesn't come back. They'll be running tests for the next few months just to make sure. He's been sleeping a lot, and I haven't really had the chance to speak with him. Most of the information I've obtained has been from his doctors. I'm hoping he's awake now, though. He'll be happy to hear that I finally found you."

Sabrina looked over to Faye, who appeared to be amazed while taking in the sight of the Palace's interior. She was smiling and her eyes were wide with wonder.

"What do you think, Faye?" Sabrina asked. "Does it bring back memories of your past life?"

"In so many ways, child," she said. "Although, the palace where I resided in Britain is nowhere near the size of this one. But yes, I'm feeling rather nostalgic at the moment."

"Do you think my parents would like it?" Sabrina asked.

"I'm not sure that they'll even believe it once they see it," she replied. "I hope we can find a way to get them out here sometime."

Marco stopped when they got to the bottom of the interior stairway. "I'll fly your parents out here, Sabrina. Just give me the word and I'll have them on a plane the same day."

"You'd do that?" she asked. "For me?"

"Of course," he said. "I'd do anything for you. Plus, I'd love to meet your parents. And also, assuming you'll still take me, we'll be getting married soon and there's no way that I'd do that without your parents being present."

Sabrina smiled at the thought of her parents getting to enjoy the island life for a little while.

"Do you want me to come with you to see Carlo right now, or should I wait until you see how he's feeling?" Sabrina asked.

"Both of you come with me," Marco said. "He'll be delighted to have the company. I'm sure he's sick and tired of getting an earful from Magdalena anyway, so we'll be doing him a favor by entering his chambers."

Sabrina and Faye followed Marco upstairs and into Carlo's chambers. When they stepped inside, Sabrina's heart sank. Carlo was sitting up in his bed, but looked weary and pale. A green oxygen tank sat next to his bed, which was connected to a hose that pumped air into his nose. He managed a smile, though, when he saw that he had visitors.

"Come in," he whispered, his voice raspy and quiet.

Sabrina and Faye approached the foot of the bed, while Marco stepped beside his father. He placed a hand onto Carlo's chest. "Father, look who I found."

"I see that," Carlo said, glancing toward Sabrina. "I'm so glad you didn't leave the island, love."

"Me too," said Sabrina. "I'm sorry for all the fuss. It's nice to be back, though. How are you feeling?"

Carlo began to cough and immediately, a nurse ran in from the other room. She patted Carlo on the back and adjusted the oxygen hose in his nose. After a few moments, his coughing fit was over and he took in a long, slow breath. Then he motioned for the nurse to leave him, which she did without question.

"I wouldn't say that I feel like a million dollars," Carlo finally said, with a smirk. "But I feel like at least a thousand dollars."

Sabrina laughed, shocked by his optimism.

"That's good to hear," she said, as she wrapped an arm over Faye. "Carlo, this is my Aunt Faye. She came from Memphis to visit me."

Carlo gazed at Faye and then sat up a little further in the

bed. He was silent for a moment, just staring at her with wonder.

"You look strangely familiar, Ms. Faye," Carlo said. "Something in your eyes. Come closer. Let me see you."

Faye did as she was asked, and walked around to the side of the bed. Carlo placed his hand onto her chin, gently pulling her close. He stared into her eyes.

"Those eyes," he said. "That color. I've only seen it on one other person's in my entire life."

Faye parted her lips to speak, right as the doors to Carlo's chambers swung open. Everyone turned to see Queen Magdalena standing in the doorway. She was dressed in formal attire, which consisted of a purple robe with golden stitching. When she saw Sabrina, she scowled immediately, but didn't say a word to her. Instead, she strolled straight up to Carlo.

"How are you feeling, Carlo?" she asked. "Would you like me to have the guards escort these intruders out?"

Sabrina's heart was pounding as she watched the queen. She was waiting for all hell to break loose, expecting that Magdalena would attack her at any moment. But she didn't.

"No, I want them all to stay," Carlo said. "They're all welcome here. They're visitors, not intruders. And they're family."

"All of them?" Magdalena said, shooting a glance toward Sabrina.

"Yes, *all* of them," Carlo responded, his voice so hoarse that Sabrina could hardly make out his words.

Faye gazed across the bed toward Magdalena. Her eyes slowly filled with tears, which quickly flowed down her cheeks. Sabrina watched as Faye wiped the tears away with the back of her hand. Faye was looking at the daughter that she hadn't seen in forty years. Magdalena noticed the old woman and scoffed.

"Who is *this* lady?" Magdalena asked. "Why is she dressed like that? Do we not have any decency in this Palace anymore?"

Sabrina didn't wait for anybody else to speak up. Instead, she took the floor herself.

"That *lady* whom you're speaking to so arrogantly is your *mother*," Sabrina said, slamming the palm of her hand down on top of the bed. "I suggest you show some respect."

Magdalena rolled her eyes and faced Sabrina. "You stupid girl, you know nothing of my life. Don't pretend as though you know who my mother is."

Faye cleared her throat and wiped the remaining tears from her cheek. "She's telling the truth, Magdalena."

"I don't know who you are, but you're clearly delusional," Magdalena said to Faye. "My mother was a poor and useless commoner who left me when I was but a child. Trust me, I would know her if I saw her. My father told me all about her."

"Your father was James Dunhill," Faye said. "And he was my husband. But I think you've got the story wrong. I never left you, Magdalena. At least not by choice. James forced me to leave the royal family. I didn't want to leave."

Magdalena turned a shade of pale and then turned to Carlo. "This woman, whoever she is, is insane. Guards!"

Two guards came running in, but Marco stopped them at the door.

"I'm happy to explain things if you give me a chance," Faye said. "But if you don't want to hear it, then I understand."

"I don't want to hear it," she snapped back, turning away

from the bed. "You're obviously insane. Besides, why are you here anyway? How did you get in here?"

"She's my Aunt," Sabrina explained. "At least, the closest thing to an actual aunt that I've ever had. She came to visit me when she heard what happened at the ball."

Magdalena looked around the room at everyone.

"Every last one of you is insane," she shouted. "I'm leaving. Please, go about your business, you group of crazies."

Magdalena then marched out of the room, stomping her feet on the way out like a child.

"I knew those eyes looked familiar," Carlo said. "It is the most auspicious of circumstances to have you standing here right now."

Carlo gazed at Faye for a moment longer, and then turned back to Sabrina.

"Why did you not tell me that your Aunt was Magdalena's mother?" Carlo asked.

Sabrina shrugged. "I just found out about an hour ago."

Marco, who was still standing by the side of the bed, seemed to be eager to speak. He was fidgeting and tapping his fingers on the headboard of the bed.

"What is it, son?" Carlo asked, coughing a few times after speaking the words.

"I know you need rest, Father, but I want to consult with you for a moment," Marco said. "Did you look into the law that says I can't marry Sabrina because she's not royal? The one that Magdalena had said she found?"

Carlo drew in a long breath and pushed himself up a bit, so that he was leaning against the headboard. "Yes, I did. And Magdalena was right. There is a law that says that."

Sabrina and Marco looked at each other and Sabrina felt her gut clench.

"Is there anything we can do?" Sabrina asked. "I want to marry Marco more than anything."

"The law states very clearly that it's not allowed," Carlo said.

"Father, can't we change it?" Marco asked. "It's a silly and outdated law, anyhow. Who would ever complain if it got changed?"

Carlo sat silently for a moment. His breathing was slow and paced. Sabrina could tell that the simple act of breathing pained him. The lung surgery had clearly taken a toll on the man.

"I've got good news and bad news," Carlo said. "The bad news, is that I can't change the law. At least, not in a timely fashion. It would take months for everything to go through."

Tears fell down Sabrina's cheeks and she ran to Marco to embrace him.

"The good news," Carlo continued. "Is that I don't *have* to change the law in order for you to get married."

Sabrina stopped crying immediately and pulled her face away from Marco's chest. She looked directly at Carlo. "What do you mean?"

"Your father is Peter Wise, correct?" Carlo asked.

Sabrina hesitantly nodded. "Yes, that's correct."

"I had one of our people look into it for me. It turns out, that your great great grandfather was the Lord of Earlshire and fought in the Battle of the Realm. His name was Arthur Wise the Third."

"I think my dad had mentioned something about that once," she said. "But I'm not sure how this all relates."

"It means, my dear child, that your father is of royal blood," Carlo explained, his eyes lighting up. "With his lineage, not only is he royal blood, but he can be knighted for his ancestor's battle bravery. If your father becomes a

Knight of Orsino, and you are his next of kin, then you are no longer considered common blood. Far from it."

Sabrina's knees went weak and she held onto Marco for support.

"You mean…" she whispered.

"Yes, you will be able to marry Marco and the law won't have anything to say about it," Carlo said. "And, on that same note, Magdalena won't be able to say anything about it either. She can try to take it to the courts, but nothing will stand up there because you won't be breaking any law."

Sabrina fell forward and wrapped her arms around Carlo's neck, pulling him in for a hug. Her heart swelled and she held him close. She sobbed, but this time, it was tears of joy that fell from her eyes. When she pulled away, she noticed that Carlo had shed a few tears of his own.

"Thank you, King Carlo," Sabrina said.

Marco dropped to one knee beside the bed and held Carlo's hand. "Father, I'm eternally grateful. You've just made me the happiest man alive."

Carlo cleared his throat and coughed once more. "It's the least I can do for my son. Now, let's get Sabrina's parents out here. We need to get this process started sooner than later. According to the doctors, my surgery went well. But I still don't know what that means as far as how much time I might have. We must make haste."

# CHAPTER 23

 *arco*

*Three weeks later...*

MARCO STEPPED out of his bedroom at the same time his father was walking down the hallway.

"Marco, you startled me," Carlo said, his voice still a bit raspy, but getting better. "I just woke up from a nap. I can't believe how drowsy these pain medications make me."

"You look like you're feeling much better, though," Marco said.

"Indeed I am," Carlo said. "The tests yesterday went well, too. I'm told that I am completely cancer free, at least for the moment. That's good enough for me."

Marco pulled his father close and hugged him,

breathing out a sigh of relief. He'd been waiting anxiously to hear about the test results.

"I'm so glad to hear," he said, squeezing his father affectionately. "Let's keep our fingers crossed that the results continue to stay that way. What do you say?"

"I'd say that's a fine plan," Carlo said, with a smile.

Carlo was starting to act like his old self again, and Marco couldn't have been happier. Just three weeks after the surgery, and Carlo was up and moving around. He wasn't able to attend to all of his duties as King, at least not quite yet. But he did manage to gather enough energy to perform one sacred ritual with Sabrina's father, who was now considered a "Knight of Orsino" because of it.

"Is Sabrina downstairs?" Marco asked. "I haven't seen her since this morning, with all the chaos."

"Yes, I just passed them, actually," Carlo said. "She's in the library with her parents."

"Perfect," Marco said, as he turned away from his father. "I'm going to go visit with them for a few minutes before we have to get dressed."

"Ah yes," Carlo said, nodding his head. "You'd better hurry, before she gets her dress on. You know how the old superstition goes."

Marco rolled his eyes. "You know I don't believe in that sort of nonsense."

"All the same." Carlo smiled, patting his headstrong son on the shoulder. "It's best not to tempt fate. After all, it's been so good to you lately."

Laughing, Marco shook his head. "All right, all right. I won't argue with you, but only because you're under the weather.

Marco turned and walked down the stairs, making his way toward the library. The palace felt different than it had just a couple of weeks ago. It felt lighter and happier. He wasn't completely sure why, but he had a feeling it had something to do with the fact that Magdalena hadn't shown her face around there in over a week.

According to Carlo, she'd gone to their summer retreat cabin a few miles north of the palace. She was there with Alonso, her not-so-secret lover. At first, Carlo was heartbroken, although he did his best not to show it. Despite her bitterness, she'd been a fixture in his life for so long, it was hard for him to accept that she was truly gone. But with the hustle and bustle of last-minute wedding preparations all around him, it was hard to stay sad for long.

Marco poked his head into the library to find Sabrina standing with her parents.

"Has anyone seen my beautiful fiancée?" Marco asked, with a boyish smirk.

Sabrina's eyes lit up and she wrapped her arms around his neck. Then she leaned in and kissed his cheek.

"Hey, love." Sabrina held him close. "What are you up to?"

"Just wanted to touch base with everyone," Marco said, looking toward Sabrina's parents. "Less than three hours... can you believe it? Does anyone need anything?"

Sabrina's dad shook his head. "I think we're just fine. Marla set out a suit for me to wear, so I'll be ready."

"I trust it's a suit that's fit for a knight?" Marco asked with a grin.

Peter nodded, his eyes widening is disbelief. "It's still hard to believe that I can call myself 'Sir Peter Wise'."

"I think it has a nice ring to it," Marco said, squeezing Peter's shoulder. "I know I've said it before, but I want to thank you again for agreeing to become a knight. It's because of you that I can marry your daughter. I'm forever in your debt."

Peter shrugged. "It's a debt that I'm not too concerned with collecting on. I'm just happy that my baby girl has found someone that treats her right."

Marco was genuinely impressed by Peter's willingness to help their situation. Sabrina's parents had flown to Orsino a week prior and Peter agreed without hesitation that he'd do whatever he could to help. In this case, it meant becoming a Knight of Orsino. He was sworn in just two days after landing on the Island.

"I'm glad both of you are here," Marco said, bringing his attention to Anna.

She was wearing a beautiful blue silk dress, which Marco had given her as a gift upon her arrival. It looked like it belonged on her and seemed more fitting than the ripped jeans she'd come wearing.

"Thank you for everything, Marco," Anna said. "You're giving my daughter a life that I couldn't have dreamed of in a million years. I'm still in shock."

"You need never thank me," Marco said, pulling Anna in for a hug. "I hope that I can give you the life that you deserve as well."

He pulled away and then stepped back to Sabrina.

"As long as you don't need anything from me, I'm going to go upstairs and get ready for the wedding." Marco leaned forward and kissed his fiancée. When he pulled away, he looked her in the eyes and sighed. He loved her so much that his heart ached. "I know I won't be allowed to see you again once you're in your dress, and I've no desire to get a shoe thrown at my head by one of the chamber-maids."

*How I got so lucky to meet a girl like her I'll never know,* he thought.

"I'll see you in a little while," Sabrina said, smiling as she gently touched his cheeks. "Can you do me a favor, though? Don't shave. I think I like the beard stubble you have going on."

"For you? Anything?" Marco said, as he scratched his chin.

Then he turned and left the library. He went back to his bedroom to get dressed. He still couldn't believe how things had turned out. What had started as a simple vacation in the United States had turned into him meeting the girl of his dreams and getting married. He was beyond grateful for the way things had developed in his life. There was a lot in his future, including his eventual rise to the position of King. But that wasn't what was on his mind at the moment. All that he cared about was spending as much time with Sabrina as possible and giving her the fulfilling life that she deserved. Because before he met her, Marco was certain that his life had had no meaning.

*I was born a prince, but thanks to Sabrina, I now know what it means to feel truly rich.*

# CHAPTER 24

 *abrina*

AUNT FAYE CONNECTED the top clasp on the back of the
Sabrina's wedding dress, then glanced into the mirror in
front of them.

"How does it feel?" Faye asked.

Sabrina brought her hands down the sides of the dress.
An intricate design was hand-sewn throughout, with
millions of tiny stitches creating a beautiful pattern.

"It feels expensive," Sabrina said, with a smile. "But also
really good."

"I can tell you're nervous," Faye said, spinning Sabrina
around to face her. "Am I wrong?"

"I'm nervous, but in a good way." Sabrina let out a sigh,
calming the anxiety in her gut. This wasn't going to be any
ordinary wedding. It was super formal, and held many traditions that were foreign to Sabrina. She'd been told the ceremony could last up to three hours, and she had no idea how

she would sit through it without bursting from excitement and nerves.

"Just take a deep breath," Faye said, her eyes glowing from the daylight that poured in through the window. "And if that doesn't work, try to keep the squealing to a minimum."

Sabrina laughed. "I'll try, Aunty. I'll try."

"Okay, well your dress looks amazing, and we have but a few minutes before we're meeting your father and the bridesmaids in the courtyard. I'd like to run to my room and change quickly. I'll be back in two shakes." Faye then turned and left Sabrina to herself in the bedroom.

She stared at herself in the mirror for a moment longer. Marla had curled her hair and applied makeup on her. She looked more beautiful than ever before. And she felt that way, too. For the first time, she felt secure. Not just for herself, but for her family, too. Sabrina knew that her old life, and her parent's old life, would be nothing more than a memory. She'd be able to take care of them. Her dreams had manifested into reality.

*It's still hard to believe,* she thought, as she sat down on the edge of the bed. *I never thought my life could get this good.*

In just a few hours, Sabrina would officially be married to Marco. The poor girl from Memphis would become a Princess. And then, eventually, Queen. She sat in that room for a moment, just pondering the way things had turned out for her. She couldn't help but to think about how one little decision had changed the outcome of her entire life.

*What if I hadn't decided to apply for that job all those months ago?* She thought. *Where would I be now? I definitely wouldn't be here, getting ready to rehearse a wedding with the most amazing man on the planet.*

Sabrina looked up, as Faye poked her head back into the room.

"You ready, Bean?" she asked. "We're going to be late if we don't hurry."

Sabrina nodded as she stood up from the bed. She walked toward the door, holding the bottom of the wedding dress up to keep it from dragging on the floor.

Out of nowhere, Marla materialized with two other girls, *tsking* loudly. "Carrying your own dress? For shame. Where are the bridesmaids?"

Faye laughed. "Where we come from, you get used to taking care of your own baggage. But you're right. I'm sorry, Sabrina, that's awfully rude of me. Let me get your train for you."

"Here, your bouquet." Marla thrust a beautiful arrangement of flowers into Sabrina's clammy palms. "Are you all right? Do you need a drink of water? Some valerian leaves?"

Sabrina giggled at the reference to the wild plant, which, she'd learned, many of the locals chewed recreationally for its calming effects. As tempting as it was, she wanted to stay lucid for the most important day of her life.

"Thank you, Marla. I'm good. But I might change my mind later."

She'd already gone through her entrance in the rehearsal, but she wasn't any more confident about it. The wedding was taking place in the massive courtyard behind the palace, backed by a breathtaking fountain and surrounded by Lilies of the Nile, lilacs, orange poppies, and sea spray – and plenty of blooms she didn't recognize. The smell was as beautiful as it was exotic.

From the balcony above the staircase, Sabrina could see the thousands of paper lanterns dotting the gardens. The ceremony itself was attended only by the royal family and esteemed guests, but even so, it seemed like there must be a million people seated there on either side of the red carpet, waiting for her to arrive.

There was only one notable absence. Magdalena, as it turned out, would not be attending.

Sabrina breathed a sigh of relief when Marco first broke the news. As far as the public knew, she was simply too ill to attend. But after her shameful outburst at the ball, most of them knew the truth.

As it turned out, though, the people of Orsino were fascinated by the idea of a "people's princess" from the American south. Ever since their engagement, the palace had been inundated with gifts. Sabrina's favorite was a little hand-carved cowboy, complete with a five-gallon hat. They didn't understand her culture any more than she understood theirs, after just a few weeks – but they wanted her to feel welcomed. They wanted her to feel at home, just as much as Marco did.

Tears brimmed in Sabrina's eyes as she waited for her cue to descend the stairs.

"Not yet," Faye whispered. "Don't cry, Bean. Or we'll all be a sobbing mess before the priest even opens his mouth."

And just like that, the music started.

# CHAPTER 25

Marco shifted his weight impatiently. He felt like he'd been standing here at the altar for a hundred years, watching the altar boys spread incense as they paced up and down the aisles. Having sat through a number of these interminably long traditional weddings in his youth, Marco knew exactly what he was in for. He would've been happy eloping with Sabrina to Las Vegas, and being married by one of those men who dress up like Elvis Presley. But this day wasn't just for them. It was for his father, and for the people of the island to share in his joy.

He had to start thinking like a king now. Thankfully, with Sabrina by this side, that no longer felt like such a burden.

But where *was* she?

"Are you sure they know when to start the procession?" Marco mumbled to his father.

"Yes," Carlo whispered. "Marla would never let this wedding go off-schedule. You know that as well as I do."

For the hundredth time, Marco glanced out over the crowd. So many faces, all of them smiling. There was Valetta in the front row, dabbing delicately at her face with a lace handkerchief. All of the diplomats and foreign royals that his father had made friends with during his reign, and of course, anyone who wanted to see or be seen at the biggest event of the year.

The press was strictly banned. All the same, Marco felt himself watching carefully for a hint of a flash bulb or any suspicious behavior.

Suddenly, the organist cleared his throat and began to play.

Marco's heart leapt into his throat. His eyes were drawn to the huge marble staircase, where Sabrina and her party were just beginning to descend. She walked slowly, measuring every step, her face covered by a long white veil. He hoped she could see all right. More than anything, he wanted to see her face.

As she reached the end of the staircase, she was joined by her waiting father. He took her elbow and smiled, wide as anything.

Her journey down the red carpet seemed to take a thousand years. White flower pedals, tossed from balconies by a few of the island's children, fluttered around her with each step.

Marco couldn't think. He could hardly breathe.

This was really happening.

He was going to be with this woman for the rest of his life.

When she finally reached him, he took both of her hands in his. His heart swelled. Now, even through the veil, he could see her glowing smile, the tears shimmering in her eyes. As the priest addressed the crowd, beginning his long call-and-response prayer that would bless their union, Marco felt everything in the background fade away. Nothing else mattered, except him and his bride.

Time dilated. Although he heard the heavy ticking of the massive, ancient clock behind them, it ceased to have any meaning. Before he knew it, the priest was saying those magic words.

"You may kiss the bride."

Marco lifted the veil with trembling hands. His wife bit her lip, a little hint of nervousness that he still found so alluring.

There were so many things he wanted to say to her. To reassure her, to tell her she was loved, she would always be loved, by him and by his people. That he couldn't wait to have her sit next to him as Queen.

He said it all in a kiss.

As their lips met, the crowd erupted into cheers.

This wasn't the end of their fairy tale, oh no.

This was just the beginning.

"I've never been more ready."

## THANK YOU!

Thank you for reading "Yours Royally"! If you enjoyed it, make sure to leave a review! Every little bit helps.

His carefree life is enviable, his kisses are intoxicating, and she can almost imagine a life with him. But all vacations come to an end. And when Cassie invites him to visit her hometown, Wyatt reveals that he can never go back. Not to her town. Not to America. Not to civilization.

Cassie leaves, confused and heartbroken, wondering just who she got herself involved with. Suddenly, her predictable life gets turned upside down when she sees her picture splashed across the Internet. And when the tabloids come looking for the mature woman who found the lost billionaire, she has no idea what to do...

...until he comes back.

Escape With Me: A Midlife Love Story

# ABOUT THE AUTHOR

New York Times and USA Today Bestseller Krista Lakes is a thirtysomething who recently rediscovered her passion for writing. She is living happily ever after with her Prince Charming. Her first kid just started preschool and she is happy to welcome her second child into her life, continuing her "Happily Ever After"!

Thank you for supporting an indie author. Anything you can do, whether it be writing a review, or even simply telling a fellow reader that you enjoyed this, helps me out immensely. Thanks!

Krista would love to hear from you! Please contact her at Krista.Lakes@gmail.com or friend her on Facebook!

Further reading:

*Bad Boys and Babies*
> Family Doctor's Baby
> The Billionaire's Baby Arrangement
> Crime Boss Baby

*Kinds of Love*
> A Forever Kind of Love
> A Wonderful Kind of Love
> An Endless Kind of Love

*Billionaires and Brides*

    Yours Completely: A Cinderella Love Story

    Yours Truly: A Cinderella Love Story

    Yours Royally: A Cinderella Love Story

*The "Kisses" series*

    Saltwater Kisses: A Billionaire Love Story

    Kisses From Jack: The Other Side of Saltwater Kisses

    Rainwater Kisses: A Billionaire Love Story

    Champagne Kisses: A Timeless Love Story

    Freshwater Kisses: A Billionaire Love Story

    Sandcastle Kisses: A Billionaire Love Story

    Hurricane Kisses: A Billionaire Love Story

    Barefoot Kisses: A Billionaire Love Story

    Sunrise Kisses: A Billionaire Love Story

    Waterfall Kisses: A Billionaire Love Story

    Island Kisses: A Billionaire Love Story

*Other Novels*

    I Choose You: A Secret Billionaire Romance

    His Every Desire: A Billionaire Seduction

    Wolf Six's Salvation: A Shifter Love Story

    Burned: A New Adult Love Story

    Walking on Sunshine: A Sweet Summer Romance

    An American Cinderella: A Royal Love Story

    Mr. Darcy's Kiss: A Contemporary Pride and Prejudice